THE SEARCHERS

Eli Bonnet came to the Yukon, during the last great gold rush, on a merciless manhunt for the killer who had savagely butchered a woman and child. Bonnet longed for a new frontier as well, and for the freedoms of the one he had lost forever.

Hannah Twigg followed, seeking a new land where she could be herself, rather than a conquest in the hands of a powerful man. She searched for love beyond lust and greed.

In an untamed wilderness of danger and desire, ripped through by a swirling river of death and gold, they found each other. . . .

WHISPERS OF THE RIVER

WHISPERS OF THE RIVER

Tom Hron

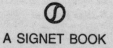

A SIGNET BOOK

SIGNET
Published by the Penguin Group
Penguin Books USA Inc., 375 Hudson Street,
New York, New York 10014, U.S.A.
Penguin Books Ltd, 27 Wrights Lane
London W8 5TZ, England
Penguin Books Australia Ltd, Ringwood,
Victoria, Australia
Penguin Books Canada Ltd, 10 Alcorn Avenue,
Toronto, Ontario, Canada M4V 3B2
Penguin Books (N.Z.) Ltd, 182–190 Wairau Road,
Auckland 10, New Zealand

Penguin Books Ltd, Registered Offices:
Harmondsworth, Middlesex, England

First published by Signet, an imprint of Dutton Signet,
a division of Penguin Books USA Inc.

First Printing, March, 1996
10 9 8 7 6 5 4 3 2 1

To Doris and Hannah Hron

Discovery

It hid there for a million years—bits about the size of sand, some bits bigger like dry beans or corn kernels, but always down in the dirt where people couldn't see. White water roared over, washed down, worked to hide it forever from snooping eyes. Rocks piled up, grass grew about, and trees swayed on top while sunshine peeked down. At the end of this sweet light, the bits that God forgot glittered enough to fire the lust of man.

This prize lay far across a savage land. Roiling water of shoreline seas, driven by tides rushing through rips into coasts, guarded its edge. Bogs with shimmering pond water and blots of black spruce reached north of points and bays and sopped the ground. Forests of birch, cottonwood, and hemlock lifted above the bogs and covered rough hills toward mountains. Snowy summits, bright white that soaked color from the sky, tore horizons to sawtooth silhouettes. All these things stood against those who wished to tramp to where the treasure waited.

This land lay gentle in places, too. Swans, beavers, and ducks dipped into its ponds and lakes. Mirrors of water, vexed by these busy creatures, wiggled with low ripples in circles around the wading wildlife. Soft shadows, silver reflections, and blue water blended with green shorelines. Brooks tumbled down from the high country and cooled sunny sides. Good timber abounded, and the rivers ran rich with salmon during summer months. Best of all, its free Indians lived as peaceful people.

One day as the sun sat on the horizon and its brassy light hung over this wilderness—and as sooty shadows reached across steep slopes like black fingers pointing the way—a blue-eyed man aided by a willow staff shuffled down, searching all around. Suddenly he fell on rubble, and then, creaturelike, snaked to a better place and stood again. Red dampness about each knee and hands dark with blood and dirt stained the rocks and marked his trail. Two Tagish Indians carrying heavier loads stepped down with surer feet and waited for his pain to pass. All three dropped from there to wash the wounds and to prospect a creek that ran below. It had been named Rabbit by someone in the past, but soon would be called Bonanza by most.

"God bless, we've struck it now!" shouted the man when he saw his first pan of gold. He'd cried that before, but it had never come true. Folks across the North had named him Lying George because of his past boasts and fibs—but they would soon regret that awful name.

His two companions, Skookum Jim and Tagish Charley, came running. They hung their heads over his shoulders and gaped at the gold in the swirling pan. Five dollars' worth rolled in its bottom, plenty for a month. At last their lives of living off the land had ended—no more poling rivers, slogging tundra, and crawling creeks day after day. It had come true, the thing they had prayed for—a fortune lay under their hands.

"Me rich Injun now?" Skookum Jim asked.

Lying George laughed. "You and Charley be the richest Injuns in Alaskee and the Yukon, too."

They staked their claims during the rest of the day, one for each Indian, two for the white man, then jumped jigs into the night. Their dancing showed how folks would feel after they learned of the strike.

The next morning Lying George, Skookum, and Charley raced down the side of the rounded mountain known as the Dome, from where Rabbit Creek ran. They launched into the Klondike River in a canoe, paddled to the Yukon River and down toward Fortymile town, yelling to men they met along the way about their strike. After hearing the news, those lucky few paddled frantically upstream pleading for the tale to be true.

When Lying George got to Fortymile, he filed his mining claims, then bought drinks at Billy McPhee's. He bragged to friends of his stake called Discovery— but no one listened until he poured the Yellow God out for all to see. Then everyone whooped and dashed for the door, abandoning the town by morning.

Whispers of the strike drifted with the wind across the wilderness like wildfire smoke. When men heard, they threw down tools and traps, nets and paddles, and stampeded toward the find. Old names of the North struck huge fortunes first—Big Alex, Swiftwater Bill, Clarence Berry. Many others got part of it as well.

Early in June 1897, whistles wailed, and two steamboats, the *Alice* and the *Portus,* chugged into the new boomtown called Dawson City, at the fork where the Klondike poured into the Yukon. Eighty-four miners got on board and began their long journey down the rolling river. They drank, danced, and most of all, gossiped about the gold stacked on deck. Three tons sat there, stuffed into bags so heavy it had taken two men to hoist each aboard.

At the end of the Yukon River, the miners boarded ships named the *Excelsior* and the *Portland* and began their sail to San Francisco and Seattle. The world would soon hear about the fabulous find.

The *Excelsior* came first and the *Portland* two days later. Mobs greeted the ships and the greatest gold stampede of all began to enchant the nation. A newspaperman named Beriah Brown described it best in the *Seattle Post-Intelligencer:* Gold! Gold! Gold! Gold! 68 Rich Men on the Steamer *Portland,* STACKS OF YELLOW METAL!

People went crazy when they read the news. This story tells of their tears.

PART I

Woebegone

CHAPTER ONE

Arizona

When jumping cholla cactus speared his fingers together for the third time, Eli Bonnet judged the desert must be the devil's forge. He'd tallied ninety-six days in the promise from hell—but not one message from the U.S. Marshals' office in San Francisco. Each day had crawled by just like each black-and-tan sidewinder had slithered by in the infested wasteland around him. Seven more snakes than days had been counted—he didn't know if that figured as a good or bad omen. Keeping score did something for him, but the purpose slipped his mind whenever he considered his habit.

As he pulled his fingers apart, he worried over which would kill him first, heat or snakes. Then the thought that both might get him at the same time made him sweat even more. Fat drops ran down until they hit muscle lines, dribbled to his sides, and stained his shirt blotchy blue. They felt like spiders scurrying across his belly and caused him to think the town of Thistles was making him mad.

Gritting his teeth, he yanked the cactus spines out of his fingers and crept farther. After one hundred paces, he peeked through devil's claw branches and signaled his hound, sneaking behind, to stay quiet. Sorrowful, a dog rescued as a beaten pup eight years before from Sioux Indian owners, had been named for his facial features. Sadness still showed in his yellow eyes, but the rest of him had grown to look like a wolf—and Eli knew all Indians now were in danger whenever they camped near.

Chiricahua Apaches, two men and two boys, crouched over a cooking fire in a rocky wash below. Madly feeding their mouths and not wanting to miss a morsel dripping off the two stolen chickens, they darted their hands in and out of orange flames catching hot grease. Seeing their ribs and hips poked against sagged skin, Eli sensed he'd discovered starving renegades running from the San Carlos Reservation.

As he watched, he recalled chasing Indians for most of his life—and getting chased back during earlier times. Now his belly was full of it. Indians and prairie lobos were alike: shot down and run off. When the few that remained wished to tread in their old sacred places, they were forced to sneak around. It was clear that the four Apaches before him were fathers and sons trying to stay alive. They weren't a threat, except to the town's chickens, and they deserved the same food coyotes had been thieving. Thistles wasn't for people who wished to farm feathers, he reflected. It existed for misfits like himself. He motioned to Sorrowful and tramped away, feeling lonely for the last wild people of the West.

This wasn't his first hot spell; it was just the most

hellish and crippling. His home had been in the Confederacy while he was a boy, and the humid South had been suffocating. But that had been a different time and place, and there had been green oaks for shade and the Tennessee River to jump into when the day became too difficult. An occasional demon's breath had blown into the Montana Territory while he'd marshaled the law there, but that, too, had been different. One could always find the shady side of a canyon and its tumbling, cold-water creek. Law enforcement up there had been in pleasant places—but now he was being asked to endure a parched purgatory for endless days and nights.

The sun sucked the life from each soul foolish enough to offer himself to the outdoors during sunny hours. Everyone with passable sense hid at home until twilight, then they and the resident pack rats, each in their own wretched ways, ran around gathering enough to make it through another day of damnation.

The town existed only because of a bitter spring and a silver prospect, but neither was very agreeable. The water tasted so sour that it made horses snort before they could dip their noses into it. Townsfolk always added whiskey or rum to mellow the sourness, but the result of this cleverness made everyone, except for those on their mother's milk, a little tipsy.

The silver seam wiggled around underground, and a few foolhardy miners, convinced that the mother lode was just ahead, kept pounding away with hammers, chisels, and blasting powder, ignorant of the stupor brought on by the spirituous water. Eli concluded that folks unlucky enough to have found their way to Thistles could never be expected to find mind or money to get away. They were condemned to drinking more and more of the damnable water—and then they were forever committed to an uncommon hell.

After backtracking to the town's saloon, he looked at the ragged *San Francisco Chronicle* on the bar, and its headline screeched at him again: SACKS OF GOLD FROM THE CLONDYKE! The smaller print confused his sunburned eyes, but the words were still clear in his mind because he'd read the story ten times. It told of a golden place named Dawson City on the Yukon River, thousands of wilderness miles to the north. But Jesse Peacock, his one-armed boss, had sent him south to a post without prospects. And the few enterprising souls that had resided in Thistles had abandoned the town in the past few days to join the gold stampede. The only people remaining were two forsaken whores and a collection of ancient miners and prospectors who would get sunk in sand forever in a short while. He'd wondered repeatedly since he first saw the newspaper if he should quit the Marshals or carry on. He judged the country to be in an economic depression, and his pay was important, but his life's work had always been in gold fields and boomtowns. Stampedes were in his blood, and he hankered to go on this one as well.

He looked at his dog resting nearby on the floor of the Good Thunder Inn. The slab boards of the saloon still stank from the spit and spill of last Saturday's celebration. Enthusiastic use of blasting powder in tunnels below had indicated a fitting name many years before he had come to the town— but it seemed better to his present mind that an explosion take place above ground and close by. Then perhaps he and a few others would be set free.

"Sorrowful, get up and let's go!" he called.

"You goin' to the horse tank?" asked a square man with a greased and swirled mustache, spoiled apron, and hostile look. Eli had shot him in the kneecap many years before, while both worked in Montana—so both could move forward with honest professions. Finley had worn a pistol in those days instead of a bartender's apron, and he had displayed an unwanted affection for other people's possessions. The administering of the law had worked well with Finley, but it was also one of the reasons for Eli's desert exile. Jesse Peacock didn't approve of his style of justice.

"My friend needs to get cool . . . and I want to stay sober!" Eli stood and turned from his table.

While he trudged to the door with his back turned, Finley pointed his finger and thumb, like a pistol, and fired a pretended shot. Sorrowful stopped, looked back, and growled a low warning. The bartender saw that his spiteful nonsense had earned him a disagreeable enemy, and he quickly returned to his bottles.

Eli walked to the round horse tank set on the edge of town, through which the townspeople had routed the bitter waters of the spring. An old prospector named Noodles had arrived there first and was sitting up to his neck in the cistern. Noodles had earned his name because of a dietary habit imposed by his toothless gums. He was a bright man who had followed gold and silver possibilities across the West throughout his long life and, though it was peculiar to Eli, had never complained about his failure to find anything to enrich his life beyond grubstake money for another prospecting trek. His faded but firm blue eyes never indicated any penitence for the paths he had chosen, and his carefree cackling told of a fulfillment that Eli blamed on the corrupted waters.

Eli threw Sorrowful into the tank, stripped, and climbed in himself. Long shadows beckoned twilight and summoned calls of quails and cries from whippoorwills. The Rosy Buttes toward the west blushed with pink from the descending sun, and the heat of the day began to creep away from the cooler evening air.

"You been at the Good Thunder again, ain't you, Eli?" Noodles asked, peering across the tank.

"I was reading the newspaper!" Eli splashed water on his head.

"You want to go to the Klondike real bad, don't you?" Noodles smiled with a wide, toothless mouth.

Eli thought about the question and decided not to reply. Somehow he knew Noodles wasn't expecting a response. The old man was about seventy years of age and seemed able to pluck answers from stares and mumbles anyway.

As he sat in silence, the water and twilight breezes began to soothe his body—but then worry crept up, mostly in his breast, and spooked him a little. Suddenly Noodles looked older than he had in the past. Eli saw a weathered white face poking above the waterline, and the spectacle made him afraid of his own future. He wanted to be young again and ride the West as he had then. But, he fretted, he'd become a hostage of Thistles, or maybe the devil.

"Why you so quiet tonight, Eli?" Noodles asked.

Eli shook away his fears, looked back across to the wrinkled old man, and said, "I was thinking of the West when I was young, and other days gone by."

"What was you doin' back in the old days?"

"My first job was with a freight master called Gabby Boy in the Dakota Territory. I was sixteen, seventeen years old." Wistful wrinkles crossed Eli's face as he recalled his old friend. He could still hear the happy freighter bellowing, "Sonny, I want you to remember four things while you're workin' for me: listen carefully, do what you're told, don't talk back, and carry all the heavy things!" He could also see the old geezer going through one of his laughing and knee-slapping sessions after hollering that sermon. He'd been smart enough to answer, "Yes, sir," and they had gotten along fine throughout the months they'd worked together.

Noodles looked at Eli for a moment. "I knowed Gabby Boy a long time ago . . . in the Black Hills . . . they was the Yellow Hills back then." Then he cackled and suddenly asked, "By Jeez, was you the kid with Gabby Boy when he got kill't by the Sioux about thirty years ago?"

"I was with him!" Eli saw Gabby Boy falling from

the wagon seat and onto the prairie as clearly as if it had been yesterday's disaster.

"How'd they kill Gabby Boy?" Noodles squeezed water from his white whiskers with one hand.

"He got shot down by a Sharps buffalo bullet, one bullet . . . he never felt the thing." Eli watched his dog paddle around. He remembered that a different dog had helped on that past, grim day. He then breathed a heavy sigh and said, "My companions and I got three of their black hearts in payment for Gabby Boy."

Old Noodles peered across the tank again. "I hear'd you was alone when them Injuns tried to get you!"

Eli smiled, picturing the night. "I had a dog and six mules with me."

"What'd them animals do for you?" Noodles squinted.

"Six of Cut Foot's warriors ambushed us. I got one by pretending to be out of cartridges. Gabby Boy's dog jumped another in the dark . . . I shot that heathen with my Colt while he was fighting with the dog. The mules ran another one down and kicked him to death. The others ran away from all the ruckus."

"Was that where you got your Sioux ceremonial jacket—the medicine coat you wear durin' troublesome times?"

Eli thought back to another time and another Indian fight. "No . . . my medicine coat came from a shaman that ran away from the Rosebud Reservation in eighty-seven. I shot his pony down at two hundred paces with my Winchester—but I was aiming for him."

"I hear'd you was good at shootin' far. How'd you miss that Injun?"

Eli laughed a little. "I believe his coat's medicine protected him from my bullet."

He remembered that fateful day: a turquoise day with cotton clouds holding over the Dakota prairie and meadowlarks whistling their songs. Suddenly the shaman had attacked on a red painted pony. He could still see the wild and angry Indian charging toward him with raven hair and white leather fringes and eagle feathers flying behind—and the horse's hooves pounding puffs of dust up through green grass.

Noodles' eyes widened. "How'd you get that jacket off of him? Them Injuns was mighty fighters and didn't take kindly to horse killin' nohow."

"When his pony went down, he took a bad tumble. He got so mad he threw his jacket off and stomped it. He didn't think its spirits had saved him. I walked over and took that magic coat for myself. He went back to the reservation without a fight. He was the only Sioux I ever saw cry. I knew the Indians were finished when I got that coat."

"You was a lucky fellow to fight off them Injuns by yourselfs. Not many folks were so favored back then."

Eli contemplated his luck and found it not that good anymore. Shooting Reuben Tugle in the knee up in Montana had turned into bad luck. Judge Bugbee had preached for an hour about Eli's crippling of crooks ... Peacock had blustered for another hour because of the sanctions imposed by the furious judge. Eli didn't understand their concern for the notorious Reuben. If he had escaped, the man would still be robbing folks at pistol point. But Peacock and the judge hadn't seen it that way, so the following day's sunrise had found Eli and Sorrowful riding toward Thistles.

"I'm presently not so favored—I got sent to this town." Scooping handfuls of water onto his face, Eli pondered his future, worrying again.

"You been hatin' this town too long. That ain't good for the soul. You best get movin' along!" Noodles stared at Eli with dark, gleaming eyes.

Eli looked back at the old white face. "Where shall I go? I've been busy with the law for more than twenty years. I don't wish to work for others, and I need the pay. I think it's best to stay till better comes along!" He rose from the tank, caught Sorrowful, lifted him over the side, stepped out himself. He slicked water from his hair and body with his hands and neckerchief and stood still to let the desert air dry the rest.

"By Jeez, let's go to the Klondike. I want to see one more herd of buffalos and one more gold stampede before I die ... maybe I could if'n you'd help me."

Eli stared at Noodles, wondering. "There's no buffalo anymore, and it's three thousand miles to the Klondike." Then he looked away, hung his head, and said, "Besides, you're too old to go and I've been told to stay."

"You don't know, might be buffalos up there—and it says in the newspaper it's the richest strike ever. I ain't too old to go. I get around good!"

"The buffalo are gone forever, old man, and so are the men who shot them down. All the boomtowns in the Dakota, Montana, and Idaho country—those places are gone, too. Now there's sodbusters and sheriffs instead. Civilized—that's what they call it. I'd like to see more wild places. I want to stop more killing and thieving before I get old like you. But what's the wisdom in quitting my duty and losing my star for a faraway place?"

"You best get over to that Joshua tree and listen to the prophets!" The old man withdrew his right arm from the water and pointed toward the sentry of the desert that stood nearby. Then he added with a yelp that knifed into the night, "You're not hearin' good counsel. You'll never see nothin' again if'n you hang 'round here!"

Eli looked into the aged eyes, then back toward the shabby town. A piano began to plunk its music, and voices sang along with melodies floating through the night. He pulled his trousers up, buttoned them, and stomped toward the revelry. He needed more, he mused, than the silence of a twisted old tree to help settle his mind—and the Good Thunder Inn had the best remedies for the end of his sad day.

CHAPTER TWO

Murder

Patches watched the stranger step through the door of the Sea Fox Tavern and search for a place to sit among the sailors and gold stampeders crowding the bar. Patrons of places edging the waterfront of San Francisco had always provided him with daily loot, and now the docks were filled with fools like never before. The rusty old *Excelsior* had steamed in from Alaska six days before with bags of gold from a place called the Klondike. Mobs of men were rushing up and down boardwalks each day trying to buy passage north, and most were easy pickings. But he'd been warned of one who needed more than a thousand dollars, and who looked to be the most dangerous of any who had come onto the waterfront.

He watched the bulldog face probe the tavern from end to end. Cold black eyes darted into every corner and ranged over every table of the darkened barroom. Suddenly the brute noticed being watched and stepped close.

Frightened, Patches snapped, "Get away from me!"

He feared the man with a fever. The black prostitute, Frissy, had told him the stranger was mad—and that he liked to kill with a knife. Patches carried a blade himself, but he dreaded blood and death. He had used his own knife for threats and escapes in the past, but never for robbery. His victims lost wallets to fast fingers, not their lives to a well-honed edge.

The bulldog face grinned and sat on a chair nearby. "I see a drunk and his purse will soon get parted!" Then after laughing at his own remark, he asked, "How much you goin' to get off these bottom fish?"

Patches stared at the stranger for a moment with cat eyes. "I'll get plenty . . . and I ain't got to cut people to death to do it!" He then scowled, thinking it would have been better to stay silent.

The ugly face sneered. "I been told you're a pickpocket. Never saw a pickpocket that was a freak before!"

Patches, his mottled red, white, and purple face enraged, reached into his trouser pocket, slipped out an ivory-handled knife, and flipped the blade open under the table. The knife's lock popped, sounding like a splitting tree branch. As the noise faded, he snarled, "You get away from me or I'll stick you bad!"

The stranger jumped away with his eyes sparking contempt. He smirked through bared yellow teeth. "You're in a bad mood today, ain't you? Got no drunk's money yet, I bet!" Then he pushed through the noisy crowd and sat on the other side of the barroom, mocking Patches whenever he glanced across.

After a few minutes, Patches got up and moved

through the bar with long, angry strides. When he reached the hallway leading to the back alley, he crouched among a stack of blackened beer barrels and spied out into the bar, waiting for the stranger to leave . . .

As night fell after the sun dipped down into the ocean, the stranger stepped out of the Sea Fox and started to march toward the outskirts of the city. He walked along, swinging his body from side to side, never looking back or to the left or right, as he climbed hills covered with castlelike homes and estates.

Later, six hours before sunup, he stopped walking and stood watching for household lights in the windows of a white mansion hovering nearby in the dark. After seeing none for several minutes, he scuttled across the lawn and slunk to the back of the home, bumping into a back iron fence on the far corner. He climbed over, stopped, listened for sounds on the other side of the wall next to him, then slid along until he felt the slant of a cellar door with his feet. He reached around, fumbled for a rusted rod he was carrying, slipped it through the loop of the door's latch, and twisted the lock free. Screws screeched as they tore from wood, but he doubted if odd noises would wake anyone at such a late hour.

He liked working in the black of night. Midnight had always been the best time to rob and kill in back alleys along waterfronts, and he thought the same hour should work well with the rich, too. Since the dock district didn't have the money he needed for the journey he wished to take, he had come up to the prosperous hills for the first time. If the night turned out as planned, he thought, he wouldn't have to come again. He just wanted enough money to buy passage to a seaport called Skagway, then to travel on to a place called the Klondike.

He levered the door open, stepped out into the black hole below, flopped the door closed over his head, and lit a Christmas candle he'd bought the previous day. It glimmered a soft light in the night, and he descended the remaining stone stairs leading into the basement with a stiff-legged bounce. The rock and mortar walls around him shone with tiny tears crafted by dark and dankness, and clots of cobwebs glittered in corners and up above in timber joists and floor planks with the same wetness.

He plodded around three separate rooms and finally found a staircase up to the first floor of the manor. He climbed the wooden steps, cringing at every creak, and pushed through a door into a kitchen smelling of baked buns and spice cakes. A doorway stood open across the room, and polished dark walnut and bright brass fixtures reflected the candle glimmer back toward him. He crept forward but saw nothing valuable and realized he would have to keep searching until he sighted a better room than this or the banquet room.

Thirty minutes passed as he moved quietly through all the rooms of the first floor. He stopped at the foot of a wide, curved, gold-banistered stairway running up along a red wall. His heart pounded as he pulled his knife from his pants pocket and held it ready in his right hand. He bounded up the steps two at a time, feeling his heart race because of the labor and the likelihood of a fight. At the top he paused for a moment to consider which room to search first as the candle glowed down the hallway. He decided to creep from door to door and listen for people along the way.

As he peeked around into empty bedrooms and storage closets, he wondered about the family's absence. At last he found an office with a massive desk, a credenza sitting behind, and leather chairs and sofas spread around. After a moment of exploring along the sides of the mahogany-paneled room, his candle's shimmer mirrored on a gray strongbox standing in a corner—but the black dial on its door crushed all his schemes. Someone would have to open the safe for him, or he would have to leave with empty pockets.

He stepped back into the hallway. A set of double doors stood closed at the end of the corridor. He padded softly to them and saw a thin streak of light through the crack in between. He stood still and listened. Moans and faint whimpers seeped through the slit. He tried the brass handles but found each one locked.

He kicked out as hard as he could against the doors' seam just below the handles. The doors split open, sounding like an explosion. At the far end of the bedroom, in the dim light of a lamp, he saw a woman with yellow hair and a nightdress of white clutching a little blond boy close by her side. They screamed as he jumped toward them, waving his knife.

"Shut up or I'll cut you!" He jumped forward again, flashing his knife with an arm thrust.

The two stopped screaming, huddled closer, then began sobbing. The stranger quickly looked around the room but saw no other person near. He wondered why the woman in white was all alone except for the boy.

"Where's your husband?" He continued to look about the bedroom.

The woman stared back with frightened brown eyes. She quieted herself a little, pursed her pink mouth, then blurted out, "He's not home!" When she sensed her stupidity, she began to cry.

"Anybody else in the house?"

The question caused the woman to burst into hysterical shrieking. The stranger leaped forward, grabbed her flaxen hair, and threw her to the floor. He slammed onto her breasts with his knees, squashing her breath away. The child darted across the room and curled bawling in a corner, wrapping his little arms around his head. The woman gasped for air.

The stranger held his knife within an inch of her eyes. "Where's the other people that live in this house? You tell or I'll kill that kid of yours—you understand?"

"There's no one. I sent them away. I'm— Please, I will do anything for you—for God's sake, don't hurt my son! I beg you, please—"

"Open the money box! Open it now! I won't hurt you or the kid if I get your money. You understand?"

The woman nodded her head in spite of the clutch of the stranger's hand in her long hair. He yanked, lifting her up without loosening his grip. She cried out in pain as she stood bent over, tethered like an animal. He yanked again, grabbed the nearby lamp, and pulled her into the hall and toward the room with the safe. He glanced at the bawling child in the corner as they passed but let the little boy stay behind.

"Open the door—do it now!" He forced the woman to her knees in front of the gray box.

The terrified woman twisted the dial back and forth. She tried three spins with unsettled hands, then two more. Shaking badly, she missed numbers each time. At last, on the fourth set of twirls, she turned and pulled the handle. Sounding like a broken bell, the door released and swung open. Astonished, the stranger sucked his breath through his teeth, whistling his surprise. Inside, three shelves sat piled high with bills and gold coins—much more than he could ever carry away just in his pockets.

He jerked his fistful of yellow hair backward. The woman shrieked as her neck and throat bowed up. Then the stranger slashed it with one flash of his knife. Instantly her shriek changed to a gurgle as blood sprayed, staining her nightdress and the floor red, then purple as her life puddled up.

The stranger pulled the woman over until her body lay flat and then dropped down on her belly with both knees. He plunged his knife into her chest and twisted the blade until a death dance began to jerk her corpse.

He dragged the body across the room and rolled it against the wall, tossing it like a ripped flour sack, but with blood pouring instead of flour. He lunged back to the strongbox, knelt down, and filled each of his pockets with ten- and twenty-dollar gold pieces and wads of bills. When his pockets bulged full, he stuffed more down the front of his shirt.

Satisfied at last, he jumped up, grabbed the light, and walked out of the room and back to the bedroom where the boy remained. The child still lay hiding his head and wailing. He grabbed the boy and cut his throat with one fatal slash just as he'd done to the mother minutes before. He then threw the bloody bundle to the floor and ran down the long hall and back to the first floor. He walked through the kitchen again, found the back door, and stepped out into the dark.

"Had to kill somebody, didn't you? You're a real cannibal, ain't you?" The voice slipped out from deep blackness.

The stranger stopped, the thrill of killing changing to shock and surprise. He grabbed his knife and snapped it open again. Its noise broke through the night with a deadly crack.

"You better get away from here, freak. I'm goin' to kill you for followin' me!" The stranger looked left and right.

Laughter bounced out of the night. Then the voice said, "You can't catch what you can't see. Better throw down some of what you took. I'll tell the police if you don't!"

"I'll tell them you did it and I took the money from

you—then they'll hang us both!" The stranger began to sneak away.

"You better give me some!"

The stranger didn't answer. He stepped out to the sidewalk and, after looking for others on the darkened street, began the long trudge back down to the waterfront.

"I'm goin' to get you—I'll make you real sorry you didn't give me some!"

The stranger didn't turn or listen. He had just enough time to repay the whore for tattling—and to get aboard the ship for the North by noon. He'd be gone to sea before anyone could catch him.

CHAPTER THREE

Turnbull

Like a courteous and alert student, Jesse Peacock faced the ebony desk with its ivory inlays and gold-leaf trim. The room around lay stone quiet, the pendulum of the great-grandfather's clock hung still, and every window stood shuttered and locked against the daylight. An electric bulb dangled down, its flare lighting the Honorable Theodore Turnbull's head as he drooped like a black and swollen bear. The Senator's wife and child were dead, murdered in the night—and Jesse supposed the call for vengeance was about to come.

He watched the Senator's features in the gloom of the room. Wrenching in pain, the face flamed with rage, then sagged into folds. Both eyes darkened with despair, and the walrus mustache drooped at the corners more than before.

"Jesse, how long have I known you . . . thirty years, maybe?" asked the Senator.

"Yes, sir . . . since the war. You were a great and courageous general to serve our nation as you did."

"You were my best officer. You never let me down. You've helped me a great deal since . . . the contributions, the votes. I want you to know how much that has meant to me all through these years."

"I've been happy to serve you, sir." Jesse sat sweating a little on his brow and under his arms.

"I've tried to help you along the way. The office you hold now—you enjoy this appointment, don't you, Jesse?" The Senator fingered his black ribbon tie.

"Yes, sir, this is a fine city, and I greatly appreciate the help you gave me in getting this office." Little sweat beads formed above his upper lip, and he tasted salt with his tongue.

Turnbull leaned farther forward and said, "I want you to think about Washington. You've served long and well as a U.S. Marshal. Your men have always been a compliment to the service. I think it's time for you to prepare for an appointment to the capital of this fine nation. How do you feel about that, Jesse?"

"It's been my wish to go there for a long time, sir."

He sensed that a killer would have to be captured before he would be invited to move. Washington had been his dream, his goal in life for many years, but now he pictured a cold-blooded murderer blocking the pathway. An ominous feeling swept his sweats away and chills chased behind.

"I want you to do something for me. I want you to find the barbarian that killed my wife and child!" Bitterness began to lift the Senator's jowls—his eyes darkened again. "I want you to find him soon. Seven days have gone by—no one knows who did it. Jesse, I want that animal arrested and hanged till he's rot-ten. I want you to get every man in your office, every man west of the Mississippi, after him. Do you understand?"

"I understand, sir!" Peacock looked away, the chill sinking deeper into his bones. Scrunching around in his chair, he asked, "Have the police told you about their investigation? Do they have any suspects?"

"They think one man did it. That's all they've said to me. They're incompetent—probably Republicans, too. They'll never help me. They can't even safeguard this city with all these gold stampeders coming in. I think one of those crazy fools did it. Every madman in this country has come to this city!" After pausing for breath, Turnbull slammed his fist down.

Jesse Peacock saw that he should calm the Senator as he had in times past. "Senator, I'll visit the chief this afternoon. He'll listen to me—I'm certain he'll help. Whoever did this terrible thing, I promise you he will be found—and soon."

Suddenly he felt his gut cramp, like it had when he and the Senator had faced Stonewall Jackson at Chancellorsville. A similar stouthearted promise had cost him dearly back then—his left arm had been blown away by cannon fire. He wondered why two ghastly murders would frighten him in the same way. He wouldn't be searching the streets himself. That assignment would be carried out by others.

Turnbull stopped blustering and fixed his eyes on Peacock. After remaining still for a moment, he whispered, "Jesse, I said earlier that you've never let me down. I want you to find the man that killed my innocent wife and boy. I loved them—" His voice choked and his eyes filled with tears. Before ducking his head, he sobbed, "You call . . . for anything . . . you just get that—"

Jesse stood, left the office, and walked out onto the street, sorrow circling his soul. Air from the ocean brushed by him, and its freshness sent shivers through his body. He pulled his coat close and turned up the crowded walkway with a choppy stride, shoving other people aside.

He soaked in the sights and sounds of the city as he plowed along, fretting about catching the killer. San Francisco sang with mobs of men preparing for their journeys to the North. Stampeders stuffed the streets with wagons and cursed at everyone standing in the way. They stacked docks with goods and screamed for stevedores to stow the stuff away—and they all called out for every woman around to come along. Every building bulged with maddened men as Jesse walked along, and he heard a hundred tooting foghorns and singing watch whistles blaring down in the ocean bay.

He turned a sharp corner, climbed cement steps, and walked through the copper doors of a gray courthouse standing alone in a town square. His footfalls echoed as he clumped up toward his office, the peaceful interior seeming to him like a funeral home after the din of the outdoors.

As he passed through the doorway, he called to a young woman dressed in a long skirt and a white buttoned bodice, "Hannah, please come to my office."

He wanted to make love to Hannah Twigg. She

was a preacher's daughter who worked hard for the U.S. Marshals' office during the week, then with her father on Sundays. High-breasted and about thirty years old, she had umber eyes, pink cream skin, and pouting rose lips that melted his spirit and made him ache inside each time he pictured touching her. But he was older, and married, and the fear of refusal had kept him silent throughout the years she'd been employed in his office.

"How is Senator Turnbull, sir?" Hannah stepped toward his desk.

"Not well and very angry. He told me to take charge . . . told me to call in every Marshal to help find the killer. I'm not sure that will be enough, there's so many gold stampeders overrunning this city." Jesse slumped into his chair and yanked at the tips of his mustache.

"What do you want me for, Mr. Peacock?" Hannah asked, smoothing her long skirt.

"Please call me by my first name . . . it's important to me. I need to talk to you." Jesse paused and looked up into her eyes. "The Senator promised Washington . . . soon . . . when I get the man who killed his wife and boy. I'll want you to come with me; you're very important. Will you think about that?" He glanced away and tried to calm himself.

Hannah's face stayed expressionless. She weighed Peacock's announcement for a long moment and then said, "I would like to continue to work for you . . . Jesse." Her face twisted as she answered, and, at the same time, she stopped patting at her skirt.

"I'm grateful you feel that way. I've worked so hard for an appointment. Have you ever seen Washington?" He looked up again and searched her eyes.

"No, Mr. Peacock . . . Jesse, I never have. Sir, why do you need me?" Hannah's mouth pinched tight.

Jesse stirred from his feelings as he recalled the Senator's demands. "The men, we need all the men to come. I want you to telegraph them—get them on the first train."

Hannah blinked. "Sir, are you certain you want them all? Do you want Mr. Bonnet? You were so angry when you came back from Montana . . . you sent him to Arizona!"

Eli Bonnet floated back into Jesse's mind. Eli remained as the last of the lawmen hired from an advertisement in the Montana Territory in 1875. The newspaper had printed, "Wanted: Young men, 20 to 30 years old, must be good horsemen and expert shots. Top pay, bachelors required." A few had been hired—and all had been killed—except for him. Long legs and Wild Bill ways had carried him through. For many years he'd been the best Deputy Marshal, but now he appeared to be a misfit. The old West had passed, and now there seemed no need for an officer who wore a Colt Peacemaker, a Sioux Indian jacket, and hair down around his shoulders.

Dropping his head, he said, "Yes, have Bonnet come, too. He'll do no good for us in Thistles. Perhaps I can use him; it seems all his old companions are passing through for the gold stampede." He then shook his head and added, "Perhaps I should take his pistol away, though. He'll likely shoot someone in the knee if I don't!"

"I'm looking forward to meeting Mr. Bonnet. You've talked so much of him. He must be an unusual man." Hannah's eyes brightened.

Peacock stared hard at Hannah, feeling threatened by her remark. He pondered the wisdom of bringing Bonnet into San Francisco. Then his pledge to Senator Turnbull ran through his mind again, and he decided not to break his word. Eli had been lucky at catching killers before.

"I promised the Senator I would see the police. You've reminded me to tell them about Eli. Send the telegrams out—I'd better do it now." He groaned as he pushed himself up from his desk.

An hour later Jesse sat across from the chief of police of the city. He suspected that the chief, an Irishman, round and gray, was not in a particularly grateful mood for the visit. Life had been fat and free for him until the *San Francisco Chronicle* had published the full-page account of the gold discovery in the North. Each day since the article, the newspaper had printed more tales of prospectors and their bags of glittering nuggets being unloaded from the old vessel *Excelsior*.

The bulletins, in turn, had infatuated everyone in the nation, except for the greasy station boss, and had caused thousands to come to the city in hopes of catching a ship. The crowds had spoiled Paddy O'Shanny's temper. And, Jesse mused, an even greater outrage had now occurred: he'd interrupted an afternoon snack.

"I've had two detectives 'signed since the lady and the wee lad got found!" The chief brushed bread crumbs from his blue coat, both hands flipping fast.

Jesse saw that he would get nothing by quarreling with the fat man. O'Shanny would just get more belligerent; then Jesse would be able to learn much less.

"I understand how difficult it must be to patrol this city. You and your men are doing splendid work. We Marshals want to help with the Turnbull investigation."

"I don't mind a wee bit of help. The Senator puttin' you up to this, is he?" Paddy O'Shanny peeked up from the front of his coat.

"He asked me to help. It isn't our wish to interfere with your good work. You must be short of men . . . there's seven or eight thousand gold stampeders in this city. We can help you find the killer in all this mess."

O'Shanny had questioned his detectives over morning coffee and plump cherry rolls. They hadn't reported any clues, their suspects had disappeared, and their tattletales had stayed quiet. He thought the Marshals might be of use—and, also, there would be someone for him to pass blame to if the search for the Turnbull killer failed.

"We've not found a man. The crowds, you know. I'll tell Jolly and O'Leary to work with you. They're fine, hardworking men, you know. They'll be glad for the help."

Jesse knew Sam Jolly and Billy O'Leary. They were not stupid and unfit detectives. The news of their bad luck at being assigned to this case sank in and made his stomach twist over; then the stitch reminded him of his other obligation.

"I'm bringing men in from other places," he told the chief. "One's worked in Montana most of his life. His name is Bonnet—Eli Bonnet. He's from the old days, still wears a Colt and his hair is long . . . like Buffalo Bill. Have your men watch out for him . . . so he doesn't trouble you."

O'Shanny let out a belch and snickered, "He'll not be a problem. He'll look like a lovely man 'mong the dregs already in this city, you know. There's bad men that have come. One cut the tongue out of a whore and beat her blind. A nasty sight it is."

"You've done good work with this city for the way it is, Paddy. I'll not take your time anymore—tell Sam and Billy my men will visit them soon. And I thank you for your time."

He stood up from his chair and reached across for O'Shanny's handshake. He then wheeled out of the room and walked back along the streets toward the courthouse, waggling his way, bouncing off people while thinking about the prostitute with the severed tongue. Sweats and chills still cursed him—and the demons that seemed always to stand in his way.

CHAPTER FOUR

Freedom

"Eli! Eli, wake up!" a voice called from the dusty hollow of the Good Thunder Inn. A hard shake on his shoulder jiggled him around, and his arm and hip ached against the boards of the floor. He opened his eyes and fought for focus, but whiskey still shaded his vision. A withered old face last seen sticking out of water came back—then his sleepy peace fell again.

"Eli! Eli, wake up! You got to wake up, Eli! You got a telegram!" yelled Noodles louder, pushing more.

"I can't read now." Eli rolled over and faced the wall of the saloon. His cramped arm prickled with pain, and his hip hurt like it would never walk again. He dreamed of a soft, quiet, and cool place to sleep in, but he didn't feel spunk enough to find it. Then the night before drifted back through his mind, and he wondered why he'd drunk so much. Finally he thought he should rouse, so he rolled once more, pushed himself up, and leaned his back against the wall, letting the sunlight shoot down and wake him.

He slid over out of the beam and blinked his eyes, clearing them to see.

Rubbing his belly and looking for his dog, he grumbled, "Get me the water bucket from behind the bar. I need to drink and wash." He then spied Sorrowful watching from across the room with unhappy eyes and pricked-up ears.

Noodles darted behind the bar and hurried back with a white-porcelain pail and a black-handled dipper. As he set the pail down, he said, "I got a telegram for you. It says you're to get to San Francisco." Then he cackled into the empty barroom, "And I'm goin' to get with you!"

Eli gulped down two dippers of water and mopped his face and neck with a sopping bar rag. He dried himself off with the same rag wrung out, looked up at Noodles' wide grin, and asked, "Where's the wire from San Francisco? I want to see it."

Noodles pulled a folded sheet from his shirt pocket and thrust it at Eli. The paper crackled as it opened, and Eli recognized the printing as fresh. The type looked black and sharp—and read exactly the way Noodles had said it would.

Date July 27 1897
    To Eli Bonnet Deputy US Marshal Thistles Arizona Assignment to San Francisco Stop Immediate transportation by rail required Stop Senator Turnbull family murdered Stop Your assistance required Stop
    From J Peacock
    US Marshals Office

Eli looked up at Noodles and said, "I've never been to a city like San Francisco." He stared at the paper and asked, "Why would they want me for murders of a senator's family?"

" 'Cause you ain't no good in Thistles and there ain't no killers out here." Noodles shook his head in disbelief and grinned again, shouting, "Get up and let's go!"

Noodles' cackling his wish to join in the journey caused Eli to study the whiskered old prospector. After a minute he asked, "Why do you want to go with me?"

"I want to go on the gold stampede, and I can get a ship out from there. That's where they're sailing from . . . there and Seattle. The newspaper says so."

"I can't go to the Klondike. Peacock has work for me," Eli complained as he walked over to a nearby table and chair, carrying the water bucket.

"Maybe you'll get to go later—you don't know! I'm goin' north anyways. I ain't goin' to stay 'round here!" Then, dancing a jig, Noodles hooted, "I'm so old I ain't goin' to stay anyplace for long, 'cept the grave." Jigging faster on the saloon's floor, he hooted louder, laughing at the same time.

Eli smiled, stood up, and tucked his shirttail into pants. "We'll go today when the light gets low. We can catch the Southern Pacific train at Cholla Flats. Go get mules from Smitty's. I'll get packs and water from Sample's after I eat breakfast. We've got a long, hard ride ahead of us. I hope you're as well as you appear to be."

"Don't worry about me!" Noodles yelled, dancing out the door.

Ten hours later they rode out of Thistles. As the mules jogged along, doves started flying back toward the horse tank, singing the end of the sun over the Rosy Buttes to the west. After an hour of trail, darkness crept down; then starlight filled the night until the sky became a frosted glow. The mules hoofed up and down the sand dunes and over the boiled rocks of the dark desert with choppy, certain feet, not needing light for sight.

At moon high, Eli pulled up and called for a cold camp for the remainder of the night. Sleeping only until the eastern sky flickered with the coming morning light, Noodles slipped out from under his blankets and started a roaring fire. Soon boiling coffee and burning bacon rolled Eli and Sorrowful from their beds, sniffing for breakfast. After eating, Eli threw their saddles, packs, and barrels of water on the mules and led the way down the trail again. The path dropped lower and traced through sages and brushes as it wove along. The sun eased up above brown, eroded mountains on the east and started to rise. When it got high and hot, they rode fast for cottonwood trees ahead and tied up in shade for the remainder of the day. Then at sundown they trotted off again.

Three nights and two mornings passed. During the third morning's sunrise, the mules tramped down a long pitch of blistering wasteland, then across a dry wash into Cholla Flats. Baked white storefronts and redbrick homes sat quietly in a circle around a sweet-water spring, a tall water tank, and a railroad station.

The station agent accidentally tipped his coffee when he saw Eli and Noodles riding toward his ticket window. A cantankerous man with a black visor and a stiff gray shirt, he liked to torment folks who needed a ride away from what he himself called "the hell-bitten land." The wet coffee stains on his clean shirt spoiled his mood even more, and he glared at the two as they marched up to his window. He didn't like the tall man with the Indian jacket and wolfish dog, and he didn't relish the dusty little prospector bouncing behind, either.

When Eli stepped up to the ticket window, the agent snarled, "What you two want?"

Eli surveyed the man for a moment and then answered, "We require tickets for San Francisco."

The agent snorted his displeasure. "You don't say! You and every mother's son think you got to go to Californy these days. Well, there ain't no room for nobody anymore, and I ain't selling tickets . . . and that dog or whatever it is can't go anyway!"

"I'm a Deputy U.S. Marshal traveling for duty. I direct you to furnish transportation for both of my friends and for myself. We don't wish to be delayed!" Eli stepped closer to the window.

The agent laughed in Eli's face, "Yes, sir, Mr. Marshal, and I suppose that dog of yours is the president of this here United States!" He then started to laugh more.

Eli's left hand shot out and grabbed the front of the agent's shirt like a snake's bite. He yanked the man forward, slamming his face against the iron bars of the ticket booth. The agent, his face squashed and bruised, shrieked and cursed but was unable to pull away. Eli removed his silver star and Colt Peacemaker with his free hand and laid them down for the man to see. Then he gave the agent another tug against the bars and said, "Your manners are bad and your arrest is near—and don't call either of my friends a dog! Now, may we have your prompt assistance?"

The blue lips blurted, "Yes, sir—I'm sorry, sir—I'll get the tickets right now. I didn't think you was a real Marshal."

"And when will the next train come in?" Eli asked, as he held tight to the man's shirt.

"Three o'clock—I can put you on the three o'clock—in a Pullman. Out at four and westbound, sir," the agent whined.

"That will be satisfactory." Eli let go of the train man and picked up his star and pistol. Then he asked, "Where can we bathe and eat before we board the westbound?"

"At Mrs. Fletcher's—over yonder." The agent pointed with a shaky finger to a house. "She's a good cook, but be careful she don't boil you in that tub of hers. She'll want to boil you like dirty underwear!"

The railroad agent produced tickets with a commotion of stub ripping and stamping. Eli and Noodles led the mules to the livery and secured an agreement from the proprietor for their return to Smitty's in Thistles. They then walked over to Mrs. Fletcher's for meals and baths.

Noodles considered traveling with Eli and Sorrow-ful a pleasant time, and he wanted to share his joy. He'd chatted endlessly since the first footfall out of Thistles; now the notion of home cooking and a train ride stirred him to one more spirited outburst as he walked up to Mrs. Fletcher's boardinghouse.

"What's to eat?" he yelled as he hit the front door.

Mrs. Fletcher, a tall, rawboned woman who had lost a husband to snakebite and children to sickness, was not afraid of anything, especially prospectors with white whiskers—and nothing made her madder than dirty men with bad manners.

"You men get out! It ain't noontime! And you two ain't eatin' here, anyways!" She raised a broom, and lifted it high enough to whack Noodles.

"Why Missus Fletcher, we been ridin' hard, and we got to eat. This here man's a Marshal. We're goin' to San Francisco to catch a murder'r. Please, ma'am, we'd be real appreciative if'n you'd help us." Noodles snatched his floppy hat off his head and held it over his heart.

"He don't look like no Marshal to me!"

"Why ma'am, this here's Deputy Marshal Bonnet from Montana. He's real famous up that way."

"I've heard the name." Mrs. Fletcher studied Eli from head to foot. "You appear to be a nice-lookin' man . . . if you'd wash, anyways." She wrinkled her nose, creasing it with little lines.

"Ma'am, I do have government work to do. We do need a meal . . . and a bath, too. I would appreciate your kindness if you could help us in any way." Eli spoke in his softest voice.

"If you want to eat, go 'round back and use the tub. And that wolf-dog's got to stay outside." Mrs. Fletcher's eyes dropped, and she started flipping her yellow-bottomed broom about the floor again.

Eli led Noodles out and around to the back of the boardinghouse. They stepped up into a closed porch with high screened windows and a stove with bubbling wash water. A giant copper tub sat in one corner, and lye soap, a scrub brush, and folded white towels lay nearby on a small four-peg table. Hooks for hanging clothes stuck out from the walls, and a green bench stood in a corner.

"Missus Fletcher don't take to dirty folks, I guess!" Noodles chuckled and walked up into the porch.

"You wash first. I need to send a telegram saying I'm on my way." Eli turned and marched back around the house again, Sorrowful padding close behind.

Two hours later, with reddened faces and wetted hair, Eli and Noodles sat down at a long dining room table. Mrs. Fletcher brought in chicken and dumplings, boiled potatoes, and a loaf of fresh-baked bread. A Baptist preacher and two merchants also appeared for the steaming meal. After the preacher's prayer, Mrs. Fletcher cleared her throat and started the meal by passing Eli the potatoes.

"Where are you bound for, sir?" the preacher asked, eyeing Eli as he picked his potatoes.

"I'm traveling to San Francisco." Eli passed the potatoes to the preacher.

"You don't look like a man of the city. What is your business there?" The preacher speared four potatoes onto his plate.

"I'm a Deputy U.S. Marshal. I'm traveling to help with the murders of the Senator Turnbull family."

The preacher and the two merchants sat up straight in their chairs and stopped passing the food. Then one of the merchants remarked, "I've read about those killings. Terrible thing! The Senator's wife and boy had their throats cut! And what be your name, sir?"

"He's Eli Bonnet from Montana. He was a real famous Marshal up there!" Noodles beamed his toothless grin.

"You're the lawman that tracked Rat Nose Red down and captured him at Poison Mountain back in 1880. Caught the meanest stage robber ever, you did!" added the merchant.

"I wanted to stop his business of robbing and killing. He was a fearless man and made a good fight of it till the end." Eli passed the chicken and dumplings along.

"What has been your work since Montana became a state and the old West is now gone?" asked the preacher.

"My work is not the same. The Indians are all gone to reservations, and most outlaws are no more. Folks are now civilized, I guess." Eli lowered his head and concentrated on his food.

"I'm goin' to the Klondike, I am," Noodles said through a mouthful of buttered bread. "It's the biggest gold stampede ever, and I aim to see it. By Jeez, it'll be like the old days up there."

The preacher swallowed food in a chunk and looked up. "Many are going, but it cannot be true that gold is lying on the ground. I believe the newspapers of this country are offering temptations to things that do not exist. Men's lives will be lost before this thing is done!"

"I want to go. The men off the *Excelsior* won't have to work again . . . and the *Chronicle* says they still have their mines!" the second merchant argued, reaching for more gravy. "I would build a saloon. That Dawson City will need a saloon, don't you think?"

"The miners make the gold and the saloons make the money. I've seen it that way since Deadwood. It ain't goin" to be different in Dawson!" Noodles cackled.

"This land must stop the evil ways of those who tempt our good men with liquor and song. I am working for the time when all liquor will be unlawful. We must stop the sins of men for the sake of their souls—is that not right, Mr. Bonnet?" The Baptist preacher's eyes narrowed.

Eli stared at the parson for a moment. "Those that you turn to prayer are those that I need not arrest." He ducked his head to his dinner plate again.

The conversation slacked as each man cleaned his plate and left the table. The merchants returned to their work, and the preacher, after bestowing God's blessings upon Mrs. Fletcher, departed to pray over a man on his deathbed. Eli and Noodles moved into a tidy parlor and waited for their meals to settle and for the train to come in. Noodles drifted into sleep, and his sniffling rhymed with the creaking of a grasshopper hiding in the room. The hours after lunch slipped by, then a lonely whistle wailed far out in the desert. The lonesome call sounded again, creeping closer in the distance.

"Old man, the train's coming." Eli stood up from his chair.

Noodles sat up and yawned. He looked around with foggy eyes and then said, "Sure had a funny dream. Dreamed about a white mountain. Biggest darn mountain I ever seen!" He sat straight up, fluffed his whiskers, and reached for his outfit sack.

CHAPTER FIVE

San Francisco

The train swayed and clacked along the tracks in an endless rhythm of sound and movement. At first it chased through desert with saguaro cactus standing tall, their odd arms reaching for indigo sky, and with pale green sage, creosote, and Joshua trees fluffing the ground and hiding the harsh earth. Then low mountains, molasses-colored, raised up as the locomotive charged west blowing black smoke and belching steam that flashed away like ghosts in hard sunlight. When the summits got high, junipers and pinyons gripped the rocks, and then, as the train rumbled down the other side, the land began to change to a plentiful green. Twisted trunks of gray oak, red poles of pine, and shiny eucalyptus covered the round hills and gentle valleys where the bountiful soil of California lay. Farms and neat, painted towns and villages looked across wandering rivers, with orchards heavy with ripe fruit on the other side. As the train thundered by, people looked up with cheerful, curious faces—and Eli thought he could see a little envy in their eyes.

The train bulged with men roaring to get to the

North. Passengers crowded into corners, tugged and shoved at each other, and shouted out a common message with their mouths. They were going for gold and would find glory and prosperity in every place and thing. Failure wasn't speculated and fear lay in the past. Coffee flowed and smoke rolled as their noisy prophecies worked into the night; the excitement ricocheting through the passenger cars made their sleep fitful.

Noodles melted into the mob, and his cackles and hoots mingled with the others in celebration of the stampede. He had been on a few before, but this one seemed best.

Eli bedded Sorrowful down in the mail car with a bespectacled postal clerk and then meandered himself. As he passed from car to car, he saw faces that had been in the Dakota and Montana Territories during gold stampedes in times past. Two were prospectors, but three others were gambling men. He had seen this before, cardsharps following spirited prospectors and miners. But he knew the fires of a gold stampede embraced all kinds, and the Klondike wouldn't be any different.

"Silent Sam and the Montana Kid are on the train," Eli said when he saw Noodles again. "I believe they've attended every gold stampede since Deadwood."

"The Montana Kid is about as old as I am. He ain't no kid anymore!" laughed Noodles. "He and Sam were in a fifty-thousand-dollar poker game in Butte one time. Biggest game in Montana that ever was!"

"They're square gamblers, but too expert for most men. They make their money running faro games, then lose it to each other in poker games."

Noodles laughed again. "Gamblin' money ain't got no home. By Jeez, those fellows ain't afraid of havin' empty pockets by mornin', I'll tell you!"

"The West must be finished. Sam and the Kid wouldn't leave for other places if there was anything waiting back there." Eli's face fell, long and frowning.

As he'd crossed the West, he recalled, so had others. He had passed from the Black Hills, through Diamond City, Butte, and Bannack. The gamblers had always followed along. They were men who clung to the freedoms of the frontier; they were camp followers, sometimes camp robbers; and they pursued their livelihood with the same passion as did the prospectors and miners that ran before them. Everyone had eagerly awaited their arrival in each new gold town. The gamblers were the money changers. They provided the amusement for the long, cold nights. Their gaming houses and saloons signaled to everyone that a town was being settled—and that the new site was ready for merchants and bankers next.

Eli and Noodles sat down in the dining car over coffee and grew more gloomy and silent. The thoughts that the gamblers were leaving the West for good, and that they, too, had crossed its boundaries, sent sadness into their souls. Each could recall their fording of the Missouri River and the timeless expanse of the land when he had first gazed west.

Their youth and energy had been spent beating back
threats thrown into their paths. Indians and outlaws,
bears, panthers and snakes, whores, poverty and pri-
vation, the chilling cold and the searing heat—they
had experienced all of those things and more. But
now it all lay behind them, far to the east, gone forever . . . and their hearts longed for another chance
at times and things they had left behind.

"I thought I'd be dead and buried before the West
was gone," Noodles said, shaking his head. "It never
occurred to me that I'd run out of places to prospect.
When I poled up the Missouri, there weren't nothing
but wilderness and Indians . . . and buffalos. By Jeez,
sometimes the prairie would turn black with buffalos. They would make so much noise runnin'—you
couldn't hear yourself thinkin'. That sure was a
sight." He stared out the window at the land going
by, and his face grew plain and white.

Eli looked at Noodles' unhappy face, and he felt
pity for the prospector. The old man was leaving his
home, and time and age would never let him return.
His only belongings were a pick, a pack, a rusty old
gold pan, and a poke full of gold nuggets found
somewhere. Eli wondered why Noodles wanted to
risk his last days and few possessions on a wild chase
toward some promised land.

"Why do you keep prospecting, old man? The
Klondike is a ways to go, and good luck may not be
there for you," he asked, frowning.

Noodles' face brightened, and his cheer came
back. "I've always found gold—a little here, some

there. Sold my mines as soon as they proved up. I just want to keep on prospectin'. I ain't no miner!"

"Then what will you do if you find gold in the Klondike?" Eli's eyes opened wide in astonishment.

"Keep on prospectin' till the money's gone!" hooted Noodles. Then he laughed and slapped his thigh. "By Jeez, ain't nothin' better than lookin' 'round the next mountain. That's why I go!"

Eli pondered Noodles' wanderlust. Prospecting for gold but not for money didn't fit well in his mind. He weighed the idea against his own pursuits of the past, but that confused him more. Most men he'd known had robbed and killed for a few dollars. Now he sat across from an old man who didn't want any riches. He wondered about Noodles' well-being in the head.

"The Klondike seems a hard direction to go. I think most men will want more than the other side of a mountain if they can make it there. They'll want the mother lode—" Eli paused, then he shook his head. "You shouldn't go, if you don't want to get rich?"

Noodles wrinkled his nose and smoothed his whiskers. "Eli, I don't need more money at my age. All I want is to keep Providence off for long as I can . . . and maybe have a good time doin' it." Then he chuckled. "I know from gold stampedes I been on before, by the time I get to the Klondike, the good stakin' will be gone and there'll be nothin' waitin' for me. It's been that way with every stampede I ever been on. I'll have to go 'round to the next mountain if'n I want to find my gold."

"In the gold towns I've been to," said Eli, "most get heartbroke and busted. Then I have to stop their robbing and killing. All that's ever around the next mountain is more outlaws running away from me."

"You never seen nothin' but the bad side of people, Eli. You best come to the Klondike with me. There ain't no more outlaws like in the old days anyways— and you'll just keep on mopin' 'round if'n you stay here. Maybe we'll get to see more buffalos, like I said before."

Eli looked hard at Noodles. "I've told you, old man, there's no buffalo anymore—and I can't go to the Klondike. I've got to do my duty!"

Seven blasts of the engine's whistle stopped their conversation as the train gathered speed running downhill. They leaned toward the windows and stretched to see ahead. An unsettled blue sea of salt water came into view first; then they saw a bright city spread all over the slopes and along the shores.

Noodles put his nose to the glass, paused, and then said, "Would you look at that? That's one of the prettiest sights I've ever seen."

The train came into the station with a great screech and roar; then its passengers flung open the doors and leaped to the platform with shouts of joy. The first part of their journey was done. Now they could get on to the North.

The platform became a mass of stampeders struggling to find their grips and gear. Eli and Noodles got off the train and fought through the maddened mobs squeezing into the station house. When they reached the center of the lofty chamber, they stopped and stood together. Eli, with his Indian jacket on and Noodles close by his side, stared at the turmoil. The many bystanders dressed in dark, vested suits, with black bowlers on their heads made him feel outlandish in spite of the disorder.

"Mr. Bonnet, Mr. Bonnet, is that you?" a woman's voice called out.

Eli spied a young woman standing apart, primly tall, dressed in dark clothes, her head topped by a gray hat. She stepped forward, leaned close, and asked, "Are you Eli Bonnet, Marshal of Montana, and from Arizona, too?"

"I am . . . and what is your name, ma'am?" Eli's face wrinkled, perplexed by the woman in front of him.

"I'm Hannah Twigg. Mr. Peacock has sent me to fetch you. How was your trip, sir?"

"Noisy and crowded, but I'm well, thank you, ma'am. And why hasn't Jesse come himself?" he asked, a little perturbed.

"He's meeting with Senator Turnbull. I wanted to meet you. I asked to come. I work for Mr. Peacock."

Eli's face wrinkled more. He had spent all his life in a land that did not permit women to work within the business of law. Most women were married, he thought, and stayed busy with their husbands, children, and homes. And others were prostitutes and gambling-hall girls who danced at night for their living. But standing before him was a woman, dark tresses, all proper with white blouse buttoned nearly

to her chin, saying she worked in the offices of the
U.S. Marshals.

Noodles, wrinkling his face also, asked, "By Jeez,
you ain't a lawman or somethin', are you?"

Hannah smiled and looked over at him. "No. I
type letters and records. I keep all the files true. I
work in the office—but not like the men. And who
are you, sir?"

"Just call me Noodles, like most folks say. I'm Eli's
friend—and I'm goin' to the Klondike."

"You and many thousands more, as well you can
see!" Hannah smiled again. "Why don't you gentlemen get your belongings, and I'll take you to the
hotel. There's a room reserved for Mr. Bonnet."

"We need to return to the mail car and get Sorrowful and my gear. Measured by most men I see here,
I've not got much." Eli waved toward the mass of
gold stampeders stacking bags and boxes nearby. "I
wonder what they'll do when it's time to carry all
they have on their backs over mountains!" He shook
his head and turned to leave.

"And who's Sorrowful?" Hannah asked, furrowing
her brow.

"That's Eli's best friend—but he's a dog!" Noodles
followed Eli out of the station, giggling through his
white beard.

All three pushed their way through the crowds to
the platform beside the mail car. Eli jumped up into
the open doorway and disappeared into the dark hollow of the car. Suddenly there was a great cry from
inside. He lunged into view again, gripped the black
iron bar next to the door, and swung out, peering

into the crowd. He cried out again, "Sorrowful, where are you? Someone has taken Sorrowful!" Then, leaping down onto the ground, he ran, leaving Hannah and Noodles to hear him call three times more, then become silent . . .

CHAPTER SIX

Folly

Hannah stood on the platform with her mouth open and her face crooked. Jesse Peacock's considerable distress over her meeting Eli Bonnet alone, his worry that something peculiar might spoil the day, ran back through her mind. She feared the price she would have to pay when he learned what had just happened . . . and after his long scolding, too. She'd just learned how to endure his unsettling affection for her while at work, but now, she thought, that might have changed forever.

"What is that man going to do, for goodness' sake?" she asked as she stood dumbfounded.

Noodles, less shocked but still surprised, mumbled his reply, "Why, ma'am . . . I guess he's run off to find his dog!"

"He can't do that. Mr. Peacock will be furious! What on earth will I say?" She balled her hands into fists, then stomped one foot.

"Ma'am, that dog's Eli's best friend. Sorrowful's saved him a few times. He ain't goin' to be happy till he gets him back."

Hannah remained angry. "We telegraphed Mr.

Bonnet so he could help find the man that killed Senator Turnbull's wife and child. My goodness, we can't have him running after a dog. He's a U.S. Marshal. He must come back!"

Noodles stared at Hannah, startled, not believing what he had just heard. The lives of men of the mountains and the prairies depended on the animals that served them. In turn, the kind and decent gave back deep and loyal affection. He couldn't understand her reasons for annoyance. It seemed odd to him that a woman would think in such a way. In his mind, a lawman of the West went his own way, answering to no one, especially not to a woman.

He shuffled his feet and tilted his head. Hannah and the railroad station noise gave him pause to reply. Finally he said, "I guess I ought to get someplace to stay." Then he hung his head down and murmured, "I'd hoped he'd go to the Klondike with me."

Hannah faced Noodles and stared back for a moment. "I think he'll go there—or to a place like that—when Mr. Peacock hears of this!" She spun, turning her back on Noodles.

They walked out of the station, Hannah leading, and caught a buggy into the city. At the hotel intended for Eli, Hannah sent Noodles up to the rented room to store his baggage. While she waited for him to return, she pondered the man she had met only a moment ago. She thought him handsome, with his sun-weathered features, flowing hair, and sturdy brown eyes that made her heart want to fidget. His white leather jacket, beaded with blue and crimson crosses and hung with feathers and fringes,

had startled her with its mysterious charm. His anguish and the quickness of his body as he hurtled
into the crowd still glowed in her mind. She thought
it must have been as quick as a panther chasing a
deer. She wasn't accustomed to men who behaved
unpredictably. The men around her plodded about
with somber faces and fretted away their days wondering what others might say. She could sense that
this man was different—but he'd caused her serious
trouble, and she felt peeved about that.

When Noodles came back down, they went into
the dining room to a blue-cloth-covered table and ordered black coffee and pumpkin pie with whipped
cream. The waiter fussed around, muttering about
Noodles' penniless appearance, but Hannah's un-
friendly mood frightened him away.

"How long have you known Mr. Bonnet?" she
asked.

"Since he came to the Dakota Territory after the
war. He was a rebel kid that fought with Stonewall
Jackson till the Wilderness, then with Jeb Stuart after that."

"How old is Mr. Bonnet?" Hannah wrinkled her
brow.

"He ain't yet fifty. I guess he was fifteen or sixteen
when he come West."

"My goodness, that means he was only ten years
old or so when he was a soldier. He was still a child!"
Her eyes blinked disbelievingly.

"Many Rebels were . . . and they 'bout whipped
the Union at that. Might of done it if'n Lee wouldn't
have ordered Pickett to charge."

"Does he ever speak of the Civil War?" Hannah stopped sipping her coffee.

"Not much. Once he said he saw a thousand soldiers layin' dead. Said they looked like logs heaped 'round, they was so many."

"Why would men do that to each other?" Hannah shook her head sadly.

"Men ain't smart. They're just God's dumb creatures. Sometimes it take a lot of death to keep 'em from gettin' too fond of killin' other people."

Noodles' reflection brought silence for a short time. They drank their coffee and Noodles chewed his pie, trying to appear poised and well-bred whenever the waiter glanced their way. His make-believe made Hannah smile. She liked the old prospector with his bright manners and quick wisdom. And it was remarkable, she thought, that he seemed spry enough in mind and body to travel on with the great stampede of men to the North.

Then Noodles' liveliness gave her an idea. She asked, "Would you go with me to search for Mr. Bonnet?"

Noodles bounced upright in his chair. "By Jeez, you bet I will. But you got to help me, too. I don't know how to get on a boat . . . ain't never been to sea before."

"I need to go back to the Marshal's office for just a moment. You wait here in the hotel until I return. Then we'll look for Mr. Bonnet and buy you passage."

Hannah walked out of the hotel and took a buggy to the courthouse. During the drive, she decided that she wouldn't tell Jesse Peacock for at least one day about Eli Bonnet's chase after his dog. She would protect him with a lie. The decision troubled her soul, but she felt compelled to shield him, and herself, from Peacock's fated outburst for a little while.

When she reached Jesse Peacock's office and looked in the door, she saw him sitting at his desk, drooping like a weary pallbearer. She cleared her throat and asked, "What's wrong, Mr. Peacock?"

He shot her a dissatisfied look. "The Senator's in an ugly mood. Paddy O'Shanny's men have nothing yet . . . and in the end, I'll get the blame. Did you find Eli?"

"Yes, he looked as you described and was easy to find. His travel was tiring because of the crowded train . . . so he's resting for a day. I felt you wouldn't mind."

Pausing before he answered, Jesse straightened in his chair. "Perhaps that's best. I'm not in the mood for meeting with Eli now."

"Sir . . . Jesse, there's one more thing. May I have the rest of the day for myself? I promised a friend of Mr. Bonnet's that I would help book passage to the Klondike. He's a nice old man . . . a real prospector from the West. I want to help."

Jesse Peacock paused for another moment and searched Hannah's eyes curiously. It was unusual for her to ask for favors of any kind. He decided the request was harmless enough. "You can if you wish. I'll not need you for the remainder of the day," He then asked, "What's the old man's name?"

"Noodles. He said people call him Noodles." Hannah smiled as she pictured her new friend.

Jesse Peacock smiled back. "I know of Noodles. He's a little bit of legend from the old days. Finds gold, then he's off for another place. Not surprising he's going to the Klondike, though I would think he'd be too old to travel that far by now."

"He seems lively enough to me. I'll see you tomorrow." Hannah turned away from the door, still feeling brightened.

During the ride back to the hotel, she wondered about her wish to find Eli Bonnet. She also weighed the sense of searching for him with an old prospector who had never been to San Francisco before. Her life had suddenly tilted to one side, and the fabric of her past, which had always held her together, seemed to be fraying apart. She had used deception and lies to make her way, and seemingly toward a man she had seen for only a moment. Perhaps, she decided, the gold stampede and the dreadful murders of the Turnbull family were affecting her judgment.

When she entered the lobby, she found Noodles close to the front desk, gaily amusing two stylish ladies with his antics. He spied her at once and came bounding over. "Where we goin' to look for Eli?" he hollered.

"We'll go down to the waterfront. I think that will be the best place to begin . . . and we can purchase passage for you to the Klondike at the same time."

"I'm ready to go!" The old man headed toward the door.

They worked their way downhill toward the docks and ships, casting about in side streets and alleys, searching through the pedestrians who scurried about. It was a new experience for both of them: Hannah hadn't visited the seaport side of the city before, and Noodles was exploring the largest town of his life. After a short time, they began to enjoy their adventure: the snooping, the chatting with strangers, and the spectacle of characters along the bay.

Daylight soon faded, and darkness crept in at the ends of alleys and at the sides of buildings, where lamps couldn't glow. Streets grew indistinct, and faces were lost to view. Sooty shadows danced, and the cries of commerce heard during the day changed to howls in the night from bars and brothels along the way.

"We need to catch a carriage away from here." Hannah peered up and down the darkened streets.

"I been thinkin' that, but I ain't seen none," said Noodles, as he, too, peered around.

"Let's walk along till we reach better light. Perhaps we can find a ride this way." Hannah pointed toward a brighter building that appeared to be a large, busy barroom. As they fronted a blackened alley on the street, two men, masked by high-collar coats and bandannas, leaped out of the dark and blocked their path. Without warning, one struck Noodles down with a blow from a club. The other grabbed Hannah with his fat arms and strangled her around the neck and chest. She shrieked as loudly as she could, but he choked her breath away, clenching three times from behind. Then he dragged her back into the alley.

"Get the old-timer in here. He's the one I saw buy the ticket with the nuggets," the fat one growled.

"Shut her up. I'll get 'im," the other man grunted as he slid Noodles like a sack.

Hannah began to twist, hit, and kick with all her remaining strength and spirit. She got partially loose and screamed three times into the night. The man cuffed her head down onto the bricks and got a better grip, a hand over her mouth, then a knee below her breasts. She tried hitting and kicking again, but the man was too heavy and strong.

"I said shut her up. Somebody'll come!" The man clutching and tearing at Noodles' pockets looked back and forth nervously.

"I will . . . I want to ride 'er when you're done."

"I don't know—somebody might come. I want to get out of here. There ain't no way out except to the street."

"Quit cryin'. Come here and help hold 'er!"

The two then began to work as one and set about spreading and pinning Hannah's arms and legs. Though she squirmed and howled under the hand crushing her face, her muffled cries sounded for only a short distance. But the noise from her fight was enough to hide the clop-clop of boots running fast up the street and into the alley.

The fat-armed man heard the threat first and turned to look. He caught a kick in the face and flew flat onto the cemented blocks of the alley. The other jumped away from Hannah's head, slipped by, and ran, bolting toward the street—and into better light. Suddenly an explosion filled the alley. Hannah screamed wildly again. Then another cry covered her shriek as the fleeing man went down and clutched his knee, where he had just been shot.

"Mr. Bonnet, you've come—" Hannah cried, recognizing Eli's jacket in the dark. "They've killed Noodles!" She rolled toward the old man, who lay a short distance away.

Eli leaped to her side. "Miss Twigg, what are you doing on the docks? Where is Noodles?" He quickly looked around.

"He's over there!" She pointed to the side of the black alley.

Eli rushed to Noodles, crumpled near the wall to which Hannah had pointed. He put his ear to Noodles' chest, then to his mouth and nose. He called, "He's still alive, and his heart and lungs are strong! I think he's just knocked senseless. Come try to wake him. I need to make sure that fellow I kicked stays down." He hurried over to the man he'd booted in the face, knelt, and poked him, but the man stayed still.

Eli returned to Noodles. Hannah was on her knees by his side, trying to revive him. She continued to sob and shake as she worked on the old man with tender persistence.

"Miss Twigg, are you hurt or harmed in any way?" Eli asked, crouching close by and attempting to study her face in the darkness.

"No—not harmed bad. But they beat and scratched me so much. I'm not able to stop crying yet. I'll be better in a moment. Oh, Mr. Bonnet, I've never been more afraid in my life."

"Quick, I want you away from here. Come with me!" He lifted Noodles' body and headed for the street. He stopped near the man who lay rolling and moaning and clutching his knee where the bullet had struck. "If your companion gets up, tell him to stay. If not, I'll shoot him as I've shot you. I'm a Deputy Marshal, and I will be back to arrest you and your friend soon!" He stepped past after hearing a moan.

Eli carried Noodles, with Hannah staying close by his side, to the Bootlegger's Inn, a bright, busy pub not far from the alley. He burst through the door, then stopped for an instant. The sight of Noodles' limp form and Hannah's bruises, smudges, and torn dress quieted everyone in the room. Eli stepped forward toward the Bootlegger's two bartenders.

"This man and woman need help—we need a doctor!"

One bartender hurried to a telephone box on a nearby wall, cranked hard, and yelled for the operator to send an ambulance. The other jumped over the bar and ran, along with several customers, to help Hannah. Eli walked forward with Noodles and laid him gently on a bare wood table, using bartenders' towels for a pillow. Hannah sat down near the table, and a pudgy waitress started dabbing and cleaning her face and pinning her torn clothing. The bartender who had telephoned pressed a fresh wet towel on Noodles' brow and probed for cuts and broken bones. Noodles stirred a bit, crying out at the touch of the towel.

Eli shouted to the people crowding around, "Care

for this old man and the lady in the best way you can. I need to arrest the two that did this before they get away!" He sprinted for the door.

"Mr. Bonnet, please come back for me. When you're done—come back. I'll wait for you." Teardrops streamed from the corners of Hannah's eyes, and she shivered again.

Eli stopped, turned, and looked back at her. He stared for a moment, then said, "I'll come back after I finish this business. You get better and see after Noodles for me." He spun around once more and pushed through the door.

CHAPTER SEVEN

Bewilderment

"Thank you for saving Hannah, but I think you caused the trouble," Jesse said from across his desk. "And I see your pistol found its mark again." He sat eyeing Eli, waiting for an answer.

Eli frowned and thought about Jesse Peacock's renewed disapproval of him. Rather than seeing their relationship grow stronger because of their shared experiences, he'd only found condemnation through the years. The dispute seemed to be centered on the handling of outlaws. Peacock had grown more compassionate as time had passed, but Eli felt more hostile. The chase and capture didn't excite him as it had when he rode as a youthful deputy on the frontier. He'd wearied of being stabbed and shot while pursuing men for their lawlessness.

He also wondered about Peacock's intolerance of Rebels like himself from the War between the States. The animosity between the North and the South seemed present during their infrequent visits, though they had never talked of it. And Eli had never told of the time he'd stood over Jesse lying with an arm blown away during a battle near Chancellorsville. He wondered if Jesse knew of that first confrontation so many years ago.

Finally he said, "I got one down, but the other was running. I couldn't leave Miss Twigg. I didn't want him to get away . . . so I shot him in the leg."

After a moment Peacock answered, "For Hannah's sake, I won't fault you for shooting, but that man will now have to live with one leg. The doctors had to remove the other."

"He'll find it troublesome to rob and assault women again. Honest work will be the best thing for him to do from this time on!"

"Eli, it's not the old days anymore. We're near a new century, and our work has changed. I've told you before to keep that pistol tucked into your belt. It's not your privilege to judge people guilty. I've told you before to bring those that you arrest to the courts— they get to decide! Your days of shooting people must stop, do you understand?" Jesse Peacock leaned angrily across his desktop.

Eli turned his head and watched drizzle squiggle down the windows of the office. He felt his own anger rise, but then he got control of it by recalling his allegiance to law and order and to the service in which he had spent so many years. And he realized it would be a waste of time to sit and argue.

"I'll not shoot unless I'm shot at. I give you my word." Eli returned his attention to Peacock.

Jesse Peacock, calming himself, said, "I accept that from you. You've broken no promises to me, or to any man I know. I respect you for that—not many people are so persuaded."

"Tell me about the murders and who might have done it. The wire directed me to come, but said nothing more."

"Servants found Senator Turnbull's wife and little boy dead in their home—throats cut—and Mrs. Turnbull stabbed once, under the ribs." Peacock pointed to his chest with his finger. "The city's detectives, Sam Jolly and Billy O'Leary, were there within an hour of the telephone call from the housekeeper. Someone broke into the cellar, went up through the house, kicked in the master bedroom door. Mrs. Turnbull appeared to have been forced to open the strongbox in the Senator's office. The detectives believe one or two men were in the home, but they think the same man did both killings. The motive seems to have been robbery. There's no clues, no snitches, and, to make matters worse, the city is filled with madmen from all around the world, any one of whom might have done it."

Eli squinted his eyes and asked, "What was in the strongbox—how much money?"

"The Senator told the detectives there were gold coins and paper bills in the box. He hasn't said an exact amount . . . doesn't want the newspapers to publish this thing . . . the amount . . . you understand. I hope you'll respect his wish and not talk about the money."

Eli rubbed his bristly beard from the day before and said, "We need to find someone who's suddenly rich but still dresses as a poor man. Someone who looks like a ragged robber but who is spending on things unlike his prospects."

Peacock shook his head. "There are many of those in this city now. I'm not sure how anyone will find the one that's guilty. And if we do—there seem to be no witnesses. Sam and Billy have questioned all the neighbors. No one saw or heard a thing."

"I believe someone saw ... or heard. This deed will come to light like most I've chased to the end."

"I hope so. The Senator is furious. He's blaming the police now, but it will be us if we don't find the killer soon. It's important that we work as hard as we can and don't do otherwise until we find the guilty one. Do you understand?"

Eli hesitated, then said, "I want to work the docks. Most of the outlaws seem to be down there. I think that's the place to find the killer ... or those that know him. And I will look the same as most of the gold stampeders, so the one I want won't be afraid."

"I've not assigned you to any place. Work the docks if you like. Your idea of stirring with the crowd may be a good one. Something might be learned that will help us. Just remember—I want no trouble, so keep yourself busy with what I've told you to do."

Eli nodded his head, stood, and began to walk out. Just before reaching the door, he stopped, turned, and looked at Jesse Peacock again. After a pause, he asked, "Where will I go when this is done?"

Peacock stared back for a moment. At last he said, "If you catch the killer, to a place that pleases you." Then he looked away and turned back to his paperwork.

Eli walked out of the courthouse and mixed in with the busyness on the streets. He felt old desires swell within him, but nagging uncertainty, too. Stalking a killer in a clogged city felt new to him, and stalking someone who killed women and children without reluctance seemed an ugly prospect. He needed Sorrowful to guard his backside—but now, with Sorrowful missing, Noodles would have to do in the pinch.

When he opened the door to his hotel room an hour later, he found Noodles napping. He called out above the old man's snoring, "Wake up, old man. I've got work for you!"

Noodles sat upright and rubbed the sleep from his eyes. "What we goin' to do? I just was takin' a little snooze till you got back."

"I want you as my deputy if your head is well. I need to find a fellow who kills with a knife . . . and I need to find Sorrowful if we can."

"By Jeez, I'll be your deputy. My head feels good, just a little sore where I got hit. That ain't goin' to slow me down none. What did that Peacock fellow tell you?"

"About a bad fellow who slashes throats, but he didn't say much else. The police haven't a notion. And perhaps I'm not required for this business."

Noodles looked puzzled, then frowned. "Why do you say that? You're the best Marshal there is—why wouldn't they want you here?"

"Perhaps the Senator said I should be. But Jesse Peacock thinks otherwise."

Noodles' frown grew deeper. "You been wearin' your magic coat all the time lately. You must be expectin' trouble if'n you're doin' that."

"Maybe for good luck, too, old man. I'll need some before I get done with this."

Eli returned to the streets, with Noodles bouncing along behind him. They moved through busy clumps of gold stampeders, hucksters, shippers, and townsmen—everyone dodging, squirming, and tumbling over boxes, bags, and bystanders. Catcalls, curses, and whistles filled the spaces between buildings and ricocheted from side to side. The noisy commotion corrupted everyone with the same madness and compelled all to shout so they might be heard by their companions.

By early evening Eli had led the way to the waterfront and stopped near the barroom where Hannah and Noodles had been attacked. He tugged Noodles close, around a corner and away from the endless noise.

"Stay near but behind me. Don't act like you're my friend. Watch those around me and yell out if you see any danger. I'll walk from place to place asking about the murders. No one will think you are with me if you're watchful. I look different from most—if the killer or someone who knows him is around, he'll follow to see who I am. You must see who he is first."

Noodles beamed his toothless grin in delight. "I can do that. But how we goin' to find Sorrowful?"

"We'll go slowly and give you time to ask about a dog. Tell everyone you want one strong and smart enough for the Klondike. Say you are old and need help. We can only hope you will be told about Sorrowful."

Both melted into the turmoil again and drifted from saloon to saloon. Eli questioned every bartender and waitress, prostitute and gambler, and any resident of the waterfront he could find. All listened, shrugged shoulders, and shook their heads. Most knew of the murders, but none seemed to know any suspect.

Eli judged San Francisco to be like other towns. Outlaws would hang together. They would favor saloons, gambling halls, and brothels with their business, and someone would know their secrets. A killer who slashed with a knife would be known by most, and his companions would give him up if they became more afraid of the law than of him.

It was a matter of time and diligence, he thought. A lawman needed to search and question, find out about money not fairly earned, and persuade those who kept outlaws as friends to tell about wrongdoing. During his time in the West, he'd found that everyone feared a killer and most would help catch one. Danger waited for anyone who gave a man the chance to kill again.

"I ain't seen a soul followin' you, and I ain't findin' out nothin' about dogs," Noodles said, yawning wearily during a rest in the dark where they couldn't be seen standing together.

"I've not learned anything from those I've questioned either. We'll go and sleep. Tomorrow we'll do as we did today. Someone knows about this thing. I'll work till I find him." Eli turned toward their hotel.

"If'n you can't, are you goin' to the Klondike with me?"

"I'll go where Peacock sends me . . . and I think not to the Klondike. And you're too old to go. You should stay with me."

"Eli, I ain't too old to go. Anyways . . . even if'n I am, I'd rather die there than here. I've lived my life chasin' gold, and I'm goin' to die chasin' it, too." Noodles followed a short distance behind Eli.

Noodles' declaration silenced Eli. He had not thought about the end of one's life. It seemed better not to tempt an end before one's time, but then spirit, determination, and the will to live on seemed most important of all. Noodles' determination to go on to the Klondike began to look sensible—and Eli began to wonder if he should go, too. There would be nothing for him after his time in the city. And Peacock would send him back to Thistles, or to some other place like that. Wherever it was, he knew he would never be able to find the West that he had once lived and loved. Those times were past, lost forever, and they had to be only bittersweet memories for the remainder of his life.

CHAPTER EIGHT

Frissy

With the purple bruises faded and the puffiness gone, Hannah felt less disgraced when people looked at her face. The assault had troubled her more than any other event in her life. At first the bruises couldn't be covered, so she had stayed at home. Later, the Marshals' office, with its infrequent visitors, became her refuge from curious gawking. But now with her appearance and spirit nearly restored, she wanted to be busy again.

Eli Bonnet had touched her heart. Hearing him cry out, seeing him run after his dog, then suddenly appear in time to save her had softened her soul like no other person had done before. She found herself dreaming through parts of her days, a habit that puzzled her because she had never been so smitten before.

The habit of worship had not rewarded her as promised by her father. She'd prayed as hard as any woman for a man who could catch her heart, but none had ever appeared. Dreary, skinny ones from church and a few merchants' sons had courted her, but the idea of marriage to any one of them had seemed repulsive. She wanted a man with a pleasant face, a strong body, and a confident manner— someone who could make her mind and body give out their joyful promise. But all the praying, waiting, and wishing had yielded nothing. She still lived and slept alone.

"You seem lost in thought, daughter. Are you feeling well?" her father asked, interrupting her thoughts during breakfast.

"Yes . . . I was thinking of Mr. Bonnet." She disliked sharing secret feelings with her father. But there was no one else to trust, and she didn't want to lie.

Her father, waiting a moment, asked, "Have you seen Mr. Bonnet again?"

"No . . . but I want to. I admire him so much for what he did. My life might have ended, and Noodles', too, if it had not been for him."

Her father frowned, then said, "You should be grateful for all your saviors, my dear, but adulation belongs only to Jesus. Mr. Bonnet is a rough and godless man . . . not one I would advise for you. Please don't fill your mind with praise for him."

"Papa, I've spent all my life in worship. I think, at this point, you needn't remind me of my obligation to Jesus. In regard to Mr. Bonnet, I shall see him if I can." She quickly rose from her chair and whirled out of the room, angry about her father's preaching.

She calmed herself after a short time and wondered about her recent moods. She wasn't often snippy with her father, but lately his opinions repelled her and drove her toward other ideas. The frenzy of the gold stampeders, Jesse Peacock's un-wanted invitation, and the turbulent introduction to Eli Bonnet had cluttered her mind and made her think she'd been sheltered too long. The thought of breaking out to another world and choosing her own destiny suddenly seemed so important. She desper-ately wanted a different life.

She dressed carefully, added a blue scarf, and walked out into the soggy morning air. Eli Bonnet hadn't reappeared since she returned to her work at the Marshals' office. She knew he would soon, and she felt determined to spend more time with him than during the two fleeting moments before.

When she reached the U.S. Marshals' office in the courthouse square, Peacock was waiting for her, looking pinched, gray and forlornly swinging his sin-gle arm.

"Mr. Peacock—Jesse—are you well?" Hannah wondered what could be wrong.

"Do you know of the woman without her tongue? The one the police found on the day of the mur-ders?"

Hannah grimaced. "I read of her. She was a whore on the docks. What an awful thing to have hap-pened. I can't imagine someone being so cruel to an-other person."

Peacock looked startled. "Please don't say that word. I don't want you to talk in that way."

"A woman can be a whore. There are many in this city now. Am I to be blind and dumb when you ask me a question?" Hannah's eyes sparked.

Jesse Peacock winced. He hadn't experienced

Hannah's anger before. And the idea that she would call an immoral woman by her real business seemed wrong to him. Suddenly the woman he felt certain he loved, though he couldn't say it, seemed like someone else. He paused for a moment, and then apologized. "No . . . I'm sorry. I want to tell you that she knows—she knows who did it."

Hannah stood perplexed. "If she has no tongue, how do you know? And if you know, what can be wrong?"

"She knows, but she can't tell. The police say she points to pictures—pictures of the Senator's wife and child. But there's no way for her to tell who did it. She can't read or write, and they say she's going mad because of her injury."

"If she does know who killed the Senator's wife and child, there must be a way for her to tell. And I doubt your fears of madness. I think the police frightened her wits away with threats and jail. They're always a mean bunch with women they catch!"

Peacock stared at Hannah. Her manner was beginning to annoy him. "The police are holding her in the city jail, but I don't think they've made any threats. And if you can think of a way to find out what she knows, you should tell me." He turned and stomped toward his office.

"I can do it. I can go to the jail and learn what she knows. But you've got to promise she will be set free!"

Jesse Peacock stopped. Any chance seemed important enough to pursue, he thought. The prostitute might respond to a woman instead of a man. He'd sent ten Marshals afield for several days, and they had found nothing. It seemed crucial to try every idea that came along.

He faced Hannah and said, "If you think you can—do it! No one else seems able to learn anything in this senseless city. If you want her out of jail, take her. I'll give you a letter for O'Shanny. But I fail to see your reasons for it. What are you going to do with a whore, as you want to call her—and one that can't talk, at that!" He shuffled on into his office, like a crippled old man.

During the middle of morning, but before the sun could dry the air and stir sea breezes, Hannah traveled across the city and walked into Paddy O'Shanny's office. His face showed his surprise when he spied her marching toward his desk, then astonishment after he had read Peacock's letter. Whenever the chief got ambushed, particularly by a woman, he had the distasteful habit of belching and scratching until he could think of a response. He began to do it in front of Hannah now.

"May I see her now?" she asked, wrinkling her nose a little.

"This be a wee bit uncommon. If Peacock wants this . . . I suppose it's lovely to me." O'Shanny burped, then scratched his side. "Why would a lass like you want dregs like her?"

"Each of us is worthwhile. I can make her well," Hannah shuffled her feet, wanting to get away from this fat Irishman and his disgusting habits.

"A Jezebel ain't dear to nobody." O'Shanny eyed

Hannah suspiciously as he scratched and burped more.

"Then why are you keeping her? What has she done? Why is she being punished?" asked Hannah, her eyes turning dark and thin.

Paddy O'Shanny sat up straight. He wasn't accustomed to anyone challenging him, certainly not a woman. He hesitated for a moment, then said, sneering, "Wasn't nobody to care, but now with you here, her troubles be over." He lunged his bloated body out of his chair and hollered, "You come with me. You and Peacock can have this lovely prize!"

Hannah followed O'Shanny down steep stairs and along a hallway of dark vaults, tramping the length of it without looking left or right. Near the end, O'Shanny turned the lock of a rusted iron door and flung it open. Hannah gasped when she saw what was inside.

"Here be the lamb you want. Get her out. Take her and be gone. Be happy with the bitch from hell!" He then stomped away, leaving his laughter behind for Hannah's ears.

A small, emaciated, black-skinned woman sat on a three-legged stool in the rear of the cell. Her hair hung down in twisted tresses of grease and dirt. A rag of red calico cotton, a stir of print and blood, covered her bony body and hung long enough to mop the floor. Pots of urine and water sat by her side, and both stunk the same. A pink oozing gauze stuck out of her mouth, and the whites of her eyes glared in contrast to the gloom of the room. Hannah, frightened, thought it must be an animal in there, not a human being.

"I've come to take you away from here. I can help you." Warily, Hannah stepped through the door; then she stopped because of the stench and darkness. She started to step forward again, but suddenly the woman snatched up the urine pot and hurled it with a mad, muted scream.

The pot hit Hannah and drenched her skirt. She jumped back through the door and quickly looked behind her, fearing a fight. When she saw there was none, she ducked to one side and peeked back in. The black woman still sat on the stool mumbling muddled things, but the message was plain that she would throw something again if Hannah came near.

"Why did you do that? I came here to help you. I've done nothing to harm you. I'll leave you here if you dare do that again!" Hannah stared into the cell.

The other pot and more crazy cries came flying through the air. Hannah ducked again so she wouldn't be hit. The second attack made her angry. She grabbed one of the pots from the hallway floor and threw it back into the cell as hard as she could. It sailed across the room, struck the opposite wall, and fell to the floor with a loud clang. The woman quickly shrank into a curl on her stool and began to sob while protecting her head with her arms.

Hannah crept close, watching the wailing woman for threatening movements. "Are you going to hit me again? What's the matter with you? I came here to get you out of this dirty hole! Why do you want to stay in this stinking place?"

The woman continued to sob. Hannah stayed still, but close by. She then reached out and patted the shoulder of the weeping woman. At last the sobs became whimpers, and Hannah felt the madness had passed. She grabbed a thin woolen blanket from the cell's board bunk and wrapped the woman in it, like a shawl, covering her head and shoulders.

She helped the woman to her feet, grasped her skinny hand, and led the way out of the cell. The woman's whimpering continued, but she offered no protest.

"Follow me and don't hit. I'm going to get you away from here and warm and clean!" Hannah led her down the hallway between the jail cells.

They climbed the stairs and crossed the office area. Chatting and laughing with one of his men, the fat chief smirked as she and the muted woman passed by.

"Heard a wee bit of clatter down there. What be that on your skirt, lassie?" The chief laughed again.

Hannah bristled but kept walking. She tugged on the hand behind her and turned quickly to the door, wanting to get away as soon as she could from the jail and its chief. Once outside, she hailed a carriage, but found that the driver wouldn't carry her and the prostitute. He and each driver she hailed afterward took one look and then drove away, meanly refusing to help. Finally she was able to gain the attention of an elderly black man running his milk wagon. He frowned and sniffed, but showed courtesy and pity as he stuffed both of them in the back and sat them on upside-down boxes among others with full bottles.

The old man trotted his horse across town as Hannah had instructed and stopped at the back of the parish home of her father's church. When she offered him a dollar, he refused, and, after giving them a kindly smile from his old, purple lips, drove away.

"Daughter, in Jesus' name, what have you done now?" shouted her father as she came through the door. He rushed over and gasped when he saw who had come into his home.

"This woman needs our help. She's had her tongue cut out. She's been beaten—maybe by the police!"

"We can't have a person like this in my house. What are you thinking, daughter? Look at her. She's filthy. How do you expect to care for her?"

Hannah stopped and faced her father. She had endured all that she could during the passage of one day's time. Her temper couldn't take any more. She shouted back at her father, "You hypocrite! When I came home ten days ago, I looked just about the same and you cared for me without a problem. For days you were at my side asking if you could help— and you did help me get well. Now it's a Negro—it seems a person not agreeable to you—and you can't see a way to help. I see you've forgotten Sunday's sermon now that it's gone from your mouth. I'll tell you this: you'll help with this woman, or I'll leave this place, and I'll never speak to you again for as long as I live!"

Her father drew back, stunned. His daughter had never turned on him with such venom before. He suddenly saw that she had fled his rule and had become rebellious—and it made him afraid. He took a step back.

"I'm sorry, my dear. I . . . I was just thinking of you. If you want to care for this woman, I will help you the best I can. I didn't mean to upset you. The housekeeper can help. I was just thinking of you."

Hannah's eyes stayed angry. "Then please move out of my way. I want to see that she's bathed and that her filthy rags are thrown away. Call Dr. Wender and ask him to come as soon as possible. This woman needs care. And send Mrs. Byrnes up to help me as soon as you can find her." She then yanked on the hand behind her and flew upstairs with pounding footsteps.

By week's end the woman was walking about the house peeking around corners, touching the smooth, dark walnut wood and other family things in curious admiration. Hannah had dressed her in clothing from the church's poor box and the housekeeper's closet. She still looked frail and weak, but the ugly gauze had been removed, and little kindnesses offered her brought brightened eyes and small smiles.

Hannah decided the woman appeared strong enough to answer plain questions with a nod or a shake of the head. The woman acted wary at first, but after a few questions she showed more confidence. She also seemed fond of Mrs. Byrnes, so Hannah kept the housekeeper near.

After a few simple inquiries, Hannah asked, "Do you know who killed Senator Turnbull's wife and child?"

The woman's eyes opened wide, and she soberly nodded her head up and down.

"Is he the same man that hurt you?"

The woman's eyes got teary as she nodded more quickly.

Hannah had thought about her next question for several days. She had the feeling it had not occurred to the police or the U.S. Marshals to ask it. "Does anyone else know about the murders?"

The answer was again a solemn nod, and then to Hannah's and the housekeeper's astonishment, the woman scampered across the room and snatched a quilt that was draped over a rocking chair. She dashed back, pointing at it.

Mrs. Byrnes, with a puzzled look on her face, asked, "Blanket?"

Hannah stared at the colorful quilt with its many squares and wondered for a moment. She then looked into the woman's eyes and cried, "Patches!" The black woman danced and nodded her head, acting crazy. Hannah laughed along because she now knew the name.

CHAPTER NINE

Calamity

Eli disliked the city, but he still fancied the hunt. It had been more than a year since he'd prowled saloons and brothels looking for an outlaw. He relished searching for lawbreakers; it pumped his blood up. But the noisy crowds on the streets of the busy city were wearing him down. The sounds of clanging streetcars, yelling people, and screeching horses were beating in his brain. In all other places in his past, investigations had been simple. The frontier towns of the West had been small; they never took long to cover. He found San Francisco a different matter.

As he sat in his room listening to Noodles' snore, he couldn't help but recall how refreshing it had been to ride away from those past frontier towns, if only for a little while, so his mind could heal by seeing mountains and trees. Many time he'd sat till nightfall nipping the ends of honeysuckle petals while gazing across unbroken land. The colors of the setting sun still glowed in his recall of those past jaunts. But now there weren't any agreeable sunsets to see, and his soul needed a rest.

A light knock on the door interrupted his memories. Noodles stirred but stayed asleep. He slipped to the door, and when he opened it, he found Hannah Twigg on the other side.

"Miss Twigg, how are you?" He scrunched the corners of his eyes in surprise.

"Mr. Bonnet, could I speak to you alone? I have something to tell you." Hannah shivered with anxiety.

"Yes. We can go down to the lobby if you like. It should be quiet there." Eli took Hannah's arm, stepped through the door, and turned toward the nearby elevator. When they reached the ground floor, he led the way to a puffy sofa under a painting of ships plowing through a storm.

As they sat, he said, "I'm glad to see you. I've worried about you getting well."

"You promised to come back, but you didn't." Hannah shivered again, still jittery. Then her face reddened, but she didn't drop her eyes.

"I'm sorry . . . I forgot that promise. When I got back to the alley, the man I'd kicked had run away. It took most of the night to catch him again." Eli looked at Hannah carefully and then said, "I forgot it was important to you . . . or I wouldn't have broken my word."

"That night was the worst of my life. The fear I felt . . . the way they beat me. I thank you for my life, and I shall repay you if I ever can."

"That's not needed. What did you want to tell me? Has Jesse other plans for me?"

"No, Mr. Peacock doesn't know I'm here. And I

don't want him to know that I ever was. Will you promise never to tell?" She stared hard into his eyes.

"I give you my promise, and this time I'll keep my word."

"Were you told about the woman the police found with a severed tongue on the morning of the murders?"

"No, I was not!"

"The police questioned her to find out what had happened. She wasn't able to tell them because of her injury. Then they found out she could neither read nor write. Later, she pointed to pictures of the Senator's wife and child when she saw them in a newspaper. That made the police think she knew who the killer was, but they were never able to get a name."

"Where is this woman now?" Eli asked, astonished.

Hannah smiled. "I've got her. The police had her in jail, but Mr. Peacock gave me permission to take her home."

Eli looked even more astonished. He hesitated for a moment and then exclaimed, "I need to see this woman. There must be a way for her to tell me something. A name—a place—something!"

Hannah smiled again. "I've gotten a name. Patches. The name is Patches."

Eli wrinkled his brow. "That's seems an odd name—" Then he laughed and said, "But no more odd than Noodles, I suppose."

Hannah described her episode with O'Shanny and the tussle to get the black woman out of the cell.

She told of the questions and of the good luck in having a patchwork quilt lying nearby. Eli listened intently, then praised her cleverness and spirit. He began to feel his heart taken the more he listened and the more he saw her charm and grace. He sensed she was unlike any other woman in his past. Then a plan suddenly came to him—one that would work for many reasons.

"Could you and your new friend come with me for a buggy ride tomorrow? I think she can show me the way to Patches. Then perhaps we can find the news we need."

Hannah brightened and nodded. "I wanted you to ask. I had thought the same. And we both want you to come along if we go to the dock again. I'm afraid of that place, and I think she must be, too."

Eli smiled. "Then we'll do it. Tell me the whereabouts of your home, and I'll be there at noon. I'll bring Noodles along as a lookout. We'll find this Patches before the day gets finished!"

Hannah rose, told Eli how to find her father's house, and walked with him across the lobby. At the hotel's door, while waiting for a rig to take her home, she asked, "Did you ever find Sorrowful?"

Eli grew sad and looked down. "No . . . and I'm worried I never will. He was my best friend. I miss him most of all."

"Noodles said he looked like a wolf but really wasn't. He also told me that he has saved your life in the past. Is that true?"

Eli looked into Hannah's eyes. "I learned long ago about man's real friend, when I lived in the wilder-

ness. Sorrowful always protected me from my enemies. I'll be in danger until he's with me again."

Hannah thought it curious to hear a U.S. Marshal
talk of his love for such a simple animal. Then she
thought of her own devotion to a spiritual faith and
wondered how foolish that might be. He had enjoyed
a friend he could touch and trust. She had spent her
time praying to something she could never see. His
way seemed better, she decided; hers had yielded
nothing but an empty heart.

Her teary eyes revealed her feelings. "I wish there
was a way I could find him for you. It would be part
payment for what I owe. Would you remember I
want to see you as much as I can. . . . I should say
good night. I'll see you tomorrow." She whirled and
ran down the steps, wiping her wet eyes.

Eli returned to his room and lay waiting for sleep.
There had always been women in his life, he remembered, mostly ranchers' daughters with their fathers
eyeing his skills with horses and rifles and ropes. But
those women's pulling and holding to just one place
had always repelled him; he wanted to keep the freedom of being a lawman without a wife worrying behind. There had also been a store owner's daughter,
but that union would have meant all indoor work
with little time to wander. There had been romances
with dance hall women, too, but those women had
been fickle and always got him into fights. Now a
woman had come along to test his feelings again . . .
and to make him worry about his present ways.

The next morning he arose feeling tired; his night
hadn't been restful. But Noodles seemed spirited,

beating about with bounce and wit, carrying their coffee and newspaper from the door, running often to windows for sight-seeing below. His commotion and chatter got Eli up and dressing for the day's promise to meet Hannah.

He groaned, stretched, and pulled on his boots. Then he sat up straight and said, "We've a different plan today, old man. It seems while we Marshals chased about the city, a woman found the clue."

"What happened? Who's got the clue about the killer?" Noodles hopped around to face Eli, his face wrinkled.

"Miss Twigg found a woman with her tongue cut out . . . it seems by the fellow who killed the Senator's family. She pointed to a patchwork quilt when Miss Twigg asked about the killings. We figure we want to talk to a fellow named Patches, and we're on our way to find him."

"How'd Miss Twigg find the woman? Ain't the police 'round here any good?"

"The police had her, but they couldn't figure a way to talk to her. Miss Twigg got her away and found out the name with sensible questions."

"How we goin' to find this Patches? He'll be livin' mighty careful nowadays."

"We're going for a buggy ride. Hopefully the woman can point out Patches—or places that he keeps to. But he's not the fellow that did it. We just think he knows the one that did."

"He's still goin' to be mighty careful. If he tells the name, maybe he'll get his throat cut the same as the others."

"I'll catch him like I've caught most men. I'll just keep at it until I do. It's my duty." Eli groaned again and stood up to leave. "Let's get our breakfast and then a buggy. I want to find this Patches before the day is done."

After eating, Eli rented a closed carriage pulled by a lone brown horse. He and Noodles drove across the city, haphazardly at first. Then they pulled up at the front of Hannah's home on time. They found her waiting by the door with her companion standing close by on jittery feet. They stared, startled. They'd not been expecting to see a black woman, and certainly not anyone looking so frightened and frail. Eli jumped down, ushered both women to the buggy, and seated them in the back where they couldn't be easily seen. He climbed up to his driver's seat again and pulled and whistled the horse around into a trot, heading toward the seaside streets.

They sped down among the barrooms and brothels and then walked the horse along the streets. Eli steered the horse and buggy through tangles of wagons, carts, and people while listening for directions from Hannah and her friend. The woman cowered in a corner of the carriage and peeked out only when Hannah begged her to do so. The black woman's hand waved them on, and a shake of her head signaled her disapproval of the places they were passing. They inched along, pressing for gaps in the traffic, and waited for some signal of where Patches might be. Suddenly the little woman's arm shot straight out, and she pointed toward a ramshackle barroom. The sign above it named it the Sea Fox.

Eli pulled the horse to a stop. "Is this the place where I can find Patches?"

The woman nodded her head hard. She then pointed to the sun and drew a make-believe line to the horizon, showing Eli nine fingers to indicate the time she meant.

"Will the bartenders know Patches when he comes in tonight? Will they point him out?"

Eli got an eager nod again. He turned to Noodles and began to pull off his Indian jacket. "I'll stay here till I catch him. Take the ladies home and wait for me at the hotel."

Noodles' face dropped. "I want to help. And you shouldn't go in there without your medicine coat. Might be trouble!"

Hannah, alarmed, leaned forward. "You shouldn't go alone. I'll go to Mr. Peacock and get him to send help."

"No . . . I'll catch this fellow like I've caught all the others. I've not had help in the past and won't require any now. I don't want to wear this coat so he can see me first." Eli folded his jacket and handed it to Noodles. "Take the ladies away before someone sees." Then he looked at Hannah and said, "I'll call you after this is done." He turned and went into the Sea Fox without looking back.

The place stank, mostly of beer but also of whiskey and urine. Tobacco smells oozed out of the wood and fabric, adding mustiness to the mix of other odors. Darkness soaked the corners of the interior. The same gloominess contrasted with the center, aglow with the shine from flaming electric bulbs. Seamen sat mumbling to painted women, their bottles and cigarettes held close. Two bartenders in bleached shirts served workmen who leaned like odd storks standing in line. A few watched as Eli walked across and beckoned to the bartenders, but most turned away and kept to their drinks and talks.

"What can we get you?" the thicker bartender asked.

"Do you know a fellow called Patches?" Eli watched the man carefully.

The bartenders traded glances; then the smaller one said, "We don't know most that come here. What do you want him for?"

"I'm a Deputy U.S. Marshal, and I require things that this man knows. Will you point him out?" Eli took his star out and flashed it for the two to see.

"He ain't here now. He comes at night," answered the first bartender. Then, after sniffing, the bartender added, "You'll know why he's called Patches when you see his face . . . but I'll show you who he is if you keep an eye on me. I don't love him none."

Eli nodded and drifted away from the bar. He circled, looking for a favorable position, and selected a table and chair off to one side. After sitting for a time and peering about, he felt a sense of foreboding, and his morning weariness came back. The place looked treacherous, all corners and dark spots, and back doors behind. He pictured an evening's crowd and saw clogs and knots that would stop him from jumping clear of trouble. Drunks and toughs stood around, and there would be more of them later. He saw none that would help him catch this man. In fact, they might kill him if they saw the chance.

He passed the remaining afternoon and evening watching and waiting. A snaggle-toothed barmaid brought coffee and hard-boiled eggs, and he sipped and chewed on those until he felt jittery and puffy in his belly. The straight-backed chair hurt his spine and made him squirm more than he wanted. He thought of the other times he had been similarly situated and remembered it had never been untroubled. Boredom and cramps were his enemies too.

His thought drifted to the outlook for his life. Noodles' hankering for the Klondike, worry over where Peacock would send him, and the loss of his beloved West to new times cursed his prospects for better duty. He had learned he wanted to stay away from big cities, but that seemed hardly a fresh idea to him. It was clear that the West appeared finished forever, and it wasn't sound to pine away, but to find a life like in his past seemed a rule he needed to remember. He remembered a story of a mountain man who had never seen a wagon. It had been told in Montana that when the coming of wagons and roads had been rumored, the old trapper had galloped away. Eli pictured the man fleeing to the North, and he wondered again if he should go there, too.

Suddenly he saw the face. He looked toward the bartenders and saw the large one tilt his head and cast his eyes to one side, signaling the sighting. Eli stayed still, not moving anything but his eyes, like a cat stalking its prey, and watched from his hiding place. The face was riveting: muddled patches of purple, white spots, and red blotches. A face that couldn't be forgotten, an awful face that got used for dishonest purposes. Patches' face spooked people into careless custody of their wallets. When they turned away from his ugly face, Eli saw his quick, long fingers snatch their money.

Eli rose from his seat and made his way through the night's crowd. Most men stood in circles, some in rows, and others stooped or sat as they tossed down their drinks, yowled with friends, and gambled with dice and cards. Racket filled the tavern, covering the sound of footsteps and soft noises. He crept forward, bumping along through the rowdiness, zigzagging toward the ugly pickpocket.

Patches glanced his way but showed no alarm. Eli stepped closer, then saw Patches' fast fingers pick a purse, and the lightning quickness of the snatch frightened him. Knots of men stood nearby, and he saw little room to jump away if any attack came up. Then, when the pickpocket stopped within an arm's length, he reached forward and grabbed a handful of collar.

"I'm a Marshal—" he began. He felt the man slip free.

Silver flashed and Patches spun around. Eli threw his left arm out and down to block the thrust, but he saw the blade get by and stick into his side. Pain shot up and he felt air burst through his throat. He leaped back, bumping against bystanders, then drew his right fist back to strike at the ghastly face. He punched hard and felt his knuckles hit nose and mouth. The pain then surged and fogginess settled in. He sank to his knees and fell sideways, hearing men hollering, feet stomping, furniture crashing—and then his senses clouded.

"Eli—" A sharp crack rang out from a small pistol. "You men get back from him—get doctors over here—do it now!" A dapper man pushed through the crowd, his black coat, red vest, and white shirt bright, and his elbows and feet shoving and kicking a path through the surrounding men.

The shot cleared Eli's head for a moment and he glanced up. When he saw who it was, he called, "Stop him—get—"

Then his consciousness passed away.

PART II

Outbound

CHAPTER TEN

Soapy

The pistol report and the sight of a shiny U.S. Marshal's star as Patches had pulled back for a second jab had persuaded him to get out on the fly. He'd simply reacted when he felt the yank on his collar, truly expecting to see that it was the angry victim of his last snatch grabbing him from behind. Later, reading in newspapers that he had knifed a Deputy Marshal during the fight in the Sea Fox scared him silly.

He understood that his face, with its conspicuous birthmarks and white blotches, was a beacon. And his busted nose increased the likelihood of being quickly identified and captured back in San Francisco if he stayed around. Policemen patrolling the waterfront had mostly tolerated him in the past, simply seizing his loot for themselves whenever they nabbed him. But an attack on one of their kind meant brutal punishment just as soon as they got their hands on him. So he had quickly fled the city, knowing he would surely forfeit his freedom if he didn't. Staying around would have been a stupid idea and would have ended with a long, painful jail sentence.

The incident hadn't been a complete disaster, though. The wallet he'd snatched just before the fight with the lawman contained a ship's ticket to Skagway. Suddenly, escape from the grasp of the law had been handy, and, anyway, it made good sense for him to follow the gold stampeders north—they were, after all, his subsistence. And the stranger who had started his bad luck had gone there also. Now it seemed important to find him and get even.

The voyage to Skagway had consisted of long bouts of sea sickness interrupted by numbing terror over getting shipwrecked on a shore with nothing but wilderness all around. Since boyhood, Patches had known no other home than the streets of San Francisco. Now he was in the middle of an endless, empty land and almost insensible with fear of such strange surroundings.

When he at last got off the ship and into the town of Skagway, he found himself in the middle of a crazy, warlike assault on rock and timber. Everywhere he looked, sweaty men were cutting down great evergreen trees, prying stumps and stones out of the way, and stringing up white canvas tents so they could shelter themselves and their trades from the cold, persistent rains. Others, more farsighted, were cutting trees into boards and then hammering the new lumber into rough, unpainted shacks with signs on the front spelling out places and professions. He found, then, the noisy bedlam to be comforting and attractive. He saw it as a welcome chance to fatten his skinny pockets and as an agreeable opportunity to distract himself from his nagging anxiety about entering frontier lands. But his amusement was short-lived—now he sat captured on a block of wood, his hands tied tight behind his back, in front of a man waving a pistol around.

"You ever hear about me? The name's Jefferson Smith—but most folks call me Soapy." The glowering man shoved the pistol against Patches' broken nose.

Patches shook his head to dodge the pain from his injured face.

"From Colorado. You know where Colorado is, don't you?" The man bounced the pistol off the swollen nose again.

Patches shook his head harder, and his eyes began to weep tears down his cheeks. He wondered if he knew of a place called Colorado.

"Boys, we got the dumbest, ugliest pickpocket on earth right here. What we gonna do with him?"

Patches watched in panic as the two men who had caught him red-handed snickered about his predicament. It had seemed so favorable to bump around inside the lumber-and-tarpaper gambling house that it hadn't occurred to him that he might be picking pockets in a bigger thief's town. And to make matters worse, he'd snatched old man Tripp's winnings, money destined to be shared with the boss of Skagway, a man who called himself Soapy Smith.

"What you suppose he's most afraid of . . . could it be gettin' his long, bony fingers cut off?" Soapy mouthed a cat's grin, and his eyes danced with delight over the pickpocket's instant horror.

Patches couldn't control himself anymore. He cried, "Don't cut off my fingers—I didn't know what was going on—I didn't mean to take your money. I was just trying to get along. Please don't cut off my fingers!"

Soapy Smith sneered, then said, "Tripp, is this sorry-lookin' scum sucker any good as a pickpocket?" Then he narrowed his eyes and stopped laughing.

An aged creature with grandpa wrinkles and stooped stance quit snickering and creased his face with soberness as well. He scratched the back of his neck, waited, then said, "Boss, I got to tell you he's the genuine artist at it—about as good as they come. Spent all his time in 'Frisco and didn't get caught much. He's called Patches, I recollect." The old face then crinkled up with snickers again.

"He must have got caught doin' somethin'—look here at his nose. Patches, how'd your nose get bashed in?" Soapy gave the swollen nose another poke with the pistol barrel.

"A Marshal grabbed me and I didn't know who he was. I stabbed him and he hit me back." Patches fretted that he had just blabbed too much for his own good.

The three men in the room exchanged stunned glances; then Soapy Smith arched his eyebrows. "It ain't a wonder you're up here. You are the dumbest pickpocket in the world. Why in hell would you stab a Marshal—they don't chase after pickpockets hardly any. What did you really do?"

"I didn't do nothing, except he might've seen me pick a fellow clean." Patches wished his mind worked fast like his fingers did.

"Nah . . . that doesn't make sense. You better tell me what you did or you're goin' to get a lot more than a bashed nose from me. Did you steal a bunch of money from somebody important?"

Patches gulped and his eyes bugged out. He wondered how he could have gone so long without figuring out the reason for the Marshal's attempt to stop him. It seemed so simple and clear; why had he missed it? The Marshal wanted the stranger—the man who'd killed the Senator's family. The whore, Frissy, must have told—but then, he thought, that didn't make sense. Why hadn't she just described the stranger to the lawman and let it go at that? His mind searched for an answer to the puzzle, but all he could decide was he'd been so busy running away, he'd misjudged the plain truth of his importance.

He looked up at Soapy Smith and saw he had better answer the last question in a hurry. Hoping for the best, he sucked in a deep breath and said, "I think I'm the one who knows who killed a Senator's wife and kid and stole lots of money!"

Soapy Smith stuck his face within an inch of Patches' busted nose. "You must be talkin' about Senator Turnbull. How come you know who did that killin'? And the newspapers didn't say nothin' about any money. How come you're sayin' a lot of the Senator's money got robbed?"

Patches instantly knew how to get free, at least

free of the leather laces around his wrists and, perhaps, free enough to escape serious harm once more. He blinked and paused, then said, "I saw the one who did it. I followed him and saw him come out of the Senator's house. And I know he had lots of money 'cause I could hear it jingle . . . it's my business to hear money when people got it."

Soapy pulled back, waited, blinked his own eyes. "Where's this fellow now?"

"I don't know. I heard he was coming up here. Maybe I could find him. You could help take the money away."

Soapy Smith cocked one eyebrow and circled Patches, humming an odd tune. He then jumped close to Patches' face again and yelled, "What's this fellow's name and what's he look like?"

Patches rehearsed his answer before giving it. "Nobody knows any name. He wasn't the kind to introduce himself polite like. He's got a bulldog face, black hair, short whiskers. I think he's crazy. Wasn't any need to kill a woman and kid. I named him Cannibal. Let me find him, and we'll split the money he's got."

"Well, boys, look here. We got the dumbest pickpocket in the world, and now he's gettin' smart on us." Soapy stayed close to Patches' face but lowered his voice. "Come up with a better description or I'll start cuttin' off your fingers one by one, I'm warnin' you!"

Patches started sweating tiny beads on his upper lip and forehead. "I can't describe him good enough so you can find the right fellow. There's a thousand that look about like him in this town already. Let me look. Let me work for you like these other fellows do. I can do just as good as they can."

Soapy Smith drew back and stared, eyes probing and squinting narrow. After a moment he said, "I've put together a committee of boys, and this is our town. There ain't no law, and I ain't gonna let there be none. They pay me a fourth of whatever they get. I keep 'em organized, out of trouble, and from stealin' from one another. We don't allow nobody else to work our town. But maybe we could use a pick-pocket . . . there's a lot of folks too smart for us to get. Maybe we could use the help. What you think, Tripp?"

The old man stroked his day-old stubble and eyed Patches. "I guess I don't mind. Me and Blue Jay here can have him work with us. We draw good crowds with our shell game, but most men won't play. They just stand around and watch. Patches could pick off a couple of 'em. He ain't goin' to be any trouble for us—he don't look to be the sort."

"He sure ain't goin' to be hard to keep an eye on. He's got the nastiest-lookin' face I ever did see." Soapy peered intently at Patches again. "How can he be a pickpocket and not get caught all the time? I just can't understand it!"

Old man Tripp laughed, scratched again. "He's so ugly folks can't look at 'im, so it gets easy to snatch their money. Then they don't think he could of been the one. It works contrary to what a fellow would think."

Soapy Smith walked behind Patches and sawed at

his bindings with a dull pocketknife. He leaned close to Patches' right ear and whispered, "It better work different than I think. Otherwise, I'm goin' to cut off your ugly head and throw it in the dump for brown bears to chew on."

Patches, more terrified than ever, jumped up when his wrists snapped loose and rubbed his trembling fingers. "You won't be sorry. You'll see that I'm the best pickpocket there is. I'll find the Cannibal fellow right away. I'll start looking right now. I think he took a lot of money and we can get it from him. You won't be sorry, I can tell you that!"

Soapy laughed, both eyes dancing. "Well, Patches, you do what you think is best. You just get out of my place now and work with Tripp and Blue Jay here. They'll get you started and introduced aroun'. Just remember I ain't goin' to give you another chance ever again. Now get out and find the Cannibal."

Patches darted through the door of the board building with a sign painted across its square front reading JEFF SMITH'S PARLOR. He went straight to the muddy road running by. When he got to its edge, he stopped and stood still. Sickness flooded up into his throat and, unable to stifle the vomit, he bent over and retched. Tripp and Blue Jay walked up behind him, chuckling as he bent double once more; they stood there clowning as they waited for his heaves to pass.

Tripp, leaning over with laughter, called out, "You needn't be so scared. Soapy ain't as bad as he comes on to you. He just wanted to get your head right!"

Patches wiped his dripping mouth and nose with his coat sleeve and inhaled as much cold air as he could. He looked back, then wiped his mouth once more.

"I thank you for putting a good word in for me, Tripp."

"No matter. Just don't steal from me again. Me and Blue Jay here's got a good thing, and you can help get more. Now let's go see if this Cannibal fellow you're talkin' about is anywheres around."

Patches bobbed his head up and down and turned onto the road dividing the scattered fields of newly raised frame shacks and smoke-sullied tents. They poked around among masses of men flowing to and from the mounds of journey goods stacked along the shoreline, and they looked over all the faces one by one.

After three hours of searching under drizzly skies, Tripp led them away from the scrambling mobs and into the town's only telegraph office. They stood squeezed together in the small one-room place, drying near a potbellied stove and trading idle talk with two men behind the busy, paper-covered counter. When their coats and trouser legs felt warm and dry, they stepped once more out onto the road and walked toward its other end, where more men were rushing about.

"How'd you like that telegraph business?" Old man Tripp grinned at Patches.

"It's more crowded than some barrooms I been to in this town." Patches looked sideways at Tripp and wondered why he would ask such an uncommon question.

Tripp crinkled his face, giggled, and nudged Blue Jay with an elbow. "You ain't reckoned what's wrong with that place, have you, Patches, my boy?"

"No . . . it makes sense that people would want to send telegraphs back to where they come from."

"There ain't no telegraph wires comin' in to Skagway from anyplace," Tripp laughed. "It's a swindle. Those boys are gettin' paid for messages that can't get sent—they make things up and get the same fools to pay collect for answers back."

Patches, his mouth hanging open, stopped, turned, and looked back toward the place he'd just stepped out of. His life had been made up of thievery and schemes for wrongdoing, mostly done by others, but a gyp as sly as running a fake telegraph office seemed clever beyond any trickery he'd known. He eyed Tripp and asked, "Who's idea was it?"

"Soapy thunk it up. It's the best swindle I've seen in a long time. That's why I'm staying with his committee. He's gotta lot of 'em like that all over town."

"Ain't there any police? I never saw any stealing last very long before the police come along."

"Soapy told you they ain't no law in Skagway—he and the committee is the police. Most people are just passin' through, so there ain't nothin' they can do about gettin' took. And the few people that live here permanent—we make sure they get lots of money for themselves, so they keep their mouths shut."

Patches turned back up the road and hung his head and watched his dirty boots squish and slip in the new black mud. His uneasiness deepened as he trudged along thinking about the likelihood of getting away from Soapy and his committee. Any attempt to board a ship back down the coast would be chancy: Soapy's men seemed to be everywhere, and they probably would catch him. Running with the ongoing stampede north through wilderness and over mountains terrified him as much as arrest and jail did back in San Francisco. Staying in Skagway with Soapy and his gang looked best, but their idea that they could be the law of the town themselves for very long seemed downright stupid, he thought. Sooner or later the real law would come, and when it did, he didn't want to be caught with them.

He lifted his head, looked at the old man walking beside him, and said, "Tripp, the law or some vigilantes will come for us someday. Ain't you scared of getting hung when they do?"

Tripp held his step steady. "I should have been hung twenty years ago, so I ain't worried about it now. And you quit worryin' about it, too. You ain't worth more than me. If we get hung—we get hung. Besides, you don't belong to nobody but the committee now, so you better quit thinkin' so much about things!"

Patches dropped his head lower and felt all his worry knot up inside his chest. He had to find a way to escape—Soapy and his henchmen were as crazy as the Cannibal.

CHAPTER ELEVEN

Swiftwater

Swiftwater Bill had saved him by firing a Smith & Wesson pistol into the ceiling of the Sea Fox in the nick of time, stopping Patches from jabbing home another blow with his knife. Because he lay unconscious, Eli had missed the following fray: Patches ducking past drunks and out into the dark streets, Swiftwater kicking and shoving onlookers back, and the crowd's cries of fear, anger, and confusion because of the nearby gunshot. He had roused by the time the police and ambulance had arrived and lay answering his old friend's questions—and blessing the day he'd helped Swiftwater get away, back in Montana Territory times.

Swiftwater made his living by persuading other people of his good and honorable intentions, even though he didn't possess a trustworthy bone in his body. He always dressed fancy: black Prince Albert coat, red vest, starched white shirt, and necktie adorned with diamond stickpins. Gold chains crisscrossed his plump belly and hung heavy with charms and nuggets and a fat pocket watch with pearly dials on the end. He kept his shoes polished to a mirror finish and wore spats over them. His hair and nails looked carved, handlebar mustache trimmed and waxed, and a fresh flower always sat on his left-hand lapel, regardless of cost.

Women thought him an attractive man, perhaps a bit small, but worldly, and, most of all, very lovable. Men liked him, too, because of his wit, his friendliness, and, most of all, the idea that they were going to get rich right along with him—all they had to do was stake him first.

Maybe Bill took their money with good intentions in the beginning, but, without fail, all former partners complained the same after a while: their money got spent on high living, card games, and women.

Eli had first met Swiftwater Bill back in Butte, during Montana boom times. Swiftwater had used his uncommon gifts to induce ten prestigious townsmen to finance a dance hall and gambling emporium, a sensible investment, given the state of the town. Men worked daily to make big money in gold mining, lumber, and gambling, but there was a sobering lack of opportunity for lovelorn men who wished to share their good fortunes with someone of the fairer sex. Bill saw the needs of the community more clearly than others (so he claimed anyway) and, therefore, won leadership in the enterprise of procuring women and a place for them to play.

Unfortunately, Swiftwater's heart lay in the wrong place, and another part of his body did too: he soon got caught sleeping with the mayor's wife. Whether she intended to play a part in the venture remained uncertain, but Bill's popularity plummeted at once.

The townsmen gathered on a railroad trestle, along with Swiftwater, held an unrehearsed legal hearing, and declared that he should be thrown off the bridge with a rope around his neck. Eli had arrived in time to stop this vigilante business, firing his Winchester .50-.110 Express over their heads to win hearts and minds to his point of view. He then pointed out that unwise investments and amorous indiscretions didn't violate territorial law. Besides, he added, the mayor's wife seemed equally blameworthy, and he wondered out loud if they intended to throw her off the trestle as well. Finally everyone agreed to run Swiftwater Bill out of town with a new suit or tar and feathers, a verdict that Swiftwater favored wholeheartedly under the circumstances, and, as an end, Eli remembered, he'd earned Bill's friendship and admiration throughout the years.

Suddenly Noodles' voice from down the ship's rail startled him. "Eli, why you so quiet tonight? Don't you like this sailing north?"

Eli shook away his daydreaming, looked over to his wrinkled old friend and said, "I was thinking of the West when I was young and other days gone by."

"What was you thinkin' about?"

"The first time I saw Swiftwater. He hasn't changed much . . . seems like he's still working old tricks. I think I'll watch the welcome he gets at Dawson City. I figure folks will be troubled when they find he did so poorly for them back in San Francisco."

Noodles chuckled into the sea breeze floating across the deck. "I think they'll get riled, for sure.

They ain't goin' to take kindly to only three beauties of the night and no dance hall furniture. I bet they skin him alive!" He chuckled more, shook his head from side to side, and added, "By Jeez, he's a slippery customer. Funny somebody ain't shot him yet."

"Folks seem to like him too much for that . . . but his two mothers-in-law might if they ever catch up."

Noodles laughed again, louder, and said, "By Jeez, they sure got riled when the crew wouldn't let them on. Maddest women I ever saw. I wonder if'n Swiftwater paid those boys to do that." He caught his breath for a moment, and then added, "I bet those two catch up, even if'n they got to swim all the way to Skagway!"

"I expect to see them soon. They appeared to be stubborn and quarrelsome women who will not let an ocean stand in their way." Eli shook his head, recalling the commotion in San Francisco just as they had first sailed away from the dock.

Swiftwater Bill possessed a penchant for younger women, ones half his age, with pink and simple faces revealing their innocence of men and money, and of negligent mothers who also could be deceived by his beguiling ways. Unfortunately he often forgot to end romances fairly and marriages, also, before beginning another, leaving broken promises scattered about and angry mothers seeking retribution. For the few who were lucky enough to catch up, it seemed Bill's charms were plenty to thaw their fury and to get them hovering around, and, sometimes, lending him additional money. San Francisco had been no exception, and two furious mothers-in-law were somewhere behind, tracking him.

Noodles' voice surprised him again. "Eli, you been feelin' good enough to make it to Skagway yourself?" He peered at Eli's wounded side.

"Yes, I'm fine. Some soreness . . . but I'm well enough to make it." Eli went back to watching the sea and to remembering his bad experiences back in San Francisco.

Patches had gotten away and no one knew where he'd run to, just that he'd certainly left the city. Jesse Peacock, neck bowed and stub arm jerking as he raged over the loss of the lead, had taken Eli's star away and cursed him till he became hoarse, not caring a bit that his deputy lay wounded in a hospital bed. Jesse's behavior had angered Hannah so much that she had gone to the U.S. Marshals' office and shouted back at Peacock till she got hoarse, quitting the job at the end of her angry tirade.

The fat O'Shanny, seeing an opportunity to remove himself from any blame, gave biting interviews to the *Chronicle*, resulting in long, blistering articles about government bumbling. Senator Turnbull, in turn, became so infuriated over it all that he returned at once to Washington to hide away, but only after damning Peacock forever to lesser offices, which sent Jesse, lastly, into sickness for days.

Eli had gotten himself out of the hospital a little early, with Noodles helping and Hannah by his side, and had healed at her father's home. She had spent all her time with him, clucking around like a mother hen scolding, cleaning, changing bandages, and, most of all, offering affection beyond his experiences with women before. It would all have won him over but for the bitterness that whipped within him, souring his soul for everything, including how he felt about the possibility of their getting together. He wanted to get even with Patches and catch the killer, and he wanted to see Peacock forced to give his star back and an apology with it.

But after a while he saw the hopelessness in remaining embittered and also in staying longer in San Francisco—so he began to listen to Noodles again. And Noodles wanted to go to the Klondike more than ever, echoing that their future lay there. Finally he drew out all his money, bought warm clothes, and acknowledged it was time to go.

Hannah sobbed out her heartbreak when he told her of the decision. He stared at his shuffling feet until he couldn't bear it anymore, afraid of the urge to hold her because he sensed it would just make matters worse. At last he took her hands and held tight, and asked her to look at him and to listen to his need to find his life once more. He couldn't live in the city any longer and stay whole, he said, and his own hopes were pushing him along, even though those hopes were only shadows in his mind. And it was a matter of manhood and respect for oneself, and an act to impede the unhappiness he'd wallowed in while back in Thistles. He didn't want to go through that again, and perhaps Noodles speculated right, maybe herds of buffalo did run across a vast, unbroken land . . . and he, too, could have the chance to die satisfied there. His explanations curbed her crying but didn't help her heart. In the end, she let him go to the docks alone, but with the pain of leaving a woman behind that cared for him more than he believed good for her . . . or him.

The beginning of the voyage north began with wild ocean smashing over the bow of the rusted old freighter and its passengers, stuffed into quarters like pigs in a pen, vomiting on one another as they fought for liberty from the filth below. Rough coasts, with round green mounds sitting on top, stood far off the starboard side, and presented little to soothe the sick when they looked that way. Ship fittings sawed and creaked day and night, screaming louder than the ruthless winds about the thrashing dangers and clearing even the foolish lubbers off the decks with noisy warnings.

One nautical mile after another, the ship plowed through the wailing storms, then into inland passages. And there, at last, the angry waves subsided, and seabirds began to wheel about. Shores soared up to green-timbered mountains with gray and snow and white misty clouds above. Shafts of sunlight shot down, like heaven's searchlights, and drew the gold stampeders out on the decks and to pointing in awe at the sights. They gazed in wonder and began to chase the breeze with their cheers—the promised land stood all around and they were close to the gold to be.

"You happy about goin' to the Klondike now?" Noodles asked a third time from down the ship's rail.

"I'm happy. This is fine country . . . the most beautiful I've seen. Like some places in Montana, but with water around." He watched translucent, soapy sea slide by the hull and sniffed at the pungent shoreline smelling of seaweed and sour seashells.

"One fellow said it's bigger than the West and mostly ain't mapped. I like that. When I'm out prospectin', it don't matter where I been, and I don't want to know where I'm goin' to." Noodles then yelled out, "By Jeez, I ain't goin' to run out of places to prospect this time!"

Eli smiled over Noodles' excitement for the new land, and after reflection he said, "I hope it's too rough for politicians, too far for buffalo hunters, and that plain and honest men get to make the laws. I don't wish to see the ruination of another wilderness before I die."

"It weren't us that ruined the West. Weren't enough of us to do any harm. And the traders and trappers didn't do it neither. The West got done in when the farmers come. Them's the ones that cut the trees down and shot the wild critters off so they could plow the prairie flowers down with dirt on top and fences all 'round. And them's the ones that brung politicians in . . . and bankers and lawyers, too."

Eli frowned. "Frontiersmen hate regulation and folks that trade in it; like Indians, they think land should be open and free. Farmers will pay a lifetime for land, and politicians always favor money and folks that pay it. They call it progress . . . but I see the true reasons."

"By Jeez, progress ain't goin' to catch me this time. Them mountains will stand in the way for a while— then Providence will take care of the rest."

Eli glanced at Noodles and then stared back out to sea, thinking over the prophecy. After a pause, he answered, "I'll have to pray for Providence . . . those mountains won't stand long and tall enough to save me."

Silence lay between them as they sighted distant mountains with even higher peaks behind them, with snowcaps on top. Then glaciers came into view, glistening white-and-blue heaps crawling down gaps, plowing brown dirt piles in front of them, and popping and groaning as they crept to the sea. Tall calves fell from their fronts and smashed green water into froth and waves that bobbed bergs like vessels in a snowy gale. Nearby, meltwater crashed down cliffs, tumbling, gouging, turning stone to sand, then pooling at the bottom before rushing away. Seals and sea lions splashed about, poking their dark heads up for a peek and then diving away from the ship chugging by. Killer whales, their black fins and white bellies flashing toward shipside, their eyes like glowing obsidian, swam on their sides for a better look; then they as well dove deep.

As the ship augered north, the foliage began to change to mellow reds up high on slopes and yellows beneath, and the woods became great patches of berries and bushes and aspens frozen by frost. Fussy passengers, worrying about the weather farther north, grabbed wool coats, pulled them close, and chattered their chills as colder air blew by. Then, at last, the night's sun sank low, and a moody pall settled upon the sea's surface, dimming the shores enough to drive the passengers, muted now, to their bunks and corners below, each whispering an idea to companions about the land all around.

Five days passed, and the mountains' snowy veils crept farther down. The ship, blowing coal smoke to the rear, stayed northwest through channels five miles wide between mountains reaching higher than ever. Then the waterways narrowed to single miles, and the ship steered, hard northerly, into a passage to starboard. Crewmen began to scurry about decks, making ropes ready, freeing anchor chains from ties, and readying ramps for overboard. The passengers, delirious and shouting, rushed to the rails and stared forward past the bow, searching for the ship's destination just ahead.

"Swiftwater, what's Skagway like?" Noodles pushed for more room among a scrambling knot of passengers surrounding Eli.

"It's the Gal-dangest place ever. The meanest, shoot-'em-down, crookedest bunch of thievin', killin' devils that ever got collected in one place on the face of the earth. When you get on shore, stay watchful. There's fellows pretendin' to be packers, bankers, telegraphers, everythin'—but they're just settin' you up. Don't do nothin' with nobody but friends you know— else they'll steal you blind—maybe kill you too!"

Noodles hooted and then said, "Eli, sounds like you got to be the law again."

"I don't wish to be the law again—but stay close, old man, and I'll see we're not troubled." Eli tugged his belt and Colt Peacemaker higher and pulled his rifle closer.

Swiftwater Bill giggled at Eli's belligerent mood. "I

see you don't figure to get stuck with a knife again. Why don't you shoot one of 'em in the knee like back in your Montana days—then they'll remember who you be."

"I'll do that if I must. No man will find me witless and with my Colt elsewhere again. I'm done with nowadays notions that bad men can be stopped with goodness in mind."

Swiftwater giggled again, then shook his head. "It's a fact that the outlaws you shot turned to honest work. Trouble was, you made it safe for government clerks, and then they made life miserable for the rest of us."

"My duty was to slow the burning and killing. I did my best. But now I see that the Indians and out-laws were not the enemies of wilderness land, just enemies of those that wanted it for themselves." Eli leaned forward and stared across the narrow channel to rocky shores, his face angry.

Swiftwater Bill whacked Eli's back with his left hand. "Don't get down on things 'cause you've had confusin' work and bad luck. You stay close to Noo-dles and me and we'll show you good times again."

"By Jeez, we sure will! But, Swiftwater, you better stop partnerin' up and pesterin' women with your promisin' ways. Folks don't take kindly to you foolin' around so much. If'n you don't, somebody's goin' to shoot you someday—but higher than in the leg." Noodles pointed his finger at Swiftwater's middle and winked one eye.

"Folks are always chasin' after me, but they'll never catch me here. It's too darn big. Wait till you see it. There's thousands of miles of wild places, not hardly any of 'em prospected. When I first came up, there was nothin' around 'cept Fortymile. Now Skagway and Dawson are being built up. Pretty soon, more gold will get found. I'm goin' to get the richest I ever been in this here Alaska land. You just ain't goin' to believe how good it is till you see it."

Eli grimaced. "I recall the same being said about the West when it was young. Now the good is gone and we're up here. Perhaps we pilgrims bring problems hitched behind."

Noodles and Swiftwater turned and stared at Eli, their eyes puzzled, wondering about the thing he'd just said.

Before either could answer, a cry flew up from the crowd at the bow, roaring through the ship's masts and ropes. Everyone leaned over the rails, stretching to see, knowing that Skagway had just been sighted.

On the far shoreline a flotilla of ships and lighters with clusters of white canvas came into view, circled by low, muddy banks, with the tide gone out. Men waded and toted boxes and bundles of freight goods, filling tidal flats toward the tent towns with their sweating bodies running wild. Horses' screams, dogs' barks, and human sounds filled the air. The newcomers could hear racket all around as the ship sailed toward the turmoil.

When the ship dropped anchor in the busy bay, Noodles reared straight up, grabbed his floppy hat, and flung it high. "Well, boys, there Skagway is—let's get goin' for Dawson!"

"Don't get yourself excited!" Swiftwater shook his head from side to side.

"Ain't we in the right place?" Noodles' eyes flared wide with bafflement.

"Yes, sir, we are, but we ain't yet where we got to get goin' to Dawson City. No use tirin' ourselves out before it's time." Swiftwater Bill waved toward a white mountain north of the tidelands. "That's where we got to get goin' north."

Noodles turned and stared for a moment, stunned. Then said, "By Jeez, Eli, that there's the white mountain I saw when I was dreamin' back in Arizona—the one that stood in my way!"

CHAPTER TWELVE

Wintertime

"Why do we have to stay in Skagway so long?" Ankle-deep in muck and manure, with sticky snowflakes pelting his coat, Noodles peered up and down the main street.

"Can't get over the Chilkoot Pass before winter sets in, and the White Pass is all clogged up with outfits coming back." Swiftwater Bill shrugged and said, "The Yukon River will be froze up . . . can't get there soon enough to float down to Dawson. Ain't smart to begin winter up in them mountains. It'll be sixty below pretty soon!"

"I've been told Dawson City hasn't food enough and folks there are trying to get down to Fort Yukon." Eli tilted his head and searched the low gray clouds hanging above. "Let's set down a good winter camp, old man. We'll start out toward springtime."

"By Jeez, I wanted to get there before it got all staked. There must be a thousand outfits headin' there—I ain't never seen so many." Noodles hung his head.

"After we get settled, we'll survey the trail for a few days and figure the best way to go. Folks coming back look whipped to me. I want to see the reason for their unfavorable times."

"I ain't traveled the White Pass, so I don't know . . . always hired the Tlingit Injuns and carried over the Chilkoot. That's the way I'm goin' about March or April." Swiftwater tugged his long wolverine coat close. "I'm goin' to find a place in town for me and my ladies. You boys come find me when you get back from your lookin' around."

Noodles' face soured. "I sure wish we could get goin' now. This is a bad place—there's more pistol shootin' here than in Deadwood before Wild Bill got kill't."

Eli pulled his right boot out of the mire and turned toward the line of hemlocks standing in the distance. "Let's find a place among the trees and close to clean water, old man . . . and a safe ways from this troublesome town."

They strung and pulled tight a Hudson Bay tent near a trickle of springwater tickling the silence of the forest. When hard puffs of rising wind bounced high off treetops at midnight, the boughs above held cover, and their sighs soothed sleepiness on moss mattresses dug from open hillsides earlier. Then a tin airtight stove knocked the nip away the next morning as Noodles fried bannock, and as Eli packed for their survey of the White Pass Trail.

A long, winding line of loaded men and animals wormed onto the rough road going north as first light brightened ashen skies sopped with snow. Moans in harmony filled the woods as everyone tottered under burdens unfit for brute or beast, then grew louder as wisdom of the quest began to rot away. The column stumbled, found grit again, slogged farther, then slowed altogether as weaklings crumpled under the audacious loads. Steam rolled off the miserable snake of travelers as all groveled together like an endless, gutted serpent meaning to find its grave. Then, one by one, more pulled out, shame dripping down their cheeks as they threw down their glory loads and turned back for the place they had just left, watching others who kept on with muddled eyes. At last the strongest fell, muscles torn, bones shattered, their cries spooking hungry, black ravens that intended to peck their eyes out, stopping for good those few compelled to carry on.

The insufferable road crossed bogs without bottom, deadfall with broken branches ready to rip bellies, loose log corduroy split apart and waiting for foolish feet, and craggy crevices wide enough to gulp down horse and man. And then it pitched up, narrowed among the boulders, spiraled, and passed close to cliffs as summits reared high ahead. Men cursed the crests by their names: Devil's Hill, Porcupine Hill, Summit Hill, and Turtle Mountain, all evil angles that knocked everyone back.

Men began to go mad along the way, raving while beating their pack animals without mercy, then torturing the poor bleeding critters with firebrands in the insane struggle to make them go with fatal loads. When their madness failed, gunshots rang out, ending everything except the lonely, sobbing sounds from demented men slumped beside kicking corpses. Snow drifted down and covered over the stiff carcasses, blocking the way with odd white heaps. But more men and animals marched on, pounding pathways through the freezing flesh, leaving animal heads on one side and tails on the other. Ravens, glutted now, flopped overhead squawking horrid, maniacal calls, beckoning black-and-white magpies and whiskey jacks to join in the feast along the rutted road.

"This is the God-awful-est stampede I ever did see!" Sickened, Noodles stared straight ahead into a snapping yellow fire. "I would never of believed men could be so sinful against helpless critters."

Eli sat thinking of the craziness and anguish he'd seen during recent days. Throughout his experience of using pack animals across frontiers, he'd seen only skilled and humane people in possession of horses, mules, and oxen. The shock of seeing unskilled and ruthless treatment by gold stampeders traveling north had angered him into silence.

At last he looked up from the smoke-blackened kettle he had just tended and said, "I think the hardship of depression times down in the Union have driven men mad with greed. They suppose that reaching Dawson City will end their poor and downhearted times. But why would they become beasts themselves and kill the ones that can get them there?" He bent his head to his work again, and stirred, letting the ruffling flames soften his fury.

"What we goin' to do tomorrow? You want to keep goin' up the trail much?"

"No . . . I've seen enough of this place from hell. We'll head back to Skagway. After we've rested, we'll cross to Dyea and see if the Chilkoot is better. I've a notion that's the best . . ." Eli's voice trailed off to his own silent thoughts once more.

They cleared and banked more snow, piled fat, long poles of spruce high on their fire for added heat through the night, then slipped into blankets covered by canvas tarp. Their dreams of cruel murder broke their sleep often—and then as the roaring fire died down, they woke again because of the coldness creeping in. Noodles, yawning and muttering about stiffness, crawled out of his bed and added more wood to the fire, setting it ablaze.

"Eli—Eli get up! Eli, get up now!"

Eli leaped clear of his bed, his Winchester raised and cocked, and peered about the camp.

"There—look at it. Right there. By Jeez, I want to get out of here!" Noodles' right arm, sticklike, pointed at a severed horse's head, bloody brown, one eye reflecting like a glassy black marble, protruding and staring from a nearby thawing snowbank.

Eli leaned his Winchester against the last of their woodpile, walked over to the head and carried it into the surrounding darkness, then threw it down. When he came back to the fire, he shuddered, brushed at the snow and bloody smears on his clothing, and stood still in front of the dancing flames for a long moment warming and drying his hands and front.

"Go back to bed, old man," he finally said. "We can't leave here safely. If we do, the same kind of men that killed the horse may kill us. They'll shoot at us in the dark, thinking we're danger. Everyone is sick with meanness and fear on this trail. We need to stay till light."

"I ain't goin' to sleep much." Noodles slipped back underneath his covers and rolled around, fidgeting. Then he said, "Eli, someday this God-awful-est road will be called the Dead Horse Trail . . . but folks will never admit what they done."

At daylight's glimmer they gathered their blankets and packs and turned back down the trail toward Skagway, trudging through snow newly fallen from an early-morning storm. On the third day, when Eli sensed that the land lay lower and that he could bear to his right across to the beach along the narrow Skagway Bay, he struck out west toward the salt water. Their spirits lifted as they gained land away from the road with its mournful, crippled procession of men and animals in slow retreat—and as a hard afternoon sun began to push its rays through breaking banks of cloud, baring bits of blue above.

It took two hours to force their way through underbrush and over snowy patches of mossy hummocks and a hump of spruce-covered land that hid the bay from sight. When they reached the cutbank of the shoreline, Eli skidded down, digging his boots into the tidal soil to brake his descent. Next, he watched, grinning, as Noodles, hooting all the way, scooted the dropoff by sledding on his backside. Then they walked the beach, kicking at driftwood stuck ashore, spying on bald eagles wheeling above, and tugging out of the snow and sand old washed-up ropes from busted nets.

They came to the edge of a small, ankle-deep run of icy water from the slopes they'd crossed. Noodles splashed in, stooped, and stirred rocks and gravel with his hands. "I brought my pan. Let's go up this creek a little ways and pan for gold. There's black sands here, might be color in it." He bounded farther upstream.

"It's not much of a creek, old man, and we'll have to break ice in places. Why would gold be here?" Eli studied the alder tangles along each side and kicked at a salmon skeleton frozen in the ice near his feet.

"When you're prospectin' you pan all these places. Sometimes gold is far away, but sometimes it's under folks' noses and they don't know it 'cause they ain't never panned to find it."

For an hour they waded along, Noodles squatting, breaking ice away, scraping the stream bottom, swirling his pan, and trotting ahead to dig in another corner. Eli followed close behind, catching Noodles' enthusiasm for prospecting, bending each time to see the bottom of the pan.

"Lookee there, there's a little bit of color—ain't much, but it's right there." Noodles probed with his finger at a tiny yellow smear. "By Jeez, Eli, we're findin' gold already."

Eli squinted hard. "We'll soon need gainful employment, old man, if we can't find more than that." He straightened, stepped sideways toward shore, then suddenly sighted and heard, too late, the danger lunging toward them. A brown bear sow and her two grown cubs, standing to see and smell, then dropping to their forelegs, charged from the nearby brush, bawling their fury loud enough to cover the sound of tumbling water all around.

Eli threw his Winchester up and fired at the sow's

head at thirty feet, knocking her down into a roll of raging, rolling fur. Leaning, twisting, he flashed his barrel sights to another bear, ten feet away. His brain burst, seeing the easy, killing shot so close but knowing that the headlong skid of the bear would knock him down. He fired and saw, slowly now, the danger upside down. Jacking the action of the rifle from habit, he glimpsed the sow, up and running away with one cub close behind, both tearing for cover upstream. He heard a distant holler, then, because he'd tipped that way, he saw Noodles splashing across the icy creek for his rifle. Falling down, flipping sideways, he bounced off the back of the thrashing bear and down to its side. A flailing paw hit him hard on the hip, tearing cloth and flesh, slapping him head over heels to the snow-covered rocks near the water's edge.

His first thoughts were of sky and sun—things above—as he lay dazed on his back listening, terrified, to the bear grunting and digging rocks with its flashing claws. Suddenly a sharp shot rang out, but he couldn't make himself sit up or roll to his side to see. He began to sort out his arms and legs, wiggling them, begging each to answer the way he wanted to feel. Slowly he began to feel happy that his limbs seemed to move the proper way. His hip hurt, and he touched it with his left hand, feeling cloth tatters and slippery wetness. Then Noodles' face popped into view just above him and broke his dreamlike study of his body and mind.

"Eli, Eli, are you all right? By Jeez, you saved us from terrible death! You don't look too hurt—how you feelin'?" Noodles' face wrinkled and his mouth hung open after rushing his words.

"Help me sit up. I'll be better in a moment. What's the bear doing?"

"You shot him right between the eyes, and I give 'im another one in the ear. He's deader than a rock now. You're lucky you was wearin' your medicine coat under your wool one. It saved you from gettin' bad hurt. By Jeez, what kind of bears where them things? They're twice as big as any grizzly bears I ever did see!"

From his sitting position Eli looked down at his hip and saw that the bear's claws had ripped through layers of cloth and leather and into his flesh, just below the joint. Blood oozed from the cuts, but the wounds seemed shallow and not a threat to his well-being. He looked up at Noodles' distressed expression and grimaced himself from the bite of pain when he moved his head and body. After catching his breath, he groaned his answer. "I don't know, old man . . . it makes no difference now. Get my pack and bring alcohol and laudanum from my sickness kit. I need to purify these cuts and slow the pain."

For an hour he bandaged his wounds, pulled and pinned together his clothing, and tested his stride by walking in circles. When he felt his wits return, he knelt beside Noodles and helped skin the dead bear. He rose awkwardly after they had cut the fur free and said, "I've got to find the wounded bear and kill her. Help me cut this pelt down to my size."

"By Jeez, why you want to go after that bear? It's gettin' late, and she'll tear you apart if you don't make a good shot. You're only goin' to get one chance. And what do you want to cut up this hide for? We can get a pretty penny for it in town. Why don't you leave her be?"

"I can't let a wounded animal suffer. It's wrongful. And if I don't kill her, she'll charge the next fellow that comes along, and he may not be so lucky as I. If I wear the hide, I figure the sight and smell will slow her down till I get the chance to make a killing shot."

Noodles looked fearful. "By Jeez, I don't know. It sounds mighty risky to me. If you got to go, I'm goin', too. You shouldn't go in that brush alone all banged up like you are!"

"No. Stay here, old man. Two of us will make too much noise, and your rifle is not big enough. I'll go alone, as I've done before."

Noodles gave his head a fitful shake, then stared peevishly and said, "By Jeez, Eli, you're too bull-headed for your own good. Don't you ever get scared anymore?"

"Fear is an impediment; it slows my purpose. But I suppose I feel the same as others. Help me with this hide. I need to get this done before dark sets in."

They sliced the hide into a crude robe, cleaned the blood away by scrubbing it with fresh snow, and draped it over Eli's outer coat by using the headpiece as a hood and the forelegs as a tie across his chest.

When he finished with his disguise, Eli followed the bounding tracks of the fleeing bear and her cub into the thick alders lining the creek bottom. After a few feet he stopped, looked about, and cocked his

Winchester so he could fire instantly. He crept farther, stopped and looked again, and felt his neck hair
prickle. Stooping and scowling because of his injury,
he twisted ahead one step at a time through low,
bent branches. Tiny red spots marked the trail, then
petered out, leaving just torn pawprints in the snow
for him to follow. The tracks closed together and
then staggered through the snarled cover, and he
knew the bears must be near. He paused, looked,
and listened as carefully as he could, then stepped
once more. A soft blow of frosty air sounded. He
froze and quickly peered around, his heart pounding
so loud it hurt his ears. He couldn't pinpoint the
sniff, but then a sinister silence settled down, tempting him to think nothing had happened. He waited,
felt the coldness prick his toes, and stared hard at a
cluster of branches on his left side, hazy in the setting sun. Suddenly a young bear stood up, snuffling
and turning its head back and forth, trying to see and
smell. Eli stood stone still, hoping his silence would
shroud his location. The cub missed seeing him,
crouched out of sight again, and sniffed and blew
from behind the bush, trying to regain the scent. Eli
hesitated, then blew air like the bear had, echoing
the animal's alarm the best he could, breaking his
own silence among the branches. The wounded sow
jumped out, stood confused for a second, then
charged roaring and frothing straight on when she
saw him flip his rifle up. He held fire, fixed the
sights between the bear's savage, piggish eyes just
above the open yellow fangs, and then squeezed the
trigger. The explosion flattened the raging bear—but

she sprang back up and attacked again. He flipped the rifle's lever open and shut, firing once more, his mind pleading for a final, killing shot that would keep the bear down. The second blast tumbled her end over end, feet flying, onto her back, her last breath blustering away in hideous, choking growls.

The young bear prowled out of its hiding place and padded toward its dead mother after the second shot faded into echoes. Eli switched his sighting, levered his rifle, and started to pull the trigger a third time. Then he paused, watching over the barrel as the beast stepped forward. He wondered if he could slip away without killing again. He stepped back one step at a time, keeping his rifle ready while wiggling backward through the branches. The young bear stopped and stared, then came forward.

"Stay back, bear, and let me go. You and I both need to walk away from here and find another place," Eli said, muttering to himself, working to get farther away.

The young bear stopped, pricked up its ears, looked at him for a long moment and then at its mother lying dead. It turned its head once more toward him and stared . . . then without a sound it padded back to the place it had come from.

CHAPTER THIRTEEN

Sorrowful

"Hannah, I want you to come back to my office and work for me again." Jesse Peacock stood on the porch of Hannah's house, hat in hand, eyes unblinking.

Hannah held tight to the doorknob, her eyes wide. She couldn't believe what she had just heard. Bitterness boiled up in her breast, and she gripped the doorknob hard while she tried to think of something civil to say. Eli Bonnet had been driven away just as she'd learned to love him, and Jesse Peacock seemed to be the person responsible. She wanted to kick and scream rather than answer him.

"I'm never coming back!" Her mind whirled, but she couldn't get out any more words.

"Please don't make me stand on this porch. Let me come in. I want to talk to you about coming back again."

"No—I don't want to talk to you. I'm never coming back. Just leave me alone!"

"Hannah, please—I'm coming in. I've got to talk to you!" Jesse Peacock shoved his way through the door and into the entry hall.

Hannah, startled by his rough behavior, screamed, "Mr. Peacock, get out! Get out and leave me alone!"

A yellow-headed broom flipped out from around a corner and slapped Jesse Peacock's face. A little black woman then hurtled into the hall and swung again, hitting his back and side as he cowered, shielding himself with crossed forearms.

"Stop. Stop it. Don't hit!" Hannah jumped toward the woman and held her tight when she saw her pull back for another whack. "It's all right—he won't hurt me!" she yelled. She turned toward Jesse Peacock and looked at his reddened face where he'd caught the blow from the broom. "You aren't hurt. You had no right to charge into my home. Now will you leave?"

"Hannah, I love you!" Jesse Peacock stood still again, his rumpled, thinning hair falling on his forehead but his eyes still firm.

Her breathing hitched as the declaration split through her mind. After a moment she answered, "That's ridiculous—insulting! You're married, and you're twice my age. What have I ever done to deserve this?"

Jesse Peacock's eyes widened, and his lips wiggled in an attempt to form words, but an odd sigh was the only sound that came out.

Hannah, frustrated, asked again, "What have I ever done to deserve this?"

"I can't help how I feel. What am I to do—keep caring and never say or do a thing? I wanted you to know how I feel and that I want you." He lifted a foot to step forward, but the black woman, grunting, raised the broom once more and made him set it back down.

"I don't care how you feel. I don't want to know how you feel. You've just destroyed what little regard I had remaining for you. Now get out and never come here again!"

Jesse Peacock paled, then red rose to his cheeks. "It's Eli Bonnet, isn't it? I wish that knife would have cut his guts out!"

Hannah shrieked, "Get out. Get out of my house, you . . . bastard!" Before she could voice another scream, the broom head flew again, hitting Jesse Peacock's face on the other side. He plunged back through the doorway and jumped off the porch, defending himself from the black woman's pursuit.

Hannah burst into tears and held her head in her hands. Her defender slipped back into the hallway, dropped her broom, and wrapped her frail arms around Hannah, hugging her like a faithful sister.

After a moment Hannah regained her ability to talk and wiped her eyes with the back of her hands. She hugged the little woman back, held her at arm's length, then smiled through her wet eyes, whispering, "I love you so . . . and I don't even know your name. From now on I'll call you Naomi . . . from the book of Ruth . . . though I'm not sure now I remember why." Hannah wiped her eyes again and wept as she said, "Oh, what am I going to do with myself? And you, too. We're both lost sheep and can't find the things we need." She clasped Naomi to her breast and bawled louder.

Each day after her clash with Jesse Peacock, she

pounded up and down the hills above her father's parish home, Naomi panting by her side, sometimes running to keep up. She wasted her afternoons chattering about colors, birds, and books she'd read—trying to hide the hurt inside her chest. It seemed the more she tried to put her forsaken love to rest, the more it gripped her very soul. She fell into bed each night, exhausted from her frenzied day, and rolled around thinking about housework and other walks to take, praying that thoughts of Eli Bonnet would be kept out of her mind. Each Sunday she knelt in church and prayed for the return of inner peace, Naomi close by her side praying as well, with hands and eyes squeezed tight. But by the next morning she found her madness had started again and her heart was begging for another way to stop the pain.

Sunny days prevailed as they continued their walks, heading out in a different direction each afternoon to visit new places. One day, after circling blocks, crossing parks, and climbing bushy hills, like schoolgirls on a class outing, Hannah led the way across a green yard to beat the setting sun home. As she rounded a clump of trees she suddenly stopped and stared at a wolflike creature tied to a white gabled house. She stood frozen, wondering, as the yellow-eyed animal with its sad face and drooping tail stared back.

"Sorrowful? Is that you, Sorrowful?" she called. Her heart pounded as she whispered a prayer.

The gray dog lifted his tail and wagged it, pulling

forward on the rope. He whined, backed, and hit the end of the rope again.

Hannah ran to the animal and knelt in front of him, taking his face between her hands. "Sorrowful! You're Sorrowful, aren't you? My God, I can't believe I've found you!" She began to laugh as Naomi ran to her side.

"Naomi, this is Eli's dog. I've found Eli's dog! I can't believe this has happened to me!"

A fat black-haired woman yelled through the screen door on the side of the house, "You two get away from that dog—he's mean. Leave him alone and get out of here!" She stepped out onto the cement porch.

Hannah stood up and asked, "Is this your dog?"

"My husband bought him, but he ain't no good. Now get, and take that nigger with you." The woman waddled down from the porch, yanked on the rope, and pulled the dog away.

"Come on, Naomi, let's go home." Hannah grabbed Naomi's hand, turned, and hurried toward a nearby sidewalk.

She continued to walk fast until she was a block away from the gabled house. Then she stopped and asked, "Naomi, do you know how to steal things?"

She watched Naomi's eyes grow wide and a small smile creep up. Then Naomi's head bobbed with a toothy grin.

After night fell they slipped out of their house and crept along walks and yards until they found the place where Sorrowful lay tethered. Lighted windows shone yellow into the yard. Hannah started toward the dog's side, but Naomi pulled her back into the darkness. Naomi held her face close and placed her finger to her lips, telling Hannah to stay quiet. She shoved Hannah down near a tree trunk, patting her shoulders to show her where to stay. Then she faded into the night.

Hannah shivered from fear and the chilly air. She squirmed and worried about Naomi going after Sorrowful alone and wondered if she should sneak along behind. Suddenly she heard a hushed panting; then a dog's warm, wet tongue licked her face. She began to cry as she hugged the dog. "We've found you, Sorrowful, we've found you! We're Eli's friends . . . you remember Eli, don't you?" The warm tongue licked faster.

She then felt a hand grab her arm and pull her up and along through the night, running with Sorrowful, and keeping to shadowed places. As they loped along, Hannah began to giggle through her tears, feeling the happiest she had for a long time, thinking she had just made the two best friends of her life.

The next morning Hannah sat with Naomi eating their breakfast, with Sorrowful resting on the floor nearby. Hannah's father scooped bran grains into his mouth, his head down over his bowl, clicking his spoon hard against the glass.

He raised his head, eyes hot, and said, "Daughter, why would you do something like this? Have you gone crazy? I can't believe it. My only child's a thief!"

Naomi moaned and frantically shook her head, pointing toward herself.

"Naomi, don't lie to me before God. Do you think

I'm ignorant enough to believe that you thought this misdeed up? After all my work to make you God's child since you've come here, you now want to spoil the love I feel for you?"

Hannah watched Naomi hang her head. "Papa, don't yell at Naomi. You're very right—it's my doing and she's not to blame. But this is Eli's dog, and I'm keeping him regardless of your feelings. Now quit fussing so much over my business. I'm not your little girl anymore!" She felt her temper rise, her lips tighten.

"Stealing a dog is not the act of a grown daughter of mine. What have you become since these Klondike people ruined this city? You're never happy anymore—you tear through each day without purpose. Daughter, you must stop this mad behavior! You're destroying your life!"

Hannah felt worried about the next thing she had to tell her father. She knew it would break his heart. She looked at him, wished for a gentle way, and said, "Papa, my life is not here with you anymore. I'm taking Naomi and Sorrowful . . . and we're going to the Klondike to find Eli."

Her father dropped his spoon on the tabletop and gasped, "My God!" He stared, white-faced, and then small tears trickled down as he sat speechless, his mouth sagging open.

"Papa, I'll write often and tell you of our travels and how much we miss you, but Naomi and I must leave here and find our lives as you did long ago."

"Daughter, please, you can keep the dog. I can't bear to have you go." More tears fell.

Hannah leaned forward and held her father's hands across the table. "Please, you must let go of us. Be happy for us. I need to go forward with my life. Naomi must find something new . . . and I must, too. And what better way than by traveling to the Klondike and finding Eli? I'm excited and happy for a change. Please don't spoil this for me."

"But why must you go to a wilderness and chase after a man as godless as Eli Bonnet?"

"Papa, you don't know that he'd godless, and even if he is, I can change that. The important thing is that I feel I love him. There's hundreds of women going to the Klondike . . . so Naomi and I will not be alone. I have all the money I need, saved from my years of work . . . so, please, don't hurt me by holding on. Help us get ready to go."

Her father sat holding her hands, saying nothing for several minutes. At last he nodded his head, let go of her hands, and forced a bittersweet smile to his lips. "I hope you will remember each day that I love you . . . and that I will always want you back. You, too, Naomi. Now I need to go over to the church for a while. When I come back, I'll help any way I can."

For ten days Hannah and her father read everything they could find in newspapers, pamphlets, and library books about the Alaskan Territory, the Yukon, and the Klondike gold stampede. They shopped for winter clothing, bought cans and boxes of food, and bundled a hammer, saw, and ax together. Naomi, smiling widely all the time, packed thick canvas bags and sewed them shut, banged tops onto wooden crates and wrapped them with wire twisted tight.

Sorrowful, with wagging tail, snooped and sat in the way until they tied him in another room.

Finally, on the eleventh day, they hired a wagon and hauled their goods down to the docks and watched as stevedores hoisted everything onto the mail steamer *Idaho*, bound for the North. As they stood near the ship's ramp, waiting to board, Hannah's father said, "This is so hard for me. I wish I could come along and keep you safe . . . but maybe my prayers can do it." He swiped at his eyes with a white handkerchief snatched from the breast pocket of his coat.

"Papa, don't worry about us—we'll be fine. I'll write you as often as I can and tell you what we're doing. And please, don't look so sad. I've never been so excited in my life. Now give us a hug and let us get on board. Remember, we'll be thinking about you, too."

Hannah embraced her father, grabbed Naomi's hand and Sorrowful's leash, and led the way up the crowded ramp. She found places for all of them against the aft rail. She and Naomi waved again and again until they could no longer see anyone back at the dock. As San Francisco turned into a smudge on the horizon between sky and sea, Hannah wiped wetness from the corners of her eyes. Then she faced Naomi and said, "I've never been away from home before, Naomi. I'm scared to death. How will I ever find Eli and Noodles in such a huge land?"

Sorrowful looked up and whined as he always did when he heard Eli's name. She patted the dog's head to quiet him and looked back across flat seas toward the place where the city had been. Now only a thin black line lay visible there. Eli Bonnet has chosen his old ways of wandering through wilderness over me, she thought. It seemed time for her to see the things that had pulled him so hard. But the idea of going into a land that she'd only read about, a land said to be full of hunting bears and wolves, a land lacking people, sent shivers down her spine. Now she had to face the truth that even though she was gladdened to be away from Jesse Peacock, and thrilled to start after Eli, she appeared ill-equipped to live on her own in a raw wilderness. She felt lucky to have Naomi and Sorrowful with her; she didn't think she could have done it all alone.

She noticed out of the corner of her eye that Naomi was fidgeting and returning the attention of someone across the deck. Hannah turned and saw a thick black man in red suspenders watching them. She also saw that his wide smile beamed for Naomi's benefit.

The man walked over with a curious, circling gait. After tipping his woodsman's cap, he greeted them. "Hello, ladies. See you goin' north, too."

Hannah smiled back. "Hello . . . yes. We're from San Francisco and hope to find two friends of ours in the Klondike."

"I'm from Wisconsin, where I cut pine logs for seven years. But I'm goin' now to get rich up there. My name's Lincoln . . . what's you ladies' names, please?"

Hannah looked and saw Naomi's eyes exploring Lincoln from head to foot. Pointing, she said, "I'm

Hannah Twigg and this is Naomi. She can't speak because of an injury, but she hears fine. We . . . my father has a church and Naomi lived with us. Is that your last name, the name Lincoln?"

The black man shuffled his feet and looked down at the deck boards. "I ain't got no last one. Where I was born and raised, we didn't get no last names. My daddy was a slave man in Alabama, and I never got no other name 'fore I went north as a tree-trimmin' boy."

"No matter . . . Naomi has none, either. You needn't always talk to me. Just remember to let Naomi answer yes or no. I'm teaching her to read and write. Soon she'll be able to tell you more than she can now."

Lincoln ducked his head down again, ashamed. "I ain' never got to do that, so it won't help me none."

"Well, then, I'll teach you, too. There will be little else to do for several days, and it will keep us busy. Naomi, do you mind?"

Naomi shook her head . . . and her lips tipped up at the corners, her eyes brightened.

"Good! Then will you stay with Naomi for a while? I need to find our cabin." Hannah took Sorrowful's leash from Naomi's hands. "This is our friend's dog, Sorrowful. I'm going to put him in our cabin—then I won't worry so much about someone stealing our things."

"Ma'am, you tell me anytime you's got troubles with anybody—I can fix it."

"Thank you, Lincoln. I think Naomi and I will need a friend before our travels are done. Neither of us knows a thing about crossing a wilderness like Alaska and Canada are said to be."

"Needn't be scared of wilderness. It's folk in it that do harm. I ain' got nobody to go to the Klondike with, so I could help you if you'd let me come along. I guess I would like to have a couple friends, too."

"You can count on my friendship. But why don't you ask Naomi about it while I'm gone? We'll decide what's best when I get back."

She turned and walked away, her shoe heels tap-dancing on the wooden decking. Finding Sorrowful, meeting Lincoln—suddenly she thought that following behind Eli Bonnet had been a wise choice. And perhaps it was going to be easier than she'd dared hope.

CHAPTER FOURTEEN

Reprisal

"Your fancy coat's gone and you don't look well. What's happened since we last saw you?" Eli studied Swiftwater Bill's fallen face and his old, woodsy garment.

"I got cleaned out—ain't got nothin' left—about as broke as I ever been." Then, his face lifting, he added, "But you and Noodles are back . . . though you don't look so good yourselfs. What'd you do, wrestle those bears awhile before you skun-um out?"

Noodles threw down the smaller hide and said, "By Jeez, Eli had to shoot two of 'em. The first one about got us—knocked Eli down and ripped 'im up a bit. Then Eli chased the big one down and kill't her. We had to camp an extra night to get the hide off'n that one. What you suppose we can sell 'em for?"

Eli frowned at Noodles. "That's not important now. Who cleaned you out, Swiftwater?"

Swiftwater Bill hung his head. "A fellow named Soapy Smith did it. He and his gang has took over this town since I was last here—calls his boys the committee. Ain't no law, so he gets to do what he wants. I was dumb enough to get into a poker game with 'im and a fellow named Tripp."

"As I recall old posters, Soapy Smith is a confidence man out of Colorado. Old man Tripp has been around cheating men with his shell game since the Dakota days . . . he's got to be sixty or seventy years old by now." Eli shook his head in disgust. "Swiftwater, you warned us about this town before landing. Why did you forget your own preaching?"

"You know me, Eli, I love poker too much. Can't never follow my own advice." His face fell again. "I'm in an awful fix. I ain't got no money and my girls are gone—I lost them, too. I can't even eat, I'm so broke."

Eli shook his head. "Take the bear hides and sell them, then get something to eat. Come over to our tent tonight and stay with us. We'll figure what to do after a night's rest."

The next morning Eli sat quietly near the tent's stove, sipping steaming coffee out of a tin cup. He'd stirred first, starting the stove and coffee early while thinking about Swiftwater Bill's run-in with Smith and Tripp.

Swiftwater, his spirits lifted by the bear-hide money, sat on the other side, joking with Noodles about frying flapjacks on a sticky frying pan. Noodles peeked outside the tent flap from time to time at more snow piling to waist-high levels and bantered back about skillful cooking.

Eli set his coffee down and asked, "Swiftwater, how did Smith and Tripp get your money? You're no fool at cards. What did they do?"

"They played me all in on a pot-limit pot and cuffed the winnin' cards. I didn't remember to count the remainin' deck until it was too late. Then I was scared to start a fuss with all Soapy's boys standin' around. They would've killed me if I'd called 'em cheats."

"Can you cheat at cards, too?"

"I can cuff and hold, crimp and deal seconds better than them—but I'm tellin' you, they'll shoot me when I win. I ain't got enough money to play again, anyway."

Eli picked his cup up, took another sip, and looked over at Noodles tossing flapjacks. "Old man, will you help me get Swiftwater's money back? I owe him for saving my life a while ago."

Swiftwater sat up straight and shook his head. "No, Eli. You saved me once before—I just paid what I already owed."

Noodles looked back at Eli, his eyes curious, and asked, "What you thinkin' of doin'?"

"Soapy and his gang won't let Swiftwater play till they think he's gotten more money. I want you to find a blacksmith's shop and get melted brass that looks like nuggets. Fill a poke and throw a few of your real nuggets on top. Pay the smithy well and warn him to stay quiet. We're going to get those fellows into another poker game."

Noodles grimaced. "If they get a close look at that poke, they'll be bad trouble."

"Don't let them touch it. If they ask, throw them a real nugget to look at. Tell them Swiftwater and you are partners—and you'll give over the poke against any losses. Set in and play yourself. I doubt they'll worry much. I figure they're a greedy bunch and think they can't lose."

Swiftwater Bill's eyes squinted. "What'd you want me to do when we get the game goin' good?"

"Play the best you can and cheat every time you get a chance ... but don't hold out any cards. Let them do that. Sooner or later a big pot will show, and you'll have to go all in with your poke of brass. That's when they'll short the deck so they've got free cards for the winning hand."

Noodles set his frying pan down on the stove with a clang. "How we goin' to get Swiftwater's money back by doin' that?"

"When we leave here to do this thing, I'm going to follow behind but stay out of sight. When you get to that big hand, play slowly and sound a ruckus so I know when to come out and call them cheats. There'll be a crowd standing around for me to hide in. They won't see me coming till it's too late. I've got a sawed-off ten-gauge shotgun I've kept for years— I'll have that and my pistol hid under my coat."

Noodles ladled flapjacks onto three plates, grinning. "That'll keep the peace sure enough ... but how you goin' to prove they're cheatin'?"

"You two just trust me, it won't be troublesome. But we need to take this camp down after breakfast. While you're at the blacksmith's, I'll hire a boatman to wait on the shore tonight with our gear. We'll need to get across to Dyea quick to be safe."

Swiftwater stood up to get the plate Noodles handed out. He sat back down again, poured syrup, and looked at Eli out of the corner of his eye. "Why you doin' this for me? I ain't much better than them. And it took me over ten years to pay you back for last time."

"You're my friend, and I may need help again. This Alaska and Klondike look like rough places—bad to live in all alone. And I never could abide the likes of Soapy Smith and the gangs he likes to run. It will do folks good around here to see him get fearful."

After breakfast they lifted the stove between two wood poles and dumped hot coals and ashes out of it. Noodles boxed up his cook gear, bagged their sleeping rolls, and carried everything outside, shoving it under a tarp to keep it dry from falling snowflakes. Then Eli and Swiftwater dropped the tent, rolled it, and tied it into a tight bundle.

After an hour of packing, they slipped away in different directions. Noodles walked into town to find the blacksmith's shop, Eli hoisted the tent pack and headed toward the shore near the front of town, and after lingering for a while, Swiftwater Bill headed the other way.

As darkness settled, they met again behind the town's livery, between the stacks of hay and grain. Eli broke the action open on his shotgun, dropped two brass buckshot into the double-barrel, and snapped it shut. He spun the cylinder of his Peacemaker, looking for five live rounds, and set the hammer on the sixth, empty chamber. After he nodded that he was loaded and ready, Noodles and Swiftwater turned away and shuffled down the frozen, rutted road along the town's frontage. When they reached a place named the Gold Pan Saloon, they walked up and pushed through its door.

Swiftwater stepped to the center of the smoky chamber, spread his arms, and shouted, "Soapy, you ain't good enough to win again!"

Except for the plunking piano, silence spread as the saloon's customers gawked at the small man who had lost so much at cards four nights before. Then the hubbub started again while they appraised his companion of similar size, who stood drunkenly nearby with a plump leather poke and a brown whiskey bottle in his knotty old hands.

"You boys sure do look ready for fun. Who's that old prairie dog you got with you, Swiftwater?" Soapy stepped out from a circle of six men.

"This here's Noodles—he's goin' to be my partner up in Dawson." Swiftwater reached for Noodles' liquor bottle.

"I ain't partnerin' up when it comes to my whiskey," slurred Noodles, yanking the mostly empty bottle away.

"You boys sit right down here, and I'll try hard to entertain you." Smith walked over to a red-felt poker table. "You don't mind if Tripp plays again, do you, Swiftwater?"

"Nope. He got some of my money the other night, too. You don't mind if we play against Noodles' poke, do you?"

"Well, now, that'll be just fine . . . but we need to weigh it up so we know what you got."

Noodles banged his bottle down on the table and clutched the poke to his chest with both arms. He shook his head back and forth and said, "Ain't no-body takin' my poke less'n they win it fair and square. I ain't lettin' you touch it—no, sir!"

"Well, Noodles, you're bein' hardheaded about this. How we suppose to know what you got in there?"

Noodles set his poke down, fumbled with the bindings, and let a few bits of yellow tumble out onto the table. He pushed the bright lumps around with his forefinger, picked up a large heart-shaped nugget, and shoved it toward Soapy Smith, asking, "Lookee there, you ain't never seen a beauty like that before, have you?"

Smith reached for the nugget, pinched it between two fingers, and held it high against the light of the coal oil lamp. He rubbed it with his thumb and then bit into it, warping his face on one side. He pulled it out of his mouth and peered at it again. After a moment he said, "I want to get this away from you, Noodles. I know a lady that would like it. Deal the cards, boys."

"Gim-me my nugget. By Jeez, you ain't won it yet!" After getting the heart-shaped nugget back, Noodles moved his poke down to his lap and held its top even with the table as he scraped his yellow lumps in. He tightened the top, then heaved the poke back up onto the table with a noisy *clump*.

Rows and circles of men, puffing on their pipes and cigarettes, stepped near with whiskey and beer glasses clenched in their fists, clucking about each card as it was flipped out. Smoke billowed around, and the lamp above sent snaking beams down to the table through the thick blue fog. Glasses clinked, shoes shuffled, and chairs squeaked, but Swiftwater and Noodles and the five they faced kept dealing and betting in spite of the racket.

Two hours slipped by as chits passed back and forth and as winning hands wrung them from one man and then another. All the players kept serious and quiet except for Noodles; he chatted and laughed with the spectators whenever he won in his turn. Suddenly everyone hushed when Tripp bet one thousand dollars on his last card and Soapy called and raised two thousand on his. Noodles showed a king and two queens face up in Seven-Toed Stud Poker. Soapy had a pair of jacks showing; Tripp had two black eights. Swiftwater, having folded two cards back, counted the hands as quickly as he could. Seven players had gotten three cards, and one had folded on the first round of betting. Six players had gotten the fourth card, and everyone had stayed through the second round of bets. He'd dropped out during the third round, and five had received last cards. There had to be nine cards remaining in the dealer's deck. But that did not seem to be the count when Tripp threw down the rest of the deck after passing out the last cards—only seven lay strewn in front. He bumped Noodles' knee hard with his own, hoping to signal him that the deck looked short.

"By Jeez, what you fellows got over there?" Noodles then slid his chair forward, its legs squawking on the rough wood flooring, and hooted, "Woohee . . . I guess I got to raise you two thousand, how you like them apples?"

Old man Tripp's face stayed straight. "I call and raise you two thousand."

"Well . . . I believe I have the best hand myself, boys. Here's your bets, and I raise two thousand. Appears you should slide your gold in, old whiskers, my friend!" Soapy leaned forward, catlike, and pointed toward Noodles' poke.

"Woohee—mighty big bets to call. You fellows rightly put your chits in . . . and it's only fair that I go all in to call." Noodles pushed his sausage-shaped bag toward the center of the table.

Eli stayed motionless, listening to Noodles' summons, and studying the risks. The ugly face he hated so much appeared in the crowd just across from him, conspicuous among ordinary faces on the other side. Patches might warn Soapy or Tripp, or threaten with a firearm himself the moment danger appeared.

But he judged it critical to move fast. With his right hand he pulled the shotgun out from under his coat, shifted it to his left, and cocked both hammers. He reached behind him for his belt knife, snapped the leather loop loose, pulled it free, and pushed forward, prodding with his gun barrels. The men in front looked behind them, wondering about the disturbance, and when they saw who was coming through, they instantly jostled sideways, clearing a path to the table. Their fright kept his approach noiseless, and he stepped up to the table before anyone could jump away. He slashed his knife down and struck its point through the last cards of the deck in front of Tripp, then shoved the double-barrel into Soapy's face.

"Let's count the cards on the table and in your hands. I've a notion we'll find more than we should, Smith!" Eli reached under his coat and pulled out his Colt, pointing it as well. He glanced at Patches and saw him still standing, watching, not moving a bit.

The piano stopped playing and the saloon fell silent; blowing breaths sounded, like unsettled, secret whispers. The men behind Smith and Tripp, in the way of the guns' muzzles, sidled off. Soapy's face bleached white as he inched his hands down until his fingers, shaking now, hung on the edge of the red cloth.

"You've just dropped your holdout cards, Smith. Somebody get over here and pick them up—they're on the floor!" Eli waved his pistol at the crowd toward where Patches stood, motioning for someone to come forward.

He blinked in astonishment. Patches pushed out and stepped to Soapy's side, leaned, then stood up with two jack face cards between his fingers, held high so everyone could see.

Soapy Smith swung his gaze away from Eli's shotgun and stared at Patches. A smile turned his mouth as he said, "Patches, my boy, you've chosen poorly."

Eli bumped his shotgun hard against Soapy's cheek. "Shut up, Smith! You're the one that has chosen poorly—and it's put you in a bad fix. Noodles, Swiftwater, count what you're owed."

The saloon grew noisy; men began to push and shove at each other as some of Smith's committee members roughed their way through to the table with their pistols drawn.

"It appears you better give up before I tell 'em not to let you go." Smith shifted his gaze to his approaching men, his smile widening.

"Get your men back, and their weapons put away!" Eli banged the end of the double-barrel off Soapy Smith's left cheekbone, and blood beaded from two half-moon cuts. "You better worry about those in here wanting to hang you rather than thinking I'll ever give up."

Shouts filled the saloon, and the crowd's brawling pressed the backs of Soapy's men, making them twist and look fearfully behind. Smith, grimacing, raised his hands and wagged them to quiet the uproar, and to keep his men back. He wiped his cuts with one hand, stared back at Eli, and said, "I'll give your friend his money back—and I'll repay any man his rightful due if he wants to step forward and show his face." He then stood up, pulled packs of bills out of his pants and coat, and motioned for Tripp to do the same.

"Them's the ones—that's the same money he got from me the other night, Eli." Swiftwater grabbed at the bundles as they dropped to the tabletop.

"We'll back out of here now. You're coming along." Eli pointed his Peacemaker at Patches, then waved it toward the door. "Keep your men inside, Smith—it'll be bad business for them to hunt me in the dark."

Eli stepped backward, keeping his ten-gauge aimed at Soapy and the men near the table. Noodles, Patches, and Swiftwater Bill bumped their way through the men behind them an jumped out of the door. When Eli reached the opening, he flipped his pistol up and fired at the lamp hanging over the poker table, bursting it into an explosion of flames. He turned and ran as fast as he could through the narrow black alley alongside the saloon, hearing the men inside holler and scramble as they rushed to get out. He turned the corner of the building and saw the tideland surf, with four shadows in it shoving on a boat. Two shots went off back in the black, and he leaped to get to the water in a hurry to help, doubting that they could row away in time to dodge a gunfight . . . and wondering why Patches had come along without a tussle.

PART III

Hardship

CHAPTER FIFTEEN

Dyea

Noodles and Swiftwater giggled like schoolboys, giggled across Skagway Bay in spite of the swamping waves that the boatman yelled to them to bail out, giggled until Eli told them to stop. They'd started their silliness after Eli had fired two blasts from his shotgun high into the night sky as the boat first rowed away on the flooding tide. The rattle of buckshot hitting and rolling off roofing had turned the thunder of footfalls from Soapy's men chasing them in the dark to a rout running the other way. Meanwhile, Patches had cowered, shivering and clutching the side slats in the hull's bottom from the moment he'd jumped aboard, hunkering away from all the laughter and bailing and Eli's glare.

Eli jumped to the middle seat behind the boatman after his warning shots, locked two more oars, and pulled in rhythm until they reached lee-side water close to winks of light from Dyea. As the boat glided onto the sheltered surface, he lifted his oars and shifted his seat over near Patches.

"Why did you give yourself up?" Eli watched the huddled shadow turn toward him.

"I read who you are and I know what you want. Smith would of got me hung or had me killed if I'd stayed back there. You come along—so I thought I could get away. You won't hurt me. You want what I know."

"I've seen men hanged for less than you've done. You may have freed yourself from death because of Smith, but you won't find it so easy to get away from me. If you try, you'll have to do it on one leg because I'll shoot the other off."

The shadow drew back, moaning, and said, "You don't need to worry. There ain't no place for me to run. I want to go back to San Francisco . . . bad . . . but I can't do that. I can't go through Skagway again 'cause of Soapy. I'm going to go wherever you're going."

"I was bound for the Klondike, but I'm turning from there now that I've found you. I want the man that killed Senator Turnbull's wife and child, and you're the one that knows who did it."

"I only saw who did it. I don't know what his name is. I called him the Cannibal a few times . . . as good a name as any." Suddenly Patches sat upright. "Why didn't you Marshals just make Frissy tell? Why you chasing me? She's the one that told me about him before I followed and saw him come out of the Senator's house."

Hannah and her friend popped into Eli's mind, and he thought the murder riddle had just neared an answer. He leaned closer to Patches and asked, "Is Frissy the name of the Negro woman that showed me how to find you?"

"Yes . . . I guess she must of been the one . . . nobody else knew about the Cannibal but her. He told her he was going to steal from a rich man's house, then she told me. She was his whore one night after he come to town."

"Why did she tell you about this man?"

"I was suppose to steal whatever he took and then share with her. But why didn't she just tell you these things herself?"

Eli hesitated before answering. "The Cannibal cut her tongue out . . . she wasn't able to tell."

Patches paused, choked, and then said, "I spent my life in San Francisco with rough men, but I ain't never seen such an evil one as him."

Eli felt the boat bump the bottom. He stood and looked back to Patches and asked, "Where is the Cannibal now? Where did he go?"

"I think he went to the place where you mean to go. He told Frissy he wanted money to go to the Klondike to strike it rich. That's where I was following him to. I know he ain't back in Skagway because Soapy made me look. He must of traveled on already."

Eli stood still for a moment, feeling the gentle bob of the boat as its owner slipped over the side into the shallows to tow it toward shore. Happy feelings surged inside him as he thought of his good fortune in being able to travel to more new places. He jumped into the water also and called, "Everybody get out of the boat and help pull. We're starting for the Klondike tomorrow!"

They carried their outfits, wading back and forth

over flooded flats, and stacked them among other piles of similar goods that lined the shore. Noodles and Swiftwater gathered scrap lumber and driftwood, kindled a blaze, and set bags of gear close to sleep on for the rest of the night. Eli sent them to their beds, pointed Patches to another one nearby, and took first watch himself.

After midnight Swiftwater roused for his turn at lookout, and Eli slid under covers near the fire. He tossed and turned because of the coffee he'd drunk during the night—and also because hope filled his mind, as it had many times before when he'd wandered across the West. The old feelings had not changed: the challenge of man hunting, the thrill of seeing mountains for the first time, the sense of satisfaction in passing through new territory and ending wrongful ways. Though, he thought, this journey looks much different from those of the past. He'd always traveled alone before, but this time he seemed bound up with a prospector, a swindler, and a pickpocket. The idea of having such odd companions puzzled him, and he rolled over again, seeking a soft spot to think more on it. At last, just before sleep, he judged he'd just grown older and now lived in a different place and time—and that he couldn't rule fate any more now then he could before.

In the morning Noodles and Swiftwater learned from other gold stampeders camped nearby that Canadian Mounties demanded that everyone have at least a ton of provisions when crossing the border at the top of the Chilkoot Pass. Eli sent Swiftwater Bill for more food, put Noodles on guard at their outfits stashed on the shore, and walked with Patches to search for the Cannibal among the men milling about the town. They poked around the jumble of false-fronted saloons and frame hotels, peering hard at bearded faces, questioning everyone willing to stop and talk. By midmorning they had circled through all of Dyea and back to Noodles, who still sat on lookout, with his rifle ready across his lap.

"I see you fellows didn't find nothin' yet. Don't know how you could—been a couple thousand men headin' by me for the Klondike this mornin' so far. How you goin' to find one outlaw in that many?"

Eli steered Patches to a seat near the smoldering fire that lingered from the night before. "I'm not sure I can. It's best we move on to Dawson City and look there. If Patches is telling the truth, I'll find the Cannibal in saloons and with prostitutes . . . or running away from more butchered remains."

"Why do you want to look anymore? You was treated bad after he stabbed you." Noodles shot a forefinger straight at Patches.

"I want to catch the Cannibal. I've never stopped following anyone like him. After I'm done with my duty, I'll stay and prospect with you, old man."

"By Jeez, I hope you hurry up. With all these men goin' north, maybe this land ain't goin' to last long enough for me, anyhow. I sure hope it's as big as Swiftwater says."

Swiftwater came back an hour later with two teamsters and their horses and sleds hired to carry their supplies up the Chilkoot Trail to the foot of the mountains. They pulled away at noon, Noodles perched on top of the first sled, with Patches hiking close behind, and Eli and Swiftwater following the last sled and watching the procession ahead. As they tramped along, Swiftwater talked about the impermanent settlements that they passed: Finnegan's Point, a blacksmith shop, saloon, and huddles of canvas five miles up from Dyea; a rest stop called Canyon City, a nook inside a two-mile-long gorge littered with rocky rubble and torn-up trees; then Pleasant Camp, the last flat place along the road, and finally, Sheep Camp, a clutter of shacks and flapping tents set in the last of the trees that could be cut for firewood.

They reached Sheep Camp after dark and cleared a circle in snow and underbrush for their tent among hundreds of others pitched in the woods. Great fires leaped into the blackened surroundings and cast quick and dancing shadows against heaped piles of snow. Men hollered in thankfulness for beating the trail behind and boasted that they could win the one ahead. While eating a sowbelly supper, Eli, Noodles, and Patches listened as Swiftwater talked more about the remaining trail. Then, slowly, the night gripped harder and chased everyone to his bed, leaving the stars winking over the smoky pall that floated overhead.

The past night's merriment shriveled as the Chilkoot Pass came into sight when the light of the coming morning crept over the mountains. Each man heaved his load onto his back and began his trudge up the steps cut out of the snow that sheeted the slope. A single black line of stampeders formed and climbed the white face with a common cry, filling the pass with wails greater than those from howling winter winds. They struggled up to a place called Stone House, a huge leaning boulder that offered shelter and rest; they struggled up until they reached the place called the Scales, where Indian packers charged a dollar a pound for their measure of the mountain; and they struggled until all of them howled for deliverance from all the suffering that lay ahead. Every man had to get his two thousand pounds up to the summit, and that seemed much more than some could do.

Eli loaded Patches with a fifty-pound pack, shouldered a larger one himself, and pushed both of them into place among the men marching by. Swiftwater Bill left the campsite to find the Chilkat Indians who had packed for him in the past, and Noodles stayed to guard the stockpile waiting behind.

As Patches stepped up the slope, Eli watched the pickpocket's long legs and bundled torso climb with strong strides, like an odd stork coming up a riverbank. Patches had stayed quiet and agreeable to his share of work since they'd camped overnight in Dyea, and now Eli could see that the man seemed willing to carry his fair part of the four tons that needed packing to the summit.

They fell out of line at Stone House and rested. Farther up, at the Scales, they twisted through knots of men begging Indian packers to take the remaining hauls up the sharpest cut of the mountain. Eli paused, caught his breath, and studied the five hundred feet slanting above. He bent his back again against the steep climb ahead and signaled for Patches to do the same.

When they reached the top of the pass, they stopped and gazed out. They had come up under clear skies tinted blue beyond the horizon by icy air; now snow-covered peaks of faraway mountains blasted sunlight back to the indigo for as far as their eyes could see. The gray inlet they'd rowed across two nights before lay below, and spruce-filled valleys reached inland. And most plain of all, long rows of stampeders stretched north down the distant side, toward the Klondike.

Patches, shading his eyes from the sun's glare, swung his head back and forth and said, "This country scares me because it's so empty, but I ain't never seen anything so pretty like this."

Eli looked at the unsightly pickpocket standing next to him. Patches had responded favorably when told to pack, and had shown unexpected strength in scaling the heights. Hearing his fear of remoteness, yet his praise for its beauty, surprised Eli. As he turned toward the two fur-clad Mounties collecting customs from each person crossing the summit, he answered, "It's the kind of country I want to stay in—and the kind where you need to learn to be honest."

They passed through customs, and registered their packs, poking a pole with Eli's bandanna fastened to the top to mark the spot against getting hidden by snowstorms. They walked back to the crest of the mountain they'd just come up and sledded down on their backsides with hundreds of other men doing the same. After an hour more of jogging downhill, they reached Sheep Camp, and saw Noodles and Swiftwater loading four Indian packers with more of their eight thousand pounds needed on top.

Noodles bounced away from the campsite and met them as they approached. "How steep is it, Eli? How long is it goin' to take to get our belongings up top?"

"It's a hard climb, a week's work with help." Eli eyed the one-hundred-pound packs hanging on each Indian's back.

"Swiftwater says he'll stay back and watch our camp so I can go. I want to pack a load with you and see the top."

"I don't want you to climb up till last . . . and I don't want you to carry a pack. It's too steep, and you're too old."

Noodles stared at Eli, long-faced, his eyes wet. After a moment he said, "I dreamt about this mountain standin' in my way and I got to climb it. If'n I can't go back and forth and do my share, I might as well die right here. I ain't goin' to be a burden on nobody."

Eli, sorry for his remark, studied his friend. Finally he said, "You've always done your share and you're no burden to anyone. Just promise to load yourself light. We started together, and it's my mind we'll finish that way, too. Go get your pack and come along."

After shouldering another pack, Eli turned again from Sheep Camp with Noodles and Patches following behind. The four Chilkats, squat, powerful, and hiking fast, disappeared ahead in streams of men carrying up the trail. Worried about Noodles' strength lasting long enough to top the pass, Eli slowed his pace. He rested for thirty minutes when they reached Stone House, and then again for that long at the Scales.

Noodles' face began to look pinched and gray like his whiskers. After standing up first and staring for a long time at the groaning men straining to climb the stairs cut up the mountain, the old man led the way from their last resting place. Patches fell in line behind Noodles, and Eli stepped in last. They moved up in lockstep with the black line of men stretching toward the summit. After two hundred steps up the stairs, Noodles began to wobble. Suddenly he fell sideways and tumbled down the steep slope with his arms and legs and pack spinning at all angles. Eli leaped out of line, threw off his pack, and skidded after Noodles' bouncing body, calling out for the men below to stop his fall.

When Eli reached Noodles, lying facedown crumpled against a snowdrift, he turned him over, brushed the snow from his face, and examined his breathing. He held his ear to his chest and listened for a heartbeat. Patches came sledding down as Eli rolled Noodles over and pulled the pack off the old man's limp body.

Patches ran over, calling, "What's happened to Noodles? I couldn't grab hold before he fell. Is he hurt bad, you think?"

"His heart and breathing sound weak—I don't know if any bones are broke. I need to get him up to the Mounties' cabin!"

Patches fell to his knees beside Eli. "I like this old man. What can I do to help?"

After throwing off his wool overcoat, Eli crouched once more, cradled Noodles in his arms, then stood up. "Collect my coat and our packs and get one load to the top. I need to get Noodles up as fast as I can!"

Patches jumped up. "I'll do it. I can get everything up by myself—you just watch and see. I'll come and see you and Noodles after my first load. You'll see you can trust me!"

Eli faced the slope and yelled for the climbing row of stampeders to break and let him in. As he started running up the mountain, fringes and feathers of his medicine coat fluttering behind, men on the lower part of the slope began to yell for the ones above to get out of his way. Soon all the men on the mountain began to cheer him up the stairs. Near the summit he slowed and stumbled. The whole mountain shouted for him to keep on—then thundered with the loudest hooray when he dashed out of sight.

CHAPTER SIXTEEN

Pluck

"How can we stay in a place like this?" Hannah stared in disgust up and down the muddy street running through Skagway. Everywhere she looked, stampeders and construction crews slopped around like foot soldiers.

Lincoln, laughing, pulled Naomi out of the muck and set her on boards laid along a building with a sign across its front reading YUKON OUTFITTERS. "Don't fret. I been livin' around timber towns, and this'n ain' no different. We just find us a dry place and pitch our tents—we be just fine, Mizz Twigg."

After looking into Naomi's eyes, Hannah thought she saw the same worry she felt in her own heart. The passage to Skagway had been thrilling, with countless seascapes and hundreds of eager faces as passengers gossiped of the gold they anticipated was waiting ahead for them. And it had been a joy to watch Naomi's and Lincoln's proud faces as they had learned to read and write simple words. But, suddenly, as she stood cold and wet in the middle of the mud, her recent enjoyment seemed imaginary and very long ago.

"Will all the towns be like this from now on?" Hannah gave a tug on Sorrowful's leash and pulled herself toward the boards, wondering why he had wagged his tail so much over the past few days.

"I suspect so. But I don't think there is more towns till Dawson City. You ladies got to dress warm and quit worryin' about lookin' pretty—and you got to stay dry so's you don't get sick. You don't want to catch cold up here."

Lincoln's indifference to the ooze and ugliness of Skagway and his easy laugh despite the icy rain chased the anxiety from Hannah's mind. She stomped clumps of mud off her shoes onto the boards and looked up at him. "Tell me how to dress. Show me how to pitch tents and build fires. I taught you how to read and write—now it's time to pay me back!"

They bought small-size woolen pants and shirts from people turning back south, two oilskins, smelly, tough, and heavy, and rubber boots, which Hannah had forgotten to buy back in San Francisco. After locating an empty area among the hundreds of tents surrounding the town, they set their two tents on angles, corner to corner, front flaps adjoining. Lincoln built a fire out in the gap in between and showed Hannah and Naomi how to cook in a Dutch oven, with beans, bacon, and molasses inside for their night's supper. They walked to trees a half-mile away and cut additional firewood—Lincoln laughing when Hannah and Naomi first tried to saw and chop. He then made them practice until each could cut wood by herself.

It was the first night in Hannah's life that she'd spent sitting next to an outdoor fire, sipping coffee, and spying on stars that peeked between broken clouds above. When it got late, she slipped into her sleeping roll and smiled about her first day in the wilderness. Her arms and back hurt, but she went to sleep feeling warm and more proud than ever before.

Just after midnight she woke and couldn't see Naomi across the tent. Then she heard rustles and murmurs in the other one and realized that she would pass the night all alone. Anger flashed through her mind, but then she decided not to judge; perhaps she would be doing the same if Eli were lying over there. Soon she slept again and dreamed of finding him and making love like she'd always wanted to do.

The next morning she remained in bed until Sorrowful whined to join Lincoln and Naomi at their breakfast fire. She let him out, stretched, and began to dress in her new trousers and shirt. Suddenly a rough voice shouted outside, "Where's the woman, niggers?"

"In the tent, suh. How can I help you-all, gentlemen?"

The voice shouted again, "You can help by shuttin' up. Ma'am, we want to speak to you. You better step out here."

Hannah buttoned her shirt as fast as she could and flew through the tent flap. She saw Naomi huddled close to Lincoln near the fire, and Sorrowful, hair raised and growling, guarding them from a gang of six men.

"Get hold of that dog or I'll kill 'im!" The man with

the rough voice stepped forward and aimed a shotgun at Sorrowful.

Hannah ran forward, knelt, and circled Sorrowful's neck with her arms, holding tight. She looked up and cried, "Why are you men here? What do you want?"

"We want to know why you're with these nigger people. It ain't right, you bein' white and campin' alone with 'em. We ain't goin' to stand for it whilst we're around!"

Hannah stared at the men in disbelief. She answered, "Lincoln and Naomi are my friends—and don't you dare call them that ugly name!" She felt her own anger build as Sorrowful growled louder.

The six men shuffled sideways, spreading their position. Then their leader stepped toward Hannah again, grunting as he said, "Woman, we ain't here to be talked back to or turned around. You get your things—you gonna come with us."

Lincoln rose from his setting log. "You don't touch the lady! She the Marshal's frien' and that's his dog. He ain' wantin' nobody to mess with them, no suh. You best get away before he hears about this."

All the men exchanged glances, then huddled together. The oldest of the gang, gray-bearded, stepped forward and pushed the man with the shotgun back with his left arm. He furrowed his brow and asked, "Ma'am, what Marshal is the darkie talkin' about?"

"I'm traveling to join Eli Bonnet, Deputy U.S. Marshal from Montana. This is his dog, stolen in San Francisco, and I'm returning him."

The old man squirmed around in his parka and

eyed his companions. He turned back to Hannah and asked, "What's Eli always wearin' for luck when he's thinkin' there's goin' to be trouble?"

"He wears an Indian shirt. He took it from a medicine man running away from the Rosebud Reservation when he was the U.S. Marshal in the Dakota Territories. I plan to see him soon, and I think he will find your behavior intolerable."

"Ma'am, I'm not certain what that last word means, but I do expect Eli to get riled when he hears. You just tell him I stopped this bad business I found myself party to. Tell 'im Fidler says hello—he'll remember who I am."

The man with the shotgun yelled, "You just gonna turn tail and run from some Marshal that ain't even here? What kind of yellow belly are you, Fidler? It ain't right this woman stays here with these people!"

Fidler swung his head and said, "Go ahead and do what you think is right, Walker. But I'm tellin' you, you trouble this woman and you're gonna have Bonnet trackin' you down until he catches up. Then he'll shoot your leg off so you can't cause trouble no more."

After hearing the old man's warning, the four men behind Walker turned and marched away, one behind the other. Fidler tipped his cap at Hannah and followed, glancing behind once at Walker standing alone.

Walker's face paled. "I . . . I ain't leavin' you here. Like I said—you better get your things." He pointed his shotgun at Hannah and Sorrowful again.

Hannah jumped up, clinging to Sorrowful's neck

hair with her hands. She stepped close to the barrel of the shotgun, holding Sorrowful back, and threatened, "Get out of here before I let this dog go. If you shoot me, I know the people of this town will hang you. If you shoot this dog, I'll tell them you tried to kill me and the dog saved me. I think they'd still want to hang you!"

Walker turned away and stomped after his companions, cursing their abandonment. When Naomi, who sat crying like a frightened child, saw that it was safe, she ran to Hannah and clung to her. Sorrowful pulled loose and stood in front barking, watching as the raving man walked away.

Lincoln stepped to Hannah's side. After a moment, he whispered, "You a brave woman. I was so scared to death of that man, I couldn't move."

Hannah felt numbness creeping into her own limbs. For some unknown reason she thought of her father back in San Francisco, and his ashen face mirrored in her mind. Then she began to wonder what had made her charge up to Walker and his shotgun. She sensed that her recklessness might have incited him to shoot. But confronting him had seemed crucial at the moment, and now her triumph tasted sweet even though the rest of her body felt deadened.

Taking a deep breath, she loosed herself from Naomi's grip and walked to the fire. After sitting down, she called, "Let's finish breakfast. When we're done, I'm going to look for Eli in town." She sat staring into the flames, shivering in spite of the fire's warmth.

"I'll go with you. Best you don't go around this

town alone. There's lots more bad-uns like that Walker fellow."

Hannah shook her head hard. "No, I want to go alone. I'll take Sorrowful to keep me safe. You go with Naomi and purchase horses for our packing— I'll give you money. I want to start up the White Pass Trail tomorrow. I've read it's best for women, so that's the way we shall go."

Lincoln wrinkled up his face, looked down, and kicked at a stray piece of firewood with the toe of his boot. Finally he said, "You don't come back by suppertime, I'll come get you, you hear?" He looked up and fixed his eyes on Hannah.

Later, with Sorrowful on tether, Hannah waded back and forth across the town's muddy lanes in her new boots with her pants legs stuffed inside. Men eyed her, grinning about her dress, as she visited stores asking if anyone had seen Eli Bonnet. Each person she asked shook his head and continued with his work, seldom bothering to look up. She slogged all through the town's center, bent on finding someone who had seen him.

As noontime chased people toward their lunch, Hannah saw a telegraph office across the street. She walked over and went inside, holding Sorrowful close to her and slipping in among the men crowding the counter.

One of the clerks, after squinting at her for a moment, yelled over the noise in the room, "Ma'am, you want to send a wire?"

Hannah squeezed through to the front and answered, "Yes, I would like to send a message to my father in San Francisco . . . and I'm looking for a man named Eli Bonnet. Perhaps you've seen him."

Before the clerk could reply, a gentle-faced elderly man shoved to her side. "Ma'am, I help administer this office. We'd be glad to help you in any way we can. We don't get many ladies up here . . . be a pleasure to do it."

"Thank you." Hannah wondered why Sorrowful flattened his ears and growled as the man stepped close. She looked down and scolded, "Sorrowful, quiet—sit down!"

"Ma'am, that's a mighty nice-lookin' dog you got there. Looks darn near like a real wolf. Where'd you get him?"

"He's Mr. Bonnet's dog. I left San Francisco to find Eli . . . and to return his dog. Do you know where he is?"

"I can't say I do, but my boss knows. Let me sit you down in back and get you comfortable. You can write your wire out while you're waitin' there. I'll go fetch him for you straightaway."

Hannah, marveling at her good luck at finding someone to help so quickly, followed the kind-faced man behind the counter. Sorrowful growled again and shied from entering a small storeroom strewn with boxes of paper at the end of the building. After sitting on a wooden bench inside, she smiled and asked, "What is your name, sir? I must tell you how much I appreciate your kindness."

"My name's Tripp, ma'am." The old face slipped backward, grinning, and the door clicked shut.

Hannah leaned down, found blank paper in one of

the boxes, and wrote a message to her father that all was well with Naomi and her. After adding a line telling how exciting she'd found her new adventure, she went to the door to return to the clerk who had first called out. She turned and jerked the doorknob, repeated the attempt, then beat on the door with her fist and yelled as hard as she could. She stopped and listened . . . then heard laughter on the other side.

She looked at Sorrowful lying with his head resting on his paws and saw his sad eyes staring back. After walking over and patting his head, she said, "Sorrowful, this will be the last time I'll fail to listen." She then sat down on the floor close by him, covered her face with her hands, and cried as hard as she could.

After a few minutes she stopped crying and dried her face on her sleeve. Her first thought had been that she'd been locked away because of Lincoln and Naomi. Now it dawned on her that her imprisonment must be because of Eli Bonnet—and that meant he must be near.

She stood and studied her jail for a way to escape or to defend herself. More than twenty boxes of scrap paper sat about the room, one electric bulb dangled overhead, and the bench she had first sat on stood against an outside wall. The room had no windows, and she could find no tools for breaking out or for use as a weapon. She thought of starting a fire with matches, but decided that would be too dangerous for her and Sorrowful. Finally she pulled the bench over to the door, turned it upside down, and wedged it against the knob. She then carried boxes over and piled them up to protect herself against anyone trying to shove the door open.

Just after she finished, she heard a yell from the other room. "Lady, what you doin' in there?" The door jiggled against the bench and boxes.

Sorrowful bounded from his place on the floor and stood against the boxes with his front paws, snarling and barking. Hannah, startled by his rage, pulled him back, telling him to quiet himself and lie down. She heard another voice as it said, "Would that beat all, she's got that door so nobody can get in—and that dog'll kill the first that figures to do it. Soapy and Tripp are goin' to have their fun with this one, for certain."

Sorrowful growled again. Hannah sat down with her back against her barricade and pulled him close. As she sat there shivering from fear and cold, she wondered how Lincoln would ever be able to find her and Sorrowful, and if he did, how he would get them free. As she whispered a prayer for their rescue, she saw Sorrowful watching, ears pricked up. He licked her face after she finished, causing her to force a smile and whisper, "I see you think we'll get away. This time I'll choose to listen." Then she hugged him and offered another plea.

An hour slipped by while she listened to men moving about on the other side, gossiping and laughing. Suddenly she heard the entry door slam and more voices—but none of them sounded clear. The muttering then stopped and someone walked to the storeroom door.

"Ma'am, I want you to come out of there!" shouted an angry voice through the door.

Sorrowful leaped up against the boxes again, raging more than before. Hannah let him carry on with his fury for a minute before she pulled him down and hushed him by gripping his nose with her hands.

"Lady, my name's Smith, and I run this town. I'll have this door cut down and your dog shot dead if you don't come out of there."

Hannah calmed herself, gathered all her wind, and yelled back, "I'll shoot the first man I see. My dog will kill another if you try it!"

"Lady, you ain't got no gun . . ."

"If you think I was stupid enough to walk around this town without one, you deserve to be shot. Ask the man who tricked me about the clothes I'm wearing. I had a pistol in my pocket which he couldn't see!"

Hannah heard footsteps move away from the door and more muttering. Then the same footsteps came back.

"Lady, you can stay in there and freeze and go thirsty. You'll want out in a couple days and I'll be waitin' right here. Just yell when you want to come out." The footsteps marched away again, and the entry door slammed once more.

The thought of drinking water struck her like a knife. She knew she wouldn't freeze to death with Sorrowful near, but they would both need water soon. Her spirits sank as she weighed their plight. Continued defiance would cost them their lives in a short time, but surrendering seemed no better. She knew the kidnappers would kill Sorrowful as soon as they smashed through the door or walls. After that she would likely be beaten and raped, then killed in the fight she intended to give her captors. She sat down against her barricade again, cradled her head in her hands, and sobbed, "Why am I so foolish? Each time I try do things, I end up in trouble and can't get out by myself." She continued to sob, unable to stop.

Suddenly, to her horror, an ax blade crashed through the back wall boards, sending splinters flying. She jumped up and screamed, seeing Sorrowful bound in front of her, barking and leaping up. Then she saw the silver blade pull out and come crashing through again, opening a larger hole. She screamed louder, realizing that two more chops would get the axman in—and then she and Sorrowful would be killed.

CHAPTER SEVENTEEN

Prophecy

Noodles reared up from his sickbed, looking and listening. "By Jeez, I hear 'em coming ... listen ... it's thousands ... there's buffalos like I said there'd be!"

Before his fears passed that Noodles lay in the throes of final dreams just before death, Eli began to hear the sound as well. Thunder filled the creekbed around their camp, creeping down, sweeping closer, growing louder, like lightning storms rolling across the prairies. He plunged through the tent's flaps, stood still, and looked around the valley. Then he saw the herd approaching, not thousands as Noodles had said, but hundreds without question, all flowing down the hills around and past their camp.

"Them ain't buffalos, but they're good enough for me. I knowed this here was new land. Lookee at 'em ... I wonder what they be?"

Eli spun backward. "Get back in bed, old man! I thought I was losing you and now you're standing barefoot in snow. For Lord's sake, take care of yourself!"

"I'll get better now. Get my bed out here where I

can see. This is a sight I prayed for and now it's come true. Looks like some kind of deer."

"Caribou, old man, caribou!" yelled Eli, running back into the tent and grabbing Noodles' bedroll from a corner. He rushed through the flaps again and laid it down facing the rumbling herd.

Noodles crawled into his covers and wiggled around, bunching up his pillow for a better view. "Go shoot one a them critters for me. Get a young, fat buck or a dry doe. I need fresh meat, and Providence has given me plenty to get well by. Get goin'—I'm hungry!"

Need for fresh meat struck Eli with a desire beyond anything he'd experienced since being a youngster in the Civil War. Back then, blockades and Rebel faults had starved him skinny; now long distances from farms and grocery stores were doing the same. Doctors on top of the Chilkoot Pass had warned that Noodles suffered from symptoms of scurvy, along with an old heart with a bad beat, and had advised wholesome foods and plenty of rest. Finding a place to rest hadn't been a problem, but canned goods and moldy salt pork were the only edibles anybody had brought along.

The Chilkat Indians had been better than the doctors in finding a remedy for Noodles' sickness. They'd dug in the snow and offered a mash of wild rose hips as a cure. Then they had pointed out the direction in which to sled to find wild game—thus providing Eli a chance to get Noodles what he needed.

He'd quickly settled with Swiftwater Bill and

Patches to finish the hauling to the summit, and to drag everything downhill to the tent city at Lake Bennett. In the meantime, he would take Noodles west on a sled, hunt for game, and try to save his life.

Leaving behind an unholy alliance between a swindler and a pickpocket worried him now and then. Mostly what bothered him was the idea of what the twosome might make their business once they reached the ten thousand stampeders who were camped waiting for the ice to thaw from the headwaters of the Yukon River. Though, he thought, this seemed the time to test their faithfulness to promises they'd made at his farewell. Once they were all launched in boats down through wild waters toward Dawson City, not being able to rely on their word could mean drowning for all.

"I'm hungry, too, old man . . . and I think I'll get one for our companions at Lake Bennett. It'll freeze, and I can come get it after you're well and back with them." Eli grabbed his Winchester and sprinted out of the campsite, toward a line of runty spruce that offered cover to shoot from.

After reaching the trees, he hid and watched for a bit, then sighted and shot the nearest plump bull. Five minutes later he selected another and shot that one, too. Then he walked out and bled both, marveling at the hundreds of animals still milling around, grunting, clicking their hooves as they trotted in circles, snorting their puzzlement.

He skinned and boned the first animal he'd killed. On the way to the second, he heard them coming.

First the valley filled with a long, mournful howl from a hillside; then others joined in from farther away. The caribou herd stiffened, pranced, then began to bound away, down toward more wooded lowlands. Before he could run back to his pile of meat, the pack had made it down around him, circling, sniffing, growling.

Wolves had shadowed him before—but none like these. Across the West he'd often seen rangy gray ones hunting in packs during the early days. But those had disappeared after the buffalo had been slaughtered, and farming and ranching had begun. This pack had black, white, and gray ones combined. And they were much larger also—well over one hundred and twenty pounds, he thought. The hair on the back of his neck prickled as it had when he'd stalked the brown bears alone in the brush back near Skagway.

He watched, thinking the pack had never seen a human before and thus would sense no danger. Judging the nearest heavy white one as the leader, he sighted and killed him with one shot in the chest. The remaining nine wolves ran for the nearby trees as the rifle blast bounced off hills and echoed back. Kneeling and aiming ahead, he swung to a black one that appeared to be the mate to the leader and dropped it during its flight. He then stood up and wondered what would have happened if he'd forgotten to carry his rifle along between the downed caribou. Shivers shook his body under his parka as he walked over to the second caribou to clean that one out, and he concluded he had better be watchful in the new land, as Noodles liked to call it.

Later, when he returned to camp, Noodles sat straight up on his bedroll, clutching his covers and yelling, "I watched through my spyglass. By Jeez, those wolfs would a kill't you if'n you wouldn't of taught 'em better. Scared me silly!"

"I don't believe they'd ever seen a man before. Probably thought I was a bear and figured on thieving my meat. I killed the two most fearless ones, hoping the others would learn to stay away. We need the food, and they can hunt for their own."

"I saw different-colored ones—never saw wolfs like that before."

Eli laid down the caribou hearts and livers he'd carried back to camp. "They're larger wolves than the ones in the West ... if there's any alive there anymore." He tipped their skillet upright, poked a bed of fire coals together, and began to slice fresh meat into the pan. "When I finish the meal here, I'll get the meat and all the hides. The Chilkats said wolf fur around parka hoods is next best to wolverine and caribou hide is the best to sleep on. If Swiftwater is truthful about winters in Dawson, we'll need them both."

After lying back down on his bedroll, Noodles sighed and then said, "By Jeez, it's good to see big herds again. I hope folks are sensible this time and don't shoot 'em all down. I can't bear to think of these caribou being killed off, too."

"This land appears poorly placed for most folks. Too far north, too many mountains, and I don't believe it can be farmed." Eli speared fried liver pieces onto a plate and handed it to Noodles. After filling his own plate, he added, "Maybe folks will figure this is the last frontier and use wild critters for rightful reasons. Most feel bad about the buffalo and the passenger pigeon being gone forever. This time might be different."

When he heard no reply, he turned and saw that Noodles had eaten his meal and slipped off to sleep. His breathing seemed to be easier, and his color looked better than it had. Eli finished his plate, readied their sled, and pulled off toward his meat piles, hoping that the fresh food would begin to restore the old man's health.

Ten days passed, and Noodles became spry again. Eli scolded the old man into careful labor around their campsite, let him ride along on the sled during caching of the surplus meat under rocks so wolves, foxes, and ravens couldn't dig it out, then let him take up cooking again.

March days fell on them as they sat in wonder under clear blue skies that never seemed to darken during the night. Eli explained the tilting of the earth and the coming of the midnight sun as spring and summer approached. Noodles sat, wide-eyed, listening, cackling as he had in the past; then he gabbed without ceasing about his prospecting across the West. Finally, when Eli thought Noodles appeared strong enough, they rolled their beds and tent and struck eastward toward Lake Bennett, hoping to get their boat built and readied for the river—and hoping that Swiftwater Bill and Patches would be waiting for them there.

After topping ridges that looked down on the stampeders ringing the lake three days later, both stopped stone still in surprise. For miles around, the trees had been cut away; a smoky white canvas city seethed with thousands of knots of men, some sawing, others hammering, and more carrying boards to finish boat bottoms. Yells, pounding, barking, saw blades screeching—it all roared up and filled the air around.

Noodles shook his head in bafflement. "By Jeez, it's the biggest boomtown I ever see'd . . . and there ain't no gold here."

"I expected this, but I can't believe it either. Finding Swiftwater and Patches won't be easy down there. Best we ask for the biggest poker game and start from there. I doubt that Bill has given that up." Eli smiled at his own guess and began to march down the barren hillside.

They tramped along the shoes of Lake Bennett for two hours asking for Swiftwater Bill. Many people knew the name, and soon one man pointed to a makeshift saloon with a sign overhead that read POKER INN.

"Gal-dang, Eli, you got 'im well. Noodles, you look fit as a fiddle!" Swiftwater reared up from his poker game as they entered the canvas-and-board shack.

"By Jeez, is this your place? You look like you got a gold mine goin' here! You won't need to go on to Dawson." Noodles bounded across the small room and shook hands with Swiftwater.

"Hello, Swiftwater. I see you're the same." Eli stepped over to shake hands also. "We've brought you and Patches caribou steaks to fry. Thought you might like meat from someplace other than a tin can."

His eyes growing round, Swiftwater licked his lips. "Eli, you can't believe the dreams I've had about steaks and gravy, onion, anythin' but this dang canned stuff we got to eat every day. But I gotta talk to you about Patches—he's been goin' crazy waitin' for you."

"Where is he? What's wrong?" Eli squinted his eyes in worry.

"Follow me. I'll let him tell you himself. He's hid away in a tent where he thinks nobody can find 'im—except for me." Swiftwater turned and walked out of his saloon opposite from where Eli and Noodles had entered.

They tramped a mile along the edge of the lake until they reached a small backwater. Hidden in brush, back from the trail, stood a lone tent, tied to two spindly trees and looking little used.

"Patches, my boy, your hopes are true. Come on out—you don't have to hide anymore," called Swiftwater, rounding the brush.

"Eli, Noodles—did you fellows get back?" Patches' ugly face peeked out of the flaps of the tent. "Noodles, you look good again. I'm glad to see you!"

"Why are you hiding here, Patches?" Eli stepped to the front.

"I saw him, Eli. I saw the Cannibal. He was over at the end of the lake. Just standing there looking down the narrows toward Tagish Lake—about a month ago."

"Did you see his camp? Is he with other folks? I need to know before I arrest him."

"He didn't see me, and I didn't stand around watching him. With my face, I stick out like a sore thumb. I'm lucky he didn't. The first he knows I'm around, he'll kill me. What good would I be then? You can't arrest him anyways. The Mounties said so—ask Swiftwater. They told me and him there ain't no law here except them, and they ain't going to allow you or anybody being the law. You gotta be a real Marshal and have papers. Then maybe they would let you do it."

His heart sinking, his mind numbed by news of his surprising worthlessness, Eli asked, "Swiftwater, is it true? Did the Mounties say such things?"

"They did. We asked when we got the chance. They come around lots to keep the peace. This is Canada, they say, not the United States, and our laws ain't no good here. You got to get your star back and warrants to make arrests."

Eli walked a short distance, stopped, and stared across the frozen lake. Its flat white reach seemed bare and empty, like his hopes for redemption. Then the sight reminded him of the willful grip the ice had on everyone. It would be the month of June before anyone could float downriver, he thought. As Noodles often said, Providence set the rules, and, it seemed, there might be time to get his badge back and a warrant as well.

He went back over to his friends. "I know the way

to settle my troubles. Swiftwater, how long does it take to post a letter back to San Francisco and receive an answer?"

"Maybe if you could make it look important enough, you might do it in a couple months."

"We've got that time and more before breakup. Noodles, you stay here and keep Patches company. I'll come back and set camp as soon as I mail a letter to Peacock. He'll send my star and return me to duty when he reads the news. He'll not take the chance that Turnbull could hear of my discovery and that I had no way to make an arrest." Eli trotted away, with Swiftwater running to stay close behind.

Back at the Poker Inn, Eli sat down and wrote his letter to San Francisco:

March 15, 1898

Sir,

I have the witness to the Turnbull murders, the man who stabbed me, in custody. He has said today he has seen the murderer nearby.

It is urgent you mail me documents and warrants letting me arrest this man forthwith. North West Mounted Police regulate this place, said to be part of Canada, and will not allow my employment without a commission.

To assist my receipt of your messages, please forward duplicates to Dawson City, General Delivery, my name.

Very respectfully, I remain
Your servant,
Eli Bonnet, General Delivery
Lake Bennett, Canada

After finishing the letter and finding a mail sled pulling back to Skagway, Eli returned to Patches' tent. He found Noodles bouncing around, done with pitching their tent, tending his Dutch oven with biscuits inside.

"Old man, I said I would set camp. You're not well yet, and I want you rested for the boat trip ahead. I'm told it's over five hundred miles of rough water to Dawson. I'll need you strong enough to help me steer."

"Don't worry about me. I'm as good as ever and ready to go." Noodles tested his baking with a whittled stick. "By Jeez, Patches says Swiftwater has five boats he's won in poker games. Maybe we could buy one."

"Swiftwater has shown me his winnings, and I've picked one I like. I hope my judgment is the same as with horses and mules. If I've chosen poorly, it'll drown us both."

Patches popped out of his tent carrying a can of syrup. "You been down a bad river before?"

"Not like the one Swiftwater tells about. He says the Yukon is a canyon with whirlpools first and four rapids after that. He's drawn a map for me. It runs flat after about two hundred miles downriver."

"I sure wish I didn't have to go. I can't swim." Patches' fingers shook as he opened the syrup.

"You'll probably ride in Swiftwater's boat, and he's run the river before. He claims if a man is careful, there's not much danger."

"By Jeez, Eli, I want you to wear your medicine coat when we start out. I can't swim neither."

"I've worn it most days since you took sick, and I've a notion to keep it on for the rest of the way. My luck seems to have turned better. I might even find gold." Eli winked at Patches, grinning, but so Noodles could see he meant to poke fun.

"Your spirit coat might work for you. You don't know. I knowed men that said they found it by dowsing with green willow sticks and brass wires."

Patches' face grew puzzled. He stared at Noodles and asked, "What's dowsing? Could you teach me how to find gold like that?"

Eli listened as Noodles gabbed to Patches about gold prospecting, dowsing, and the required good luck to strike it rich. He thought of his own fortunes and smiled about his recent deeds and the peace he had found in living in the new land. Seeing boundless horizons of a new frontier and sensing that this time he would die before men could destroy it inspired him to look forward again, rather than back.

He stood up, stretched, and looked across the lake. Black specks were coming over the ice toward him. He stared, blinking, not believing what he saw far off in the distance.

CHAPTER EIGHTEEN

Deceit

The letter from Eli Bonnet stunned Jesse Peacock. Jealous, undecided, yet pleased, he sat at his desk trying to formulate in his mind the best plan to seize the opportunity offered him. Eli's luck hadn't changed, he thought—and if that luck got used correctly, Senator Turnbull's favor could be won back again.

It seemed wise to mail Eli's badge and to send along the required documents authorizing him to arrest the murderer. But the Senator would be much more grateful if he, rather than Bonnet, returned to San Francisco with the prisoner. And newspapers would write columns applauding the capture—printed words that would help him to earn the Washington assignment he had wanted for so long.

But if Eli arrested the man at Lake Bennett and moved him back through Skagway, which was the likely event, Soapy Smith's committee would certainly butt in. The *San Francisco Chronicle* had printed several articles describing the lawlessness of that town. And he wasn't ready to argue with Bonnet for sole custody of the killer and then have to battle to get away from Smith's gang next. A bargain like that meant a gunfight with outlaws, and he wanted no part of it. That seemed Eli's kind of duty.

He had to persuade Bonnet to take the man to a more suitable place, but he had no idea where that might be. Peering out his office door at Hannah Twigg's replacement, he called, "Etta, please come here" and watched as she pattered in. Etta wasn't as bright and intuitive as Hannah by anyone's judgment, but she looked more shapely and tempting, and he intended to bed her soon,

"What would you like, Jesse?" she asked.

"I need you to bring me a map of the Canadian and Alaskan Territories. In particular, the regions around a place called Lake Bennett. One of my Marshals is camped there and wants to arrest the killer of Senator Turnbull's wife and child. I need to determine the most sensible place to travel to after the arrest so I can secure the prisoner for return to jail here. Can you do that for me, please?"

Jesse watched as she smiled again, nodding and swinging out of his office, her bottom teasing him.

After eating the noon meal together, he and Etta worked over the maps she'd found. Measurements and the logic of following the Yukon with the gold stampede downriver to Dawson City made up his mind as to the kind of message he would write to Eli Bonnet. But he puzzled over how he would get himself there. By the looks of the size of the Yukon River on the maps, and because of river's rip through the center of Alaska toward the seas near a place named

Saint Michaels, he guessed he would be able to travel by water all the way.

Although bothersome operators kept him waiting for too long, an hour of telephoning around the city provided answers to his questions about how to travel to Dawson City. He learned to his pleasure that he could board a ship out of San Francisco, sail across the North Pacific, through islands called the Aleutians, into the Bering Sea, and on to Saint Michael. Once there, he could change to a steamboat and ride upriver past the frontier town of Fort Yukon and on up to Dawson City, about three hundred miles beyond. All this could be done in comfort, and he'd been promised special attention because of his prominence as a U.S. Marshal.

He reached into his desk, pulled out paper for his letter to Eli, and wrote his instructions:

April 20, 1898

Deputy U.S. Marshal Eli Bonnet, General Delivery
Lake Bennett, British Columbia Territory, Canada
Reinstatement: U.S. Marshal Status

Dear Mr. Bonnet:

Thank you for your vigilance and continued devotion to the U.S. Marshals' office. I want you to know of my appreciation for your diligence in locating the men essential for the prosecution of the murders of Mrs. Turnbull and her son.

Your badge is enclosed within this envelope. The accompanying documents will certify you as an authorized lawman of this office and in possession of United States Government Warrants and Extradition Certificates. Please complete and submit these documents to officers of law appropriate to your location and requirements.

It is very important that you comply with my following instructions. Your arrest of the person or persons your letter reports must include the best likelihood of moving each to a United States line of demarcation. You are therefore directed to take any prisoners to Dawson City, Yukon Territories, Canada, for transportation by steamboat down the Yukon River to Territory of Alaska, USA.

Upon arrival in Dawson City secure your prisoners with assistance of any available law enforcement agency in that town. U.S. Marshal personnel will arrive at the earliest possible date to join you in moving said prisoners to San Francisco, California, for trial. Please wait for their arrival.

With best wishes for your success and safe travel,

Regards,
Jesse Peacock
U.S. Marshals

Wishing to send the packet to Eli with every prospect that it be delivered swiftly, and because he wanted to purchase passage north for himself, Jesse hired a ride to the seafront rather than spending the time necessary to walk. The docks continued to throb with thousands of people wanting to go north to the gold fields. He found a ship sailing for Skagway on the following morning, forced his way to the captain by flashing his Marshal's star, and de-

manded that the man send the message to Eli Bonnet at Lake Bennett by the fastest possible means.

He then found another ship's ticket office selling
passages over water all the way to Dawson City and
asked about costs and comforts available to Saint
Michael and up the Yukon River. Pleased with the
special attention he received, he purchased a stateroom on a ship departing on the first day of May,
picked out handbills describing the voyage, and paid
the office manager with a government voucher.

Smiling and feeling cheerful for a change, he
strolled back toward his office, thinking over his
plans. He wouldn't bother sending copies ahead to
Dawson as Eli had requested in his letter. He suspected Eli would float down to that point regardless
of whether he received the packet at Lake Bennett
or not. That was Eli, he thought, keeping on, following the murderer at all costs, doing his duty even
though there was little sense in it.

And when Eli did get to Dawson, he would be surprised to find who stood waiting and prepared to
take the prisoner away for himself. Jesse wondered
how long it would take for the Senator to ask him to
come to Washington after he got back to San
Francisco with the killer shackled behind him. Soon,
he thought, very soon.

"Etta, please come here," he said, smiling as he
went back through his office door.

"What is it, Jesse? You look so happy. I've never
seen you act this way before. What is it? Please tell
me."

"The maps you found this morning—the maps of

Alaska and Canada—I bought a ticket to go. I'll see Dawson City and the gold fields this summer."

"Are you going because of the murders of Mrs. Turnbull and her little boy, and the Marshal you sent mail to?"

"Yes, and God willing I'll be back at the end of summer with the man that's guilty and another that will testify against him. If I can make this arrest, it means an appointment to Washington for me. All my working life, I've hoped to go there. Now I've got the chance—and, it seems, I'll have a good adventure besides."

Etta wriggled with her hands clasped in front of her. "I see why you're so happy. That's so exciting to be able to do things like you're planning. I wish I were a man."

Jesse laughed, watching her bright-eyed envy. She always appeared so happy and eager—like a teenager, he thought. Then he remembered she wasn't much older than that—middle twenties, maybe. He wished he could capture the headlong spirit of her youthful excitement. Since the start of the Civil War most events had seemed so important to him, of life-or-death magnitude—he'd forgotten how to feel carefree enthusiasm.

He then, his body jittery, puffed up his courage and asked, "Why don't you come with me—you could go—I'll take you." His face reddened, and he tried to slow his pounding heart. At least, he thought, she isn't the kind of person who will make me feel like scum if she refuses. She will just brush it away by laughing and teasing, leaving my feelings intact.

"Jesse . . . you're tempting me. I've never traveled anyplace, ever, but . . . I should say no. There's nothing holding me here, you understand, but . . . I don't want to upset your life . . . or mine either."

He stepped close. "Please come with me. My life is my own . . . you needn't worry . . . I'll see that nothing harms you. When we get back, you could go on to Washington with me. Think of the things I could give you . . . the parties we could go to. I need something special in my life, and I want it to be you."

Etta reached forward and fingered the gold watch chain stringing across Jesse's vest. After a moment of silence, she whispered, "I'll go with you . . . but you let me leave work now. You need to tell everyone I gave up my employment here . . . or you can tell them you made me go away if you like. When you leave this evening, come to where I live and talk to me again . . . and think about the promises I'll make you keep."

Jesse stiffened. Suddenly he saw Etta as more than he'd supposed only moments ago. Even though he felt thrilled by her acceptance, he nonetheless began to worry about her quick strength. Prickles raced from his toes, through the pit of his stomach, and up his spine as his mind raced for a reply. Then it struck him to say nothing and just seal the bargain with a kiss. He reached out with his arm, pulled her close, and kissed her, brushing her lips with his, testing her. After a moment he relaxed his hug and whis-

pered back, "I'll want you to keep one promise, too."
Then he let her go, seeing her smile and shiny eyes
as an agreement to his wish.

They boarded and sailed out of San Francisco on
the first of May, laughing, holding hands like sweethearts sworn to romance. Jesse thought his life
changed forever. He'd found lovemaking with Etta an
uncommon joy compared with the intimacies of his
past. She acted soft, sensitive, touched with her
fingers at the right moment, gave him pleasure beyond any experiences gone by. Yet she seemed hard,
pushy, making him perform again and touch her until
she reached her high moment. Easy laughs filled
their time in between. Her sweet cheerfulness soon
melted him into ongoing happiness also, something
he'd never experienced before. It all made him feel
ten years younger.

When the pitching ocean tired them during their
daily exercise around decks, Jesse would take her below and bury his face between her breasts, or in her
tummy again. He had never felt such gladness before
to be with a woman. When he couldn't make love
anymore, he would tow her around on his single arm,
strutting her good looks and friendliness in front of
the stampeders packed aboard. She charmed each
she met to mumbles with her smiles and good-
hearted ribbing about the riches that must lie ahead
for everyone. Soon he knew he loved her—more
than his own life.

At last islands—foggy, rainy, windy outcrops of
green land—came in view against the dullness of

nothing but North Pacific seas. The passengers soon
rumored that the ship had made the Aleutians and
would dock at Dutch Harbor for delivery of freight
and mail. As the ship rounded pincers of coastline
and dropped anchor, skin boats with dark, tattooed
people, squat and thick under walrus-gut garments,
surfed out on the ocean swells to trade. Called
Aleuts, they offered ivory walrus tusks, whale teeth,
tanned seal hides, and stone and bone weapons. Bartering stampeders handed over clothing, knives, pots,
and tobacco for the things that struck their fancy.

Jesse traded his pocketknife for an ivory comb for
Etta, grinning as she toyed delightedly with the sou-
venir after he'd surprised her with the gift. They
walked the railing watching other stampeders drop
personal items and then catch trade goods that the
natives tossed aboard. Laughing and cheering, everyone marveled at the quick skill of the boatmen as
they darted about in their skin-covered kayaks, spinning and rolling with the flip of a paddle, not
minding their own deliberate dunking.

By blowing watch whistles, the captain and first
mate warned off lighters and the skin boats, pulled
up anchor, and turned the ship out of the harbor,
stampeders and Aleuts waving good-bye like long-lost
friends. Excitement swept the decks as the ship's
crewmen told passengers the Bering Sea lay just
ahead and Saint Michael only a week northward.

The ship passed more masses of black rock bursting from the sea, topped by windswept green and
necklaced by white waves pounding their sides. After
unrolling the maps he'd brought along, Jesse identi-

fied the first two as the Pribilof Islands, Saint Paul and Saint George, and the next beyond by two days as Nunivak Island. Etta never seemed to tire in the ongoing daylight, declaring the midnight sun as her favorite part of the voyage north. They leaned against the ship's railing for hours with Jesse's field glasses spying on whales and seals and hundreds of kinds of seabirds. Using a borrowed book, they made a game of identifying species by their English and Latin names, laughing together at Etta's attempt to pronounce some.

Jesse's love for Etta deepened as time slipped by in a blur because of the absence of darkness to mark the days. He admitted to himself that he'd begun the journey as an interlude from a troubled marriage and an unbroken burden of work. But his affair with Etta had shown him a picture of love between men and women that he'd never seen before. In his spare time he began to worry about the distress that divorce and remarriage would bring to Etta and himself. But he felt certain of one thing—he couldn't bear to lose her and the happiness she'd brought him.

"I want to marry you when we get back to San Francisco," he said on the morning of the day the ship was to reach Saint Michael.

Etta, surprised, waited a moment, then said, "Jesse, you're already married. You should think more about what you're saying."

"I just meant to talk to you about how much I care . . . and I don't want to ever lose you. I'm going to ask for a divorce as soon as I can." Embarrassed, he ducked his head.

"That's not one of the promises I asked for. And you're spoiling our day by being serious about things that are months ahead. You know how I hate worry and planning and all the things you do to make life unhappy. Please don't spoil our travel! It's been so exciting! I don't want to change ourselves before it's time, Jesse."

"Sorry. I didn't mean to slip back to old ways." He forced a smile. "Let's hurry and find the best place forward on the bow so we can see Saint Michael first." He turned and led the way out of their stateroom, thinking that Etta's reply seemed unusual . . . and wondered what she'd meant by it.

Avoiding low, dirty seas, the ship stayed off from the mouth of the Yukon River. Jesse and Etta used their field glasses to spy flat, bushy tundra far to the east, along with countless river channels pouring silt into the sea. Stampeders standing nearby gossiped that gold colors could be panned from the soiled water flowing out, so rich were the gold fields inland. Then, at last, the ship swung around to the east, staying out from points and bays of the mossy land, and sailed into a broad harbor filled with other vessels of all kinds, each stuffed with passengers waiting to unload for their journeys upriver.

"Are those the boats that will take us up the Yukon River?" asked Etta, pointing to two white sternwheelers anchored near shore. "They look just like pictures of steamboats I've seen in history books back in school."

"I'm certain they're the ones . . . and they'll be like their history, too. You'll see dining and dancing in the evenings like in the Old South on the Mississippi River before the Civil War . . . and gambling like faro and poker just as in those days." Jesse smiled over his memories of travels before the war.

"How far is it to Dawson City?"

"It's a long way. As I recall, the distance upriver is about two thousand miles. We'll be on board a long time before we reach our stop."

"This seems like it will be the best part. I want to see animals and Indians and the mountains that many of the men have been talking about. They say they're covered by snow all year around and are taller than any others in America. I read about the West when I was a little girl and always wished I could see the frontier. Now I can see this one and live in it, too."

Jesse looked at Etta. What did she mean by "live in it, too," he wondered. She must be thinking of the summertime ahead before they could return to Saint Michael. He gazed across the water to several log cabins, an old Russian church, and hundreds of tents pitched about the flat surrounding the little village up above the tideland nearby. He reminded himself not to spoil their happiness with worries anymore. That's what she had warned him about, he brooded.

CHAPTER NINETEEN

Rescue

Two black hands gripped the handle that swung into Soapy Smith's back wall on the next blow from the ax. Then both disappeared and came smashing through the boards again, chopping a hole large enough for Hannah to duck through.

Lincoln's head popped in, yelling, "Come on, Mizz Twigg, we got to get out of here. Come on, they're comin' 'round the back."

Hannah dove through the hole, close behind the tip of Sorrowful's tail, and skidded facedown in the muddy snow of an alley. Before she could get to her hands and knees to run, she felt herself being grabbed around the waist, lifted, and bounced violently as Lincoln ran with her on his side like a sack. The pounding on her ribs and stomach from Lincoln's grip sickened her and made her cry out as he sprinted away, his boots splattering mud up into her face. Suddenly she heard two gun blasts close by and a man's scream, then more shots and boots slapping in the muddiness.

A voice that sounded like the man named Fidler

called out, "Walker, you okay? Walker, was that you shootin'?"

"Help—they're goin' to kill me!" screamed a voice back toward the building they'd just dashed out of.

Another volley of gunshots rang out, and then two blasts from a larger firearm shook the night. Sounds of running and cries broke out again.

"You boys come up this way again and I'll shoot more buckshot down there!" shouted the voice like Fidler's. Then someone else yelled, "Walker, you still with us?"

A low groan answered as Lincoln ducked around a corner, with Sorrowful running behind, and set Hannah down. "You well enough to run, Mizz Twigg? We got to keep goin' fast!"

"Let me catch my breath. Those men with you—one sounded like the old man from this morning!" Hannah held her stomach and side, bending over to ease the pain.

"There're the devil's disciples, sure enough—" Lincoln grabbed her hand, pulling, running again.

Fighting for breath, Hannah choked as she asked, "Why are those men helping us?"

"Best you shush till we get out of here!" huffed Lincoln, trotting among tents and shacks set on the edge of downtown.

He led the way to an enormous tent with oxen and horses tied nearby and lanterns hung inside and out, lighting the surroundings. When Hannah stepped inside the front flap, Naomi ran to her, hugging her and crying, hanging on to her like a child.

As Hannah looked around the interior and saw

Sorrowful pad in and sniff the clothing scattered about, many questions raced through her mind. She hugged Naomi back and asked, panting, "Lincoln, how did you get these men to help you?"

"I spend all the money you give me and bought all the horses and oxes out there. I got to haul the freight for them to Lake Bennett. They said if I do it, they would get you free for sure."

"How on earth did you know where Sorrowful and I were?" With Naomi's help, Hannah rubbed the mud off her face and clothing.

Lincoln hung his head. "I snooped behind and saw you go in there. Pretty soon you don't come out. I look in front and then listen in the back and figure you in bad trouble."

The gray-bearded Fidler shoved into the tent with his men close behind, carrying a limp and bloody body. He grinned and called, "I see you made it, Missy. Got excitin' back there, didn't it?"

"My God, is he dead?" Hannah stared in horror at the motionless man. "How can you laugh now?" She burst into tears and shivers, wailing a little.

"He ain't dead yet . . . might be soon though. Walker always liked gunfightin', and he's been shot before—but maybe not so bad as this time." Fidler shrugged, seeming undisturbed as he pointed to the bedroll to lay Walker on.

"Get away from him and let me look!" cried Hannah as she rushed to Walker and began to tear at his clothing, trembling. A moment later she fell to her knees, held her head in her hands, and said, "He's shot in the stomach and chest—we've got to find a doctor. I can't help!"

Fidler shrugged again. "Lady, how we gonna find a doctor? And if we do, how's he gonna do any good up here in the wilderness? There's no hospitals or nothin'. And we gotta get movin', too! Walker knew what he was gettin' into . . . and nobody likes 'im that much, anyways!"

"My God, what kind of men are you?" Hannah asked, sobbing again.

"Appears a lot rougher ones than you been around. What you doin' up here if you can't abide a little trouble? You been in church all your life?" Fidler stared at her, his forehead creased.

"Suh, that's a fact. Her daddy's a preacher and she ain' been around folks like's up here." Lincoln pulled Hannah away from the dying man, and added, "But don't worry—she be just fine soon enough."

Fidler turned, surprised. "I'll be derned! Might of figured Eli would hitch up with a churchgoin' woman. Well, Missy, don't mean to be so hard on you, but we been outlaws 'most always. We just come up from the Hole in the Wall country and there's been Marshals and sheriffs and Pinkertons shootin' at us since I don't remember. It don't bother us that much anymore. I suggest you buck up and face things like you did this mornin'. You gonna need to if you gonna cross this land and live to find Eli."

The dare shook Hannah out of her crying and set her to wiping her runny nose and tears on her sleeve. She looked up, paused briefly, then stood and asked, "Lincoln, can you get my medical kit from our camp

without harm to yourself? I'll give him enough laudanum so he can die in peace and without pain." She
walked back to Walker and pushed a pillow under
his head. "Mr. Fidler, how long before we leave for
Lake Bennett?"

"Ain't no hurry. They ain't gonna come and start a
gunfight among a thousand tents and five thousand
stampeders tonight. Be the last one they'd ever get
into. Everybody would get riled and start shootin' at
'em. Take your time, ma'am—we'll pull out tomorrow." The old bearded face grinned.

"Why did you men help us? Are you going to steal
our things and kill us later?" Hannah watched Lincoln step out of the tent. She feared the outlaw's answer.

"No, ma'am. You'll be safe. We were busted and
needed help to get packed over the White Pass.
Can't rustle critters or steal from folks here and not
get caught. There's only two trails and no place to
hide except in snow-covered mountains. And the
first you get tracked down, folks are goin' to hang
you—no trial or nothin'. Lincoln come along at a
lucky time and made us a fair bargain, so we'll keep
our end. I'll see to it."

"Then may I have Walker's gun? I think he'll not
need it by morning, and I'm not traveling further
without one."

Fidler stared at Hannah for a moment, then
laughed and said, "Missy, you sure harden up in a
hurry. Best let me show you how to use it, though."
The old man chuckled again, shook his head, and
reached for the shotgun nearby.

Within a few minutes Lincoln returned with the laudanum and helped Hannah pour trickles of it down Walker's throat. They covered his body with blankets and found places for themselves to rest. Fidler crawled into his own bedroll after he'd posted two of his men on guard outside.

The night crept by. Hannah lay awake listening to men snoring—then, she thought, to the sounds of Walker dying just as daylight began to creep under the cracks of the tent. She cried, muffling her head in blankets, unable to stop. For the first time, she felt homesick, and she wondered what had tempted her to travel north into such an uncivil land. She thought of Eli—his reasons for leaving, his failure to say that he loved her, his fondness for frontiers. None of it made clear sense to her, yet she saw the summons for such a man as he to defend simple people living in such a lawless wilderness. But she wondered how hardhearted he must be to match the meanness of the men who slept around her. All of it frightened her, making her pray she could harden up in a hurry, as Fidler had said—instead of just acting that way.

When Fidler rolled out of bed in the morning, coughing and snorting his wakeup, Hannah rose as well and went over to Walker's bed to feel his wrist for a pulse. The moment she touched his icy, taut skin, she knew he had died. She pulled the covers up over his face, tucked in the edges, and turned to Fidler, and demanded, staring dry-eyed, "Get him out and dig a grave. I don't want him in this tent any longer!"

"Missy, I'd like to get coffee and bacon goin' before I see to buryin' somebody."

"My name is Hannah, not Missy. I'll say prayers when the grave is ready. He lost his life saving mine, now I'll ask the Lord to help him. Each of us is worthwhile!"

"You're not bossin' me around. I'll eat if I like. Walker can wait!" Fidler reached for the camp's coffeepot.

Hannah leaped forward, tore the pot out of the old man's hands, and flung it across the tent, splashing cold coffee on the walls. Flaming, she threatened, "You'll do as I say or I'll stand here and scream until every man for a mile hears me. Guess what I'll tell them, and what they'll do after hearing it. Now do what I want!"

Stunned, Fidler stood still for a moment, staring at the spilled pot on the tent's floor. Then, cursing, he kicked around the tent, yelling for his men to get up. They, along with Lincoln, rolled over and jumped out of their blankets, everyone awakened by the crash and the bellowing old man. Grumbling and in a hurry, three outlaws lugged the body outside. Fidler followed close behind, still cursing his fury at being bullied into something he didn't want to do.

An hour later Lincoln poked his head inside the front of the tent and asked, "Mizz Twigg, we done diggin' the grave and got it ready to fill. You want to pray now?"

Hannah nodded, picked up her Bible, and with Naomi and Sorrowful trailing behind, followed Lincoln to a shallow hillside dotted with dirt piles and wooden crosses, all marking recent burials not yet covered by the snow. She stopped at the foot of Walker's open grave, waited until Fidler and his men circled around, still grumbling, and then cleared her throat to silence them. Flipping her Bible open to marked pages, she read loudly:

To every thing there is a season, and a time to every purpose under the heaven:

A time to be born, and a time to die; a time to plant, and a time to pluck up that which is planted;

For who knoweth what is good for man in this life, all the days of his vain life which he spendeth as a shadow? for who can tell a man what shall be after him under the sun?

God shall judge the righteous and the wicked: for there is a time there for every purpose and for every work.

For God shall bring every work into judgment, with every secret thing, whether it be good, or whether it be evil.

Who knoweth the spirit of man that goeth upward, and the spirit of the beast that goeth downward to the earth?

All go unto one place; all are of the dust, and all turn to dust again.

For to him that is joined to all the living there is hope.

Truly the light is sweet, and a pleasant thing it is for the eyes to behold the sun.

Then she snapped her Bible shut, leaned forward, clutched a fistful of dirt, stood straight, and pitched it down onto the dead body. She looked around at each man, cleared her throat again, and said in the same strong voice, "Cover him up. Naomi and I will cook breakfast now. After that's done, I want to leave for the North." She spun around and marched away, clutching her Bible to her breast.

After eating, the outlaws, with Fidler staying silent, watched as Lincoln heaved boxes and bundles onto the pack animals he'd purchased, binding each load with ropes. Hannah and Naomi helped by skidding baggage over to him and lifting on opposite ends of the heaviest packs. Then, abruptly, Fidler stood up and yelled at his men, "Get up and help load. I can't stand to see two women workin' and you sittin' on your rears. I want to get north like Hannah said!"

At noon they joined the ribbon of men, a smattering of women and children, and thousand of horses, mules, and oxen, all twined together in a single row tramping up the White Pass Trail. As they moved along the narrow path toward the mountains, Hannah began to see everything in black and white: each snowfield contrasted with the barren, dark trees; peoples' faces pale against their heavy clothing, caps and hats scrunched down against the cold; every pack animal shadowed or bleached light by workborn sweat; and the endless mud track through the snow, looking inky and, she thought, stretching forever through the leafless forest ahead. Having lived all her life in San Francisco, she found wintertime relentless, colorless and hushed in its permanence away from the sides of the trail. And she felt chilled by more than the cold as she tramped behind her pack train, led by Lincoln. The solemn, resolute eyes of each person she saw reminded her of pallbearers bending forward to their task.

Soon she began to realize the price paid for the promise of new gold—and of loads too heavy for man and beast. Outfits lay on each side of the trail, thrown down in despair; people sat, crying out in pain from sprains and breaks; at last, animals lined the roadside, standing, broken down, sometimes lying dead with their blood staining the snow. She turned back and fastened her stare on the rumps of her own animals, horrified, fretting about the weight they lugged, trying to forget the agony all around.

Fidler slogged to her side. "Hannah, why'd you say those things over Walker—about hope and light?"

Grateful for the distraction, she saw uncertainty on the outlaw's face and wondered about his recent brooding. "That was for you and me . . . and for the others gathered with us. We should cherish each day as an opportunity and thank the Lord for the light."

The outlaw continued walking by her side, staying quiet for several minutes. Finally he said, "We're just bandits. Most folks don't want us to see another day. Surprised me to hear you say such a thing with us standin' around."

"I told you this morning each of us is worthwhile. Change your unlawful ways and become something useful. How can you bear to rob and hurt people who have worked so hard for what they have? Have you no honesty at all?"

The old man's eyes sparked. "I've always kept my

bargains with my friends—and I'll keep the one I've made with you."

"I think you should do more than that. Look at all these people suffering so much to get to the Klondike—how could you think of stealing from them?"

"We don't trouble poor folks like these here on the trail. They ain't got much money to steal. We rob railroads and banks—that don't hurt nobody—except maybe those that want to get into a gunfight about it."

Hannah blinked, disbelieving the reasoning she'd just heard. Exasperated, she said, "You're hopeless—and perhaps you can't be changed after all!"

The old outlaw marched along, quiet again for a time. Then he said, "Hannah, look at these folks workin' away to get north. They're just like me . . . most tryin' to find one more frontier. None of us come this far so we would change."

Fidler's reply knifed through her. His insight into the stampeders' reasons for traveling north chilled her further, adding something she hadn't thought of before: Eli wouldn't want to change either. She wondered if she had come into a new land for poor reasons—reasons that might break her heart later on.

Up the trail at a knot of tents and log cabins named White Pass City by a crude sign, Lincoln stopped to feed and rest the animals. He explained that he'd learned there was no hay or grain ahead, and that for more than thirty miles, through the mountains, the horses and oxen would have to travel without feed. Hannah helped unload and pitch the night's camp, unhappy that they'd traveled only a few miles on their first day out of Skagway. Enviously, she puzzled over how Lincoln upheld his spirit and strength in spite of the cold and misery all around. He seemed able to overlook the hardship and horror they had just passed, and he seemed unafraid of what she feared would lie ahead as they climbed higher.

The next morning they broke camp early and turned northward again, joining the snaking column once more. All night the endless procession had crawled by in wisps of light cast by a late moon. Hannah, sleeping fitfully, had listened to wails floating down from the mountains and had wondered if the noise was wind or something else. Now, as she followed their pack animals up, she passed the sources of the past night's cries—even more horrors than the day before had provided.

The trail hooked back and forth in notches between falling mountainsides. Snags, boulders, and holes in the road ripped flesh and broke bones as people and animals tried to squeeze through, most of them hauling too much for the roughness of the trail. The whole line then stopped for cripples that clogged the path, infuriating all those trapped behind. Sticks, whips, and clubs beat helpless animals as everyone tried to get them up or out of the way. Fights, gunfire, and screams sounded when those behind, unwilling to wait, pushed the injured aside or just marched over them. Blood, guts, and carcasses lay left and right.

"Don't know how folks could do that to simple critters!" Lincoln cried as they set their second camp. "Tomorrow we get over the top and maybe free from the devil's doin's—pray to the Lord for that!"

Fidler knelt to help his men stake their tent. "I'm an old man and have heard about worse back in the West. The Trail of Tears, Injuns dyin' like the critters here, the Donner Party, folks eatin' each other. This isn't so bad as that. Everybody just wants to get to the gold first."

"The things I've seen today are wrong and not worth all the gold in the world. I hope I never see another stampede as long as I live!" Hannah threw down an armful of cooking pots in disgust. "How can men be so heartless as I've seen today?"

Fidler reared up, plain-faced. "Hannah, you read a sermon over Walker. Maybe you should think more about what you said. Strikes me your preachin' fits. Things will look better tomorrow, and hell will look smaller from up on the mountaintop."

The old outlaw's remarks stuck with Hannah, quieting her for the rest of the evening. She sat near the night's fire toasting herself and thinking about what he had said. His comments made sense. They didn't excuse or make the wrongness leave her mind, but they did cause her to recall her recent grit and her past wish to begin a new life. She promised herself that she would push forward, stop crying, and look beyond the problems that surely would impede her progress in the days ahead.

Fidler's prophecy rang true the next afternoon. At the top of the trail, people's spirits soared, animals lifted their drooping heads and arched their backs against heavy loads for the first time since Skagway, acting lively for a change. The air all around filled with chatter and laughter as everyone realized that the hardest part had been won and the rest of the journey lay downhill and downriver.

The next day they turned westward, dropped out of the timbered hills at the foot of a lake called Lindeman, turned north again along a short stretch of river, then finally reached Lake Bennett. The huge body of water stretched to the north, looking endless, Hannah thought, running off out of sight between wooded hills and low mountains.

"I want to keep on and find Eli," she told Fidler. The noise and size of the tent city along each shore had convinced her he had to be camped nearby, waiting with all the other stampeders for spring breakup.

"Go on if you like—but me and the boys are stoppin' right here. I ain't walkin' another step till I get to Dawson. I'm floatin' the rest of the way!" Fidler flopped down on his side on the snow-covered lakeshore, grinning. "You don't need us now, anyways, Hannah. You're hardened up and can take care of yourself. Just remember to keep that shotgun you took off Walker close by and don't trust no one you don't know. You're a good-lookin' woman, and men'll want you for one thing and another, mostly for no good . . . so be careful as you travel along."

"The shooting and Walker's death scared me so that I forgot to thank you for saving me from Soapy Smith. I hope to see you in Dawson City—changed to an honest man, of course." Hannah smiled, respecting the old man even though she couldn't settle in her mind why.

"I hope to see you, too. But I ain't likely to be honest if I see any banks first!" Then the crusty robber laughed and waved good-bye.

Hannah turned and led the way, Sorrowful fronting her, Lincoln and Naomi following, leading pack animals carrying their share of the food and equipment. She turned back and waved good-bye again a short distance down the lake, still smiling and feeling good, wondering what her father would think if he could see her marching along in a wilderness, dressed in boots and pants and carrying a shotgun. He wouldn't understand why, she thought, and he wouldn't approve either.

After several miles of crisscrossing the lake, searching for Eli Bonnet in the tent camps, Hannah saw Sorrowful stop, point his ears and nose, then sniff the wind. Suddenly he yelped wistfully and raced toward a lone figure standing on the ice at the edge of the lake. She stared at the silhouette, fearing a fantasy. Then, breaking her earlier promise, she cried out herself and ran after Sorrowful.

CHAPTER TWENTY

Reunion

Sorrowful knocked him over, yipping and dancing, licking his face. Eli rolled, laughing and crying at the same time, not believing his dog had somehow crossed an ocean and a mountain range to find him. As he tipped over in the direction Sorrowful had come from, he glimpsed someone the size of a small man running toward him. He bounced to his knees, grabbed Sorrowful, and faced the person, wondering why the man was laughing and crying, too. Then he recognized Hannah in men's clothing. His mind slipped into a muddle.

"Hannah, where did . . . how did you find me? How did you find Sorrowful? I can't believe you've followed—"

"They locked me away in Skagway . . . The White Pass . . . I saw a canyon filled with dead horses." Hannah tried to smile and wipe her tears away at once. "It's been the hardest thing I've ever done. I always believed I could find you . . . but I . . ." She broke into sobs and covered her face with her hands, shaking her head.

Eli stood up, wrapped his arms around her, and

rocked her back and forth. After a moment of gathering his own wits, he whispered, "Hannah, I . . . I'm so happy you're here. And to bring Sorrowful with you . . . I'll never be able to repay you for what you've done."

Hannah leaned back in Eli's arms, rubbing her face, trying again to smile. "You . . . you saved me once . . . now I've paid you back."

"You surely have!" Eli wiped his own eyes dry on his coat. "I can't believe you came over the White Pass. Noodles and I scouted that trail and climbed the Chilkoot instead. We couldn't abide the beating and the killing . . . and it was all stopped up with dead horses, like you say."

"I found Sorrowful tied to a house not far from my father's and stole him back. Then I decided to follow. I missed you so much . . ."

"I should have known you were strong enough. Getting that poor woman out of jail, getting me well. I saw it before. But I was troubled and didn't want to ask you to come along."

"I've named my friend Naomi. It's been even harder for her, she's so tiny. It's good the Lord found us Lincoln, or we wouldn't ever have got this far." Hannah pointed across the lake to the pack train ambling toward the shore, Lincoln leading and Naomi perched atop a horse, holding on with both hands.

Grabbing Eli's hand, she led him toward Lincoln, Sorrowful still hopping around close by. As they came close, Lincoln dropped his lead rope, bounded forward, and called, "Suh, I glad to meet you—

hearin' so much about you from Mizz Hannah . . . and from that old outlaw Fidler, too!"

"Fidler!" Eli's mouth fell open as he grasped Lincoln's powerful hand. Startled, he said, "Hannah, you met Fidler? He's the only outlaw I couldn't catch—a fearless and ornery one, too! I can't believe he's come north!" Sighing and shaking his head, he added, "But it appears that most of the old outlaws have."

"Fidler and his men saved me from Soapy Smith and a man named Tripp who fooled me into believing he would help find you, then locked me in a storage room. Lincoln traded pack animals for Fidler's help to get me free. One of his men named Walker was killed during a gunfight when Smith's men heard Lincoln and me getting away. I'll never forget that night—it was the most frightening of my life!"

Eli's face paled. "I never wanted you to see such troubles. I should have shot them both while I had them at gunpoint. They're the worst I've seen on this stampede!"

"You fought with them, too?"

"Those two cheated my friend Swiftwater out of all his money. Noodles and I helped get even, but we had the same kind of troubles as you did getting away. If I'd known you were following, I would have figured out how to rid Skagway of those two forever."

Having sighted the pack train, Noodles came bouncing down onto the lake, hollering at the top of his voice, "By Jeez, Hannah, you come to see us!" He ran to Hannah and hugged her, nearly knocking her over in his joy. "You goin' to the Klondike with us?

Eli's got two boats and Swiftwater Bill's got three more!"

At last able to brighten, Hannah laughed, and then said, "I want to if Eli will take me. I've decided to see the gold fields for myself. You won't mind if I come along, will you?"

"You sure look fit to go. Lookee at you, all dressed in pants and boots!" Noodles stood back and gestured at Hannah's clothes.

Eli touched Hannah's arm and said, "Let's get over to the tents and set yours up. Noodles, say hello to Lincoln. He saved Hannah from Soapy Smith, and we owe him for it. Help him come up and tie the critters. Patches and I will help unload."

"Patches! You've caught Patches and he's here!" Hannah's eyes widened.

"Yes . . . I found him the same night Noodles and I helped Swiftwater get his money back. He was so afraid of Smith and Tripp that he willingly came with us." Eli wondered about Hannah's sudden fright. When Lincoln walked back and lifted Naomi down off the horse, he understood. The black man seemed to be in love—and he must not know anything about her past. A troublesome problem, he fretted. He didn't know how to stop Lincoln from learning about it in the next few minutes.

Eli led everyone up the shore toward the campsite, holding tight to Hannah's hand, his mind spinning, searching for a way to keep Lincoln from being hurt, and Naomi and Hannah, too. But his turmoil didn't matter—Patches popped out from behind the tents and shouted, face cockeyed, "Frissy, what are you doing here? Eli said your tongue's cut out. I never thought I'd see you again!"

Hearing Hannah's moan, Eli grimaced, knowing she'd only done what any loyal friend would have done. But as he looked back at Lincoln's face, he sensed that Hannah's merciful prudence wouldn't make any difference to the black man—everyone would feel his pain.

As the last of winter passed, the sunlight lasted longer and longer, puzzling even the most diligent timekeepers. Everlasting May days came and melted the snow thin and completely away from the sunny hillsides and the north shore for as far as the eye could see. The sounds of boat building echoed along the long, narrow lake. Ripsaws raged and claw hammers banged around the clock, reflecting every stampeder's frenzy to float down the Yukon to the mouth of the Klondike River.

Eli and Noodles had asked Lincoln to share their tent, trying their best to lift him from his despair. Hannah had taken Lincoln aside after Patches called Naomi by her former name, the one Hannah hadn't even known about. She told him what she knew of Naomi and how much she wanted Lincoln to forgive them both for their deceit. Since that hurtful visit, however, Lincoln had lost his spirit and he refused to acknowledge either woman. Finally, dispirited himself, Eli sent him back into the mountains with Noodles for the cached caribou, hoping that the old man's endless stories of gold prospecting might mend the problem.

The departure of the two men from Eli's tent allowed Hannah and Eli to spend unbroken hours together for the first time. They sorted through their feelings toward each other, talking about fears and pledges and hopes, melting their intimacy into a bond that only a man and a woman could make. They quarreled over Eli's worries about their age difference and, most of all, about his sense of duty toward the U.S. Marshals and toward the new land he'd learned to love so much. Hannah cared nothing about the differences in their ages; she thought it silly even to discuss it. But she did care about his devotion to the Marshals and the wilderness. Both of those things angered and frightened her; she thought each unjust, cold, mean-spirited, not a bit easy to live with. But by sharing their thoughts and fears, Hannah and Eli fell more deeply in love, sealing their fate by kissing like eager young sweethearts.

They made love for the first time that night. The midnight sun crossed along the north skyline, shining its shadows through the canvas, casting light on their nakedness in ways that Hannah in her shyness could bear. Touching, kissing, then fumbling as their minds and bodies flamed, they were drawn together by desire, Eli thrusting up and down, glowing in the warmth and wetness of Hannah's body. Then he stopped for a moment, yearning to make their lovemaking everlasting, wondering why his hardness had never felt so good before. He watched as Hannah's eyes widened at the sensations she'd just discovered. And he watched her lips curl up at the corners as she learned how to move against him while he held still, then with him, then how to make him move faster, and, at last, how to make him lose control and thrust wildly, crying out as he reached his end.

Afterward, they lay still, wrapped together. Hannah cooed her desire to stay close and make love again. She whispered about her awakening, the sensation of having him inside, her selfish need to capture him again. She giggled that she could now hold him under her spell, make him love her more, make him want her again—make him give her the pleasure she'd just enjoyed any time she wished. He laughed and teased back, but kissed her and held her with a passion he'd not known before. Somehow this young woman had just won him away from his many years of proud loneliness. Somehow she had just made him feel whole for the first time in his life!

Then he lazily began again, kissing, petting, willfully exciting her as high as she could go before he entered her. He stayed on top, thrusting into her stubbornly, teaching her how to come to her own end. Finally it burst, her eyes widening more, brightening, her face radiant, her body losing control, pounding up as she broke free and whimpered from the spasms that stormed inside.

The next morning, sunlight scorched into the top of the tent, heating them, nudging them from the sleep furthered by their second coupling. After kissing Hannah awake, Eli rolled out of their bed, pulled his clothes on, hiked down to the lake, and hauled buckets of water from a hole in the ice. Back at camp he slid a tub into the tent and heated the water. When the hot bath was ready, he carried Hannah over, lowered her into it, and bathed her, both of them cherishing the event and making it last. He trickled warm water down onto her as she rinsed her hair, something she'd not done in many days. Finished, she stepped out, now proud in front of him, and both of them patted her body dry with towels that Eli had found packed in her bundles of clothing. After wrapping her to keep her warm, he took her back into his arms, cradled her, and whispered about the love he'd found. Whispering her love as well, she held on, clinging, both finally finding the promises they'd wondered about for so long.

When they went outside after Eli had bathed, they found Naomi, Patches, and Sorrowful all sitting in a row, waiting for them. Everyone made and ate a midday meal, Sorrowful nuzzling Eli for attention after having been banished to Naomi's side the previous night. Afterward, Eli and Hannah zigzagged along the trails leading to Swiftwater's makeshift gambling hall, Sorrowful circling, sniffing for rabbits and other dogs. Eli had visited the poker room each day, asking for his mail, hoping Jesse Peacock would answer before the Yukon River began to flow again.

"You got your package from Peacock brung in today—I got it over here," Swiftwater said when he spotted Eli ducking through his door. When he saw Hannah follow, he whistled and asked, "Where did you find this beautiful lady way up here in this Galdang place? Tell me she's come to marry me and make me a happy husband forever!"

"You're presently married—I believe to three or four, as I recall. You seem to forget to end any before you begin another!" scolded Eli, laughing at Swiftwater's remark. Turning and bowing, he added, his eyes twinkling, "Hannah, this is my friend Swiftwater Bill Gates, the man who saved me from Patches, the man who discovered the first gold on the Fortymile River down from the Klondike, the man who charms women out of their money and their innocence the moment they meet him. Stay close to me if you wish to remain free of this old swindler."

Hannah stepped forward and offered her hand, smiling. "Your name tells me of your reputation, Mr. Gates—so I'll watch out for you! But I'm still pleased to meet you, and I thank you for saving the man I'll love rather than you."

Taken aback at Hannah's witty answer, Swiftwater blinked. "Gal-dang, Eli, this pretty woman is the one that nursed you back fit as a fiddle back in San Francisco, ain't she?"

Eli rested his right hand on Hannah's back, up near her neck, grateful, and surprised, too, at her cleverness. "Yes . . . hopefully I won't be fool enough to bother her like that anymore." After glancing at her, feeling proud again, he turned back to Swiftwater Bill and said, "Get Peacock's package for me. I'm wondering what his plans are now. Hopefully, they're sensible—"

He and Hannah walked to a table and sat down as Swiftwater hurried over with a lumpy, yellow envelope soiled from its travels. Eli ripped it open, worrying about its contents, but he saw that his anxiety appeared needless. His Deputy Marshal's star fell out first. He read the letter, clutching his star and staring straight ahead at the paper. At the end, he folded the paper, pinned his star to his medicine jacket, and said, seemingly to himself, "I'll arrest this one . . . for the boy and his mother . . . not for Peacock. I think he has disappointments waiting for me at the end of the river." Then he stood, pensively looking down at the star hanging shiny on his chest. "Hannah, let's walk back. I want to talk—" He reached over, took her hand, and turned to leave.

"Eli, what's wrong?" Hannah worried about his sudden unhappiness.

"All my life I've lived alone. Now that you're with me, now that I have my star back, my heart says to choose you rather than my past. And Peacock said less in his letter than I wanted, but perhaps more than I wished to hear. I don't trust him anymore . . . not in the least. I'm tempted to write him to come catch the Cannibal himself."

Hannah flushed with happiness and fear in the same instant. Eli's heartfelt words thrilled her, but she dreaded Jesse Peacock's arrival also—and she didn't trust him a bit herself. And the thought flashed through her mind that if he'd learned she had traveled north, he would surely try to hurt them. Yet even though she wanted Eli to quit the Marshals and stay with her always, she knew that might be wrong and, perhaps in the end, damning for her. Personal feelings were less important than the clear need to capture the man responsible for the death of a mother and a boy, both helpless during that long past, fatal night.

She reached out and tugged Eli to a stop, facing him. "You need to arrest the man who killed Mrs.

Turnbull and her son—and who hurt my friend Naomi. In my heart I want you to quit and not do it . . . but I know you must for the good of everyone. I can't abide thinking that this man is still free and now close by as well. You must go arrest him!"

"I know . . . and I'll do it tomorrow. But I fear the trouble it will bring. I don't want you in danger all the way downriver." He walked a few steps and stopped again. "But now you're with me. You'll have to help—and I hope you understand how much. This Cannibal looks as cold-blooded as any I've ever chased in my past."

At Eli's warning, both happiness and fear flashed through her once more. She had come north to start a new life. In achieving that purpose, she'd seen beauty and ugliness—then beauty again in Eli's arms. She had cried too many times, but she had grown much stronger because of it. Could it be that greater tests awaited her now that she lived with the man she loved? She doubted it! But Eli seemed so instinctive about the remaining hardships. What did she face, she wondered? Fright crept into her soul as she watched his face grow hard and unforgiving on the walk back to their camp.

CHAPTER TWENTY-ONE

Apprehension

Chain, padlock, nuts and bolts, arrest documents, pistol loaded and loose in his belt, medicine coat for good luck, Eli rehearsed for the capture of the man he'd chased for so long. He saw Sorrowful whipping his tail around like a hungry cat, his yellow eyes dancing, and sensed his dog's readiness to go on the manhunt, too. Shifting his attention to Patches, he saw the pickpocket fidgeting with buttons, swiping with one hand at his sniffles, squirming inside his coat. Reluctantly, Patches had conceded that he should go along, agreeing that Naomi didn't seem fit for the task of pointing out the Cannibal, but the mood around camp reeked of his fear.

Eli faced the pickpocket. "Walk around so he can see you. Talk to everyone near the place where you last saw him. Tell folks you want to find a man who's been spending gold for things he wants. I've a notion we'll see the Cannibal show himself before coffee-time."

"I know we can find him—my face is like a flag. And he'll come after me for following him. My worry is he'll kill me before you can save me. Just wait—you'll see he's not afraid of you!"

Eli studied Patches, puzzled by his terror. The pickpocket was lanky, strong, quick as a wink, a man unlikely to be so afraid. Wanting to reassure him, he answered, "He will be when he sees who I am, and what I can do—and you'll see Sorrowful stop him the moment he appears. You need to stop being so afraid."

"You weren't that tough when I stuck you."

Eli's eyes flared. After a moment of cold silence, he said, "I lost my common sense in Arizona, Sorrowful in the city, and gave my good luck to Noodles instead of wearing it that night. You won't see the same foolishness today. And reminding me that you're not square with the law or me isn't helpful toward realizing your wish for freedom."

Patches winced, his inky, sullied face remorseful. "Eli, I'm sorry—didn't mean to make you mad. I get a stupid mouth when I'm scared. Just want you to keep the Cannibal away from me."

"I will, and Sorrowful will, too. Now let's go and get him in chains. Then he'll not seem so bad."

Sitting nearby at the campfire with Naomi clutching her hard, Hannah asked worriedly, "Won't he shoot at you or Sorrowful? I should go along with my shotgun and help."

Eli glanced at Hannah, surprised, proud of her willingness even though she looked as afraid as Patches and Naomi. Smiling, he answered, "Sorrowful and Patches and I will be safe by ourselves. If there's trouble, I'll shoot him down like others who've refused to come along peacefully. Peacock can have one more one-legged outlaw to complain about as far as I care. I think he'll not protest too much about the Cannibal being a cripple when I write him to come and take the man back to San Francisco by himself."

Suddenly Patches' face lifted, his eyes hopeful. "Do you think I'll get to go back myself? Can I go back and talk to the police about me seeing him come out of the Senator's house?"

"You'll be taken back for your testimony in court. Without it, the Cannibal might go free. If you help me today and I see no mistakes, I'll write a letter so the police don't jail you for stabbing me. I'll give you a copy and send the original to Senator Turnbull. That will keep Peacock and the police mindful of your helpful ways. And I've a notion they'll need to be reminded when they first see you back."

His blotchy face brightened, and Patches grinned. "I'll do what you say. I want to go back home. Naomi, don't you want to go back, too?"

Shaking her head, Naomi tilted it toward Hannah, signaling her wish to stay. Hannah, smiling at Naomi's loyalty, asked, "Will they make her go back, Eli? I don't think it's wise. And she loves Lincoln so. Isn't there a way we can keep her with us?"

"Yes—for as long as she wants. She would be treated as badly as I've seen Indians treated before. The lawyers would submit that she's not American and unable to talk. I doubt the judge would consider her worthy."

"I love her, and I'm sure Lincoln does, too. We just

have to remind him of it!" Hannah hugged Naomi, miming the relief that now calmed the black woman's face.

"I'll try my hand at settling Lincoln's unhappiness if Noodles fails. But now I need to settle my own. Patches, it's time. Walk out ahead of me and don't look back. Act the same as I've said. Don't worry a bit about the Cannibal getting near you—the moment you signal you see him, Sorrowful will knock him down and hold him helpless."

They hurried mile after mile down the lake to a cluster of tents and shacks clumped near the narrow passage leading out of Lake Bennett into Tagish Lake and Marsh Lake beyond. Eli stayed behind Patches, keeping himself at a distance from the pickpocket, keeping Sorrowful at heel and on watch. As they neared the campsites ringing the outlet, Eli doubled his vigilance and signaled for Sorrowful to do the same—and to listen for every command.

Patches slowed down, drifted left and right among the camps and the pole platforms. Sweaty men whipsawed spruce logs into lumber, while their partners feverishly pounded nails and tar caulking into newly built boats. Most of the men Patches spoke to, repelled by his ugliness, backed off from him, shook their heads, shuffled their feet, nodded, waved arms. Others shrugged and pointed across the slim passage out of the lake. After working up and down the one side for an hour, Patches began hiking across the ice to search the other side.

Suddenly, as the pickpocket neared the bushy alders covering the opposite shore, a bearded, heavyset man scrambled down the lake bank onto the ice three hundred paces to the north of Eli. The stranger, bundled in a purple pea jacket, heaved after Patches as fast as his thick legs could chop up and down, and as quick as his burly arms could pump. Patches' howl when he spotted the man coming after him confirmed the stranger's identity. Then Eli saw blinks of sunlight flashing off a shiny object as the man's right arm shot forward at each stride.

"Get him!" Eli couldn't believe his luck in finding the Cannibal so easily—and catching him so defenseless against Sorrowful out on the middle of a frozen lake channel.

The Cannibal didn't see Sorrowful streaking toward him until the attacker had closed to within a few feet. Running after his dog, Eli saw the killer's shock as the wolflike creature lunged at his leg. Sorrowful snapped a mouthful of trouser as he hurtled by, swinging his whole body free of the surface, flipping the Cannibal off his feet and flat on the ice. Before the man could roll over and right himself, Sorrowful hit him again, clamping his fangs around the hand that held a silver blade and knocking it onto the ice a few feet away. Cursing and crying out in pain, the man pulled away from Sorrowful's teeth and rolled to his hands and knees. Raging, Sorrowful hit him once more, biting his left biceps and knocking him onto his belly. Stunned, the Cannibal pushed himself up, trying again to stand and defend himself—but Eli's pistol blow to the back of his head left him senseless and still, facedown on the ice.

"Get over here and hold his head down!" Eli waved to Patches, who had begun to creep away.

Eli watched as Patches jumped forward to help and as Sorrowful ran to the Cannibal's ankles, biting and pulling on one pants cuff, keeping the leg outstretched. Smiling, seeing that his dog remembered his training, Eli whipped leather laces around both of his captive's wrists in a cowboy's tie, binding the arms hard together behind the waist and to belt loops.

"Get off his head now. Sorrowful, let go!" Seeing Patches' knee on the Cannibal's neck, Eli worried that he would press too hard and kill the man.

Patches jumped up, grinning. "Sorrowful got him good. I'm glad I never had that dog come after me. That Cannibal never had a chance, like you said. I would of never believed it if I wouldn't of seen it happen with my own eyes!"

"My friend hasn't forgotten his duty, and he's still as quick as ever. And you'll see him keep the Cannibal peaceful for as long as I say. We'll be able to sleep at night—no prisoner can stir without him telling me."

Moans and choking sounds from the Cannibal's mouth prompted Eli to roll his captive over. As the killer opened his eyes, Eli knelt in front of him and wiped snow away from his nose and mouth, clearing his clogged air passages.

"I'm arresting you for the murders of the Turnbull woman and boy and for the theft of their money. My name is Eli Bonnet, Deputy U.S. Marshal. Do you understand me and why you are my prisoner?"

The Cannibal blinked at Eli, focusing. Then, when he saw Patches again, he pivoted and kicked at Eli, cursing and raging, "Gonna kill you—gonna gut-cut you and pull your innards out! You bastard freak, you gonna get it worse—"

Sorrowful attacked again, catching one flying leg in his teeth and yanking the Cannibal away in loops opposite to the direction of the first kick. Eli jumped out of the way and listened to his prisoner's outburst change to screams of pain as fangs sank deeper into flesh. A moment later the screams changed to cries to call the dog off.

"Sorrowful, stop!" Eli stepped forward and knelt near the bearded face again, asking, "Do you wish to come along peacefully, or would you wish for my friend to drag you all the way up the lake and to my camp? Which is it? My patience is gone—"

"I'll stay still . . . for now. The first chance I ever get I'm gonna kill you . . . all three of you!" The Cannibal's eyes burned even in the daylight.

"Stand up. If you ever trouble me again—or anyone else—I'll shoot you down. And I advise you to shut up. My friend may choose your throat to chew next!"

Eli stood up first, then heaved on the pea jacket's collar, lifting the heavy man to his feet. Giving him a hard push toward the shore they had both come down from, he said, "Show me your camp. I'll search and clear it before I take you to mine. I don't want to bother the men near here with questions of where you've camped. Now let's not waste my time!"

The Cannibal led the way up the side of the lake, plodding toward a circle of spindly spruce at the foot of a small hill, far from other campsites. He bled in three places and favored the leg Sorrowful had bitten. When he reached the front of his tent, he plopped down on an oblong stone near a cold fire and sat staring down the narrow exit to Tagish Lake, his eyes narrowed and brooding.

Eli searched inside the tent, leaving Sorrowful on guard and Patches outside snooping through piles of firewood tossed nearby. Sorting through the dirty dishes, smelly clothing, blankets, bags of dried foods and canned meat, Eli couldn't find any evidence or any money that appeared to have been owned by the Senator or his family. He threw each article out the door flap into a heap as he worked, finally emptying the interior. Then he pulled down the tent, draped it over the items he'd examined, and peered around the ground it all had rested on. Seeing nothing disturbed, he looked around, wondering, eyeing the Cannibal.

"Get up!"

Not moving even an eyelid, the Cannibal continued to stare in the same direction downstream.

"Sorrowful . . ." Eli watched the brutish killer jump up and scramble away from his sitting place in a blur, cursing again.

"Patches, come over here with a block of wood."

When Patches carried the cut of firewood over, Eli threw it down next to the seat the Cannibal had used and, using a stout pole he picked up nearby, pried the heavy rock over. Crumbly chunks of dirt lay underneath, hinting that someone had dug under the rock once before.

Using his knife blade to break the soil loose, Eli pawed with his hands through a foot of ground cover. Then, smiling, he lifted out a leather sack, ringing and clinking as he dragged it up. When he opened it, he saw the bagful of gold coins with thick wads of paper money on top.

"Your carelessness matches that of those I've arrested in the past. A bag of gold will surely help persuade a jury of your guilt. I doubt they'll think it was fairly earned after they've seen the sight of you. Now turn around and get down to the lake. We're going back to my camp!"

After telling Patches to follow with all the Cannibal's belongings on a sled that he found tipped over nearby, Eli grabbed the leather sack and led the killer away, Sorrowful growling his watchfulness just behind both of them.

In two hours he had marched his prisoner the distance back, up the shore and near the fire circle used since he pitched the campsite many winter days earlier. The Cannibal burst into another fit when he spied Naomi, threatening and cursing again, sending her dashing into Hannah's arms in tears. Sorrowful, angered by the fuss and the kicking, nailed the bleeding leg once more, quieting the brute instantly.

Eli forced him down on the ground against a cottonwood snag and chained his wrists, his waist, and his feet to the trunk, using the padlock and bolts he'd gathered. After he had completed the chaining, he hammered each bolt's threads, smashing it so no one could twist the nuts free.

"I'll freeze in a few hours and die here all chained up like this!" The Cannibal's face paled for the first time since his arrest.

"I'll leave wood for you to keep a fire with. That will keep you warm through the night. We're nearly to breakup, so I doubt you'll freeze—unless you're as lazy as you are dishonest."

"Then I ain't ever goin' to get much sleep, and I ain't got hardly any slack to throw wood on a fire either."

"My aim is to keep you sleepless—perhaps then you'll remain tired enough to stay peaceful. And you have enough slack to feed a fire. You have all that you'll ever get from me." Eli stomped away with the leather sack he'd found, his face set.

Three days later Lincoln and Noodles returned with the caribou meat. Lincoln's spirits seemed better, and after hearing the Cannibal's awful curses hollered at Naomi and himself, he began to speak and help around the camp in a friendly manner. He set up his own tent and took Naomi into it on his third night back, thereby letting Eli and Hannah sleep together again. Patches and Noodles remained in their bachelors' tent, each pestering about the day the other had guessed the ice would thaw away.

"By Jeez, it's sure good Lincoln's strong! We didn't have much snow to slide back on. Saw fast water running back in the mountains. . . . The Yukon'll be open tomorrow or next day after. It's about the end of May. Got to go out soon!"

Seeing everyone gathered around, listening, Eli said, "I've a notion by tomorrow. The lake is black with needle ice. If we get wind it will be out by evening time." Looking at Lincoln, he added, "I'll carry Hannah and Sorrowful, with Cannibal up front so I can watch him. You take Naomi, Patches, and Noodles. I'll carry more gear to balance the loads."

"Folks tell there's fast water when we get to the river. I been down rivers before, but I hope this'n ain' bad."

"I've boated down rough water in Montana. Let's try to stay close so we can pick our way down rapids together. And if we tip over, we can save each other."

"By Jeez, I hope! I can't swim a lick!" hooted Noodles. "I ain't had a bath for a while—but I don't want one that way."

Eli looked at the old man, then at Hannah, Naomi, Lincoln, and Patches. Regret shot through him when he saw all their fearful eyes staring back, wide, white, unblinking. Even the Cannibal's eyes across from them looked afraid. He wondered if he should have let the dangers stay unspoken until they'd reached the head of the river. The first miles down the three lakes would be a drift with the wind behind, as explained by Swiftwater Bill. At least everyone could have had peace of mind for a day or two more, he thought. Now he'd probably alarmed everyone needlessly.

CHAPTER TWENTY-TWO

Downriver

Eli and Hannah wrote the date on the first blank page after the front cover of her Bible. Neither could explain why the day of May 29, 1898, meant so much to them. And neither had yet pledged their union as eminent as wedlock or birth, but they wrote it down nevertheless and added: "ice out, Lake Bennett, bound for Dawson City," followed by Hannah's flowery signature and Eli's scribbled one. Perhaps, they said to each other, it seemed important because of their being trapped for so long waiting for open water. And now their bond needed to be shown as bravely as all the other bargains made by the stampeders who had just ceded their lives to the ways of the Yukon River.

Both then shared their thoughts about the trip ahead. Eli recited Swiftwater's description of the river: Miles Canyon at first, a trough boiling inside hundred-foot rock walls, then the Whitehorse, Squaw, Five Finger, and Rink Rapids, chutes of tumbling froth between rocky edges. After that, a long, favorable passage flowing down to the Klondike through timbered hills and mountains.

Sensible and seasoned, he talked about rowing and steering through fast water, about routes through rocks, about meeting standing waves head-on. Unwise and green, she talked about being brave, about trusting him, about meeting God's will head-on. He teased about her choice of faith over worry; she teased about his choice of worry over faith. But by the time they had finished their breakfast, their ceremony with the Bible had blossomed into merrymaking over sailing down Lake Bennett, Tagish Lake, and Marsh Lake to the top of the river.

After everyone had joined and pushed each of their boats into the water using wooden rollers, Eli and Lincoln took command over their assigned passengers. Each crew hauled and balanced cargoes and rigged square homespun sails. Then, just before shoving off, Eli and Lincoln led the Cannibal to the prow of Eli's boat and chained him by his wrists with enough length for him to move about and help balance the bow.

As they pushed off from shore, Noodles tossed his floppy hat up above Lincoln's boat, hooting his happiness, joining his howl with thousands of others. Peppering the surface, boats of every size and shape floated out toward the middle of Lake Bennett.

Eli surveyed flat bottoms, round bottoms, high-sided, low-sided, pointy ones and square ones; no craft seemed more favored than another. He saw hundreds sailing his way from the south, most from Lake Lindeman, he thought. Thrilled by the sight, he smiled at Hannah, silently sharing his joy at being off once more on a gold stampede. It had been a long since he'd sensed such excitement . . . back when he first rode west into beautiful Montana, he recalled. He hesitated to figure the years that had passed by since then; it seemed a number he wished to forget.

He kept Hannah nearby in the stern, and Sorrowful on top of the freight in the center, guarding the Cannibal. Lincoln's boat sailed as fast, and the crafts stayed side by side as they rode warm, northbound breezes through the headwater lakes of the Yukon. Yelling across, everyone soon slipped into a festive, holidaylike spirit, fun-filled and restful. Then Hannah practiced steering with the aft sweep, shoving it back and forth, testing her strength, setting the oar to angles, and bringing the nose to new headings. She laughed aloud, crying out her delight in her new skills to Noodles and Naomi.

The next day Eli crawled up beside Sorrowful with his field glasses and spied scores of men doing the same. When the shore near the head of the river became visible, he sat studying the river's entrance and the other boats that had landed and anchored around the outlet.

"Hannah, steer for shore and keep us out of the river. I've a notion Lincoln and I should walk a ways down and look the water over. Something is wrong below—there's too many boats and men beached for me to think it's safe." He then waved to Lincoln and yelled for him to follow, watching him wave back and turn toward the shore also.

After dropping sails, tying up, and telling Noodles to cover the Cannibal with Hannah's shotgun, he led Lincoln along the banks of the river. They saw unskilled men shooting fast water for the first time—and watched most of them whirl around and around in Miles Canyon. Hiking the riverside for hours, Eli and Lincoln lost count of the swampings, the wrecks smashed and stuck against rough rock walls and scattered along boulder banks and below in shallow water. Then they saw the drowned bodies floating by; moments after that they saw the corpses' partners sitting dazed on the shore that they had swum to. The horror of the disaster along the river silenced and sickened both of them all the way back to their own boats. They were both determined to avoid the same fate.

"Hannah . . . Noodles, take Naomi and Patches along the river on this side, past the canyon and Whitehorse Rapids. Take your time; it's a long way. Lincoln and I will take the boats through and wait. The river's too dangerous for any of you to come along." Eli slumped down inside his boat to rest.

The Cannibal's eyes blinked. "You not gonna keep me chained, are you? Let me go—I ain't wantin' to drown!"

Eli glanced at the killer. "You're staying up front. I'll give you length enough that you can help paddle and steer. If you want to stay alive, help me keep the boat straight all the way through."

Alarmed, Hannah asked, "Are you and Lincoln sure? Isn't there something else we can do?"

"Lincoln tells me he can swim like a fish. I'm more like a duck myself." He winked at Hannah, wanting to reassure her and Naomi. "Please don't worry. We'll be fine. Now get going. We'll wait for you at the foot of the Whitehorse."

After their companions had disappeared into the woods, Eli and Lincoln lowered and stored their makeshift sails and lashed the rigs down. Shoving off again, each man heaved and fought to pole the heavy vessel by himself over to the river channel and to head it properly downstream. Gathering speed then, each jumped over to his sweep oar and pushed and pulled to steady the bow of the boat against the crosscurrents jostling below.

Eli signaled Lincoln to stay close behind and on the same course through the roaring water as he. Shouting over the cauldron ahead in the canyon, he ordered the Cannibal up and paddling to help steer as whirlpools and white water slurped and crashed everywhere. Seeing terror in the killer's eyes, he wondered if his own eyes looked as fearful. Then he suddenly saw the man's wild flapping with the oar as futile; he would be just thrown overboard and drowned in his chains. Even Sorrowful, still standing guard, perched splayfooted on top of the load against the pitching, pounding, and whipping of the boat. Eli screamed at both of them to get down, hunker low in the bottom. Twisting and leaping, Sorrowful dived down. The Cannibal, slower and not hearing at first, finally saved himself by dropping to his knees and grabbing on to the floor slats.

Eli's mind flashed back to his experiences of shooting raging waters before, the Flathead during a Montana spring, but this river ran much worse and this boat felt much more clumsy. He fought for his steering, ripping at the river one way, then the other with his aft oar. Rolling, clawing waves smashed aboard, wetting everyone and everything. Bucking, tipping, banging, the hull bounced again and again over rocks and tree stumps hidden below the surface. Glancing back, he saw Lincoln coming through also, his mouth crying out soundlessly, white eyes on black face, trapped, riding down regardless, one way or the other.

He prayed one of Hannah's proverbs, crying out to be saved himself. Then he saw it, slack water, just ahead to the left, and he aimed for it with the hardest heave on his oar yet. Shooting forward, the boat obeyed and slipped into the gently pool, bobbing, suddenly tame again.

"I ain' been so scared in my life, never. I rafted logs down rapids before—but I ain' done nothin' like this!" Lincoln's mouth stayed hanging after his outburst.

"We're past the canyon. The Whitehorse is next. Let's bail the boats and rest. Have faith—I do believe we'll make it safely now." Eli smiled, picturing Hannah's self-satisfied nod and laugh over his sudden religious rebirth.

The sun and wind began to dry the soaking Eli had gotten from the descent through the canyon. Sorrowful and the Cannibal shook themselves off as best they could and returned to their assigned places, each eyeing the river off the right side. Sharing hardtack and jerky all around, Eli rested, demanding that Lincoln do the same after seeing him tinkering needlessly with his boat.

After two hours Eli pushed off again, leading the way. The river ran flat for more than a mile, then broke into a torrent of booming, tumbling whitecaps rearing four and five feet high. Whipped around a sharp corner in the channel, he barely missed a hidden reef; then he pushed madly on his sweep to swing the other way and line up for the worst water just before the bottom. He saw two points of heaped stones choking the river to a narrow chute between them, thundering a flume, spilling the water out into a wide basin he could see waiting below. He hung on, holding his point, then threw the steering oar over, balancing the boat on the roll of water, hanging, waiting, at last falling to the quiet water, rocking side to side, slowed again. Quickly turning, laughing, he glimpsed Lincoln splashing into the basin alongside him, grinning from ear to ear, holding his fists high.

The midnight sun had set north before Hannah and the others skidded down a steep bank and boarded the boats again. Eli, unsettled about their weariness and appearance, helped brush spruce needles and bits of twigs from their clothing, then dabbed Noodles' homemade poultice on the bug bites on everyone's faces and hands. After setting Hannah on the floor of his boat next to Sorrowful, and watching Lincoln seat his passengers likewise, he shoved off into the river once more, peering ahead for the Squaw Rapids roaring just around a bend.

The next rush down the river lacked the speed and danger the raging waters he and Lincoln had come through earlier. Nonetheless, the women screamed and held tight while Patches cowered sulky-faced in the bottom—but old Noodles reared straight up and hooted and yipped all the way down, riding like a kid on a race.

At the foot they floated into a wandering flow unlike anything upriver. Hannah curled up and fell asleep against their gear in a corner, Sorrowful snuggling alongside her, but still on watch. The Cannibal leaned back and slept, too, resting along the slant of the bow. Eli hung his upper body over his oar and swayed with the whispers of the river as it washed northward. He passed a new settlement named Whitehorse, after the rapids. A few hours later he swung into the top of Lake Laberge, also marked on Swiftwater Bill's map. Anchored in the mirror of turquoise between low, wooded mountains, after waving Lincoln over, he finally lay down himself, thankful for free breezes to brush the mosquitoes away.

The next day they ate their first meal late and afterward let the two women sneak away to bathe themselves. Eli studied his map once more and shared the names and places Swiftwater had scratched out. He then listened as Noodles, Lincoln, and Patches jabbered about the sunniness, puffs of warm wind, and endless daylight from the northern sun.

"By Jeez, tonight's weather is goin' to be sunny and mild!" Noodles then cackled, causing everyone to laugh at his wit.

"Folks in the South where I come from won't never believe this. They would say it's winter all the time and not for a darkie like me. I can live in this land just fine, yes, suh!"

Patches, less happy, complained, "I still want to go back to the city. It's nice here now that it's spring, but there ain't nothing but trees and mountains, water and bugs. I sure don't like so much water—or these bugs, neither." He swatted at the myriad mosquitoes buzzing around his motley face.

Eli smiled. "Judging by the sum of folks coming through, I believe Dawson will soon be large enough for you. Noodles and I have run stampedes before, but not like this. We'll see most men with long faces when they find there's not enough gold to go around." He gazed out at the hundreds of boats sailing past.

"By Jeez, then let's get goin'. I'm older than most. I better get there first before I run out of time!" Noodles hopped into Lincoln's boat, hooting and laughing.

They rafted down the winding river again for thirty miles after floating from the bottom of Lake Laberge; then at a newly constructed Northwest Mounted Police post called Hootalinqua, they saw the Teslin River run in from the east. The Yukon River changed to a broad, steady rush northwestward, clenching their two boats like a devilish giant, pushing, rolling, never wanting to let go.

Three days passed drifting with the rowdy currents of the river. The boats slipped through braided channels gouged between islands, past tangles of tree roots looking like tentacles clawing at the waterline, around bends piled high with sand and stone, and seemingly forever between lands that reached toward far horizons of low hills amid round mountains, all painted green by forests of springtime bursting out.

Then four blocks of earth carved out by the relentless water raised up from around a bend. Seeing the odd islands that forced the Five Finger Rapids just ahead, Eli called for Lincoln to come behind once more for the run down the cuts foamy with fast breakers. He watched as the black man pushed and pulled on his sweep, trying to angle over against the flow of the river, fighting, using his strength to overcome the draw of the clumpy hull.

Suddenly Lincoln's steering oar snapped. The boat swept sideways and swirled downstream toward an overhang of rock wall on the east bank. It bounced once off the headland, spun again, and pitched into white water churning between the mainland and the nearest island. Twice more its sides crashed against cliffs, ugly faces with roots and snags sticking out over the water. Breaking free, the boat then scrubbed along the shore again, crunching, banking its way past.

Eli steered to stay near, hearing dreadful, mingled human sounds, seeing Lincoln thrust again and again at rock walls with his broken pole to push off, daring to save his boat and passengers. Eli then watched as the boat smashed under a huge spruce tree lying flat just above the waterline. The sweeper jammed the starboard side and tipped the hull, flipping the boat's topside down into the Yukon.

Naomi, tiny and frail, tumbled out first; Lincoln plunged after her like a sea creature. Noodles, then

Patches, fell out next, each thrashing, trying to stay afloat. But the rolling currents sucked them down, away, out of sight.

He heard screaming. "Save him. Save him!" Screams close, in his ear. He looked. Then Hannah pushed at him, pointing at Noodles, up again, not far away. She hit him again, screaming, "I'll steer and stop when I can. Save him—go!"

He leaped as never before. Hitting the water, then breathless from the icy wash, he stroked twice and caught the old man by his collar in a spin downstream. Seeing more sweepers just ahead, he side-paddled as hard as he could, twisting fast, reaching high, and catching hold of the first one.

Seeing Noodles awake, clear-eyed, he hollered, "Grab to the tree. Get on the tree, old man—quick, now!"

Noodles, not strong, not fast, but sure-handed, wrapped himself around the dead tree and locked his arms. Eli hooked the log with his free arm, heaved up to his belly, pivoted, and sat astride it with both legs looped around, steadying himself. He leaned, clutched the old man, and lifted as quickly as he could, pulling Noodles out of the river in a swing, throwing him up like a soggy sack.

"Hop back with your hands—we've got to shinny back to shore. Hurry up!" He watched as Noodles nodded his head. He saw Lincoln dragging Naomi from the water down the shore where the river banks slanted shallow. Peering left and right, he couldn't find Patches. He instantly worried that the pickpocket had drowned, slipped forever into the selfish Yukon, the very serpent he had feared so much.

"Old man, turn around and hang on. I'll piggyback you up top—we're next to shore now. We've got to build a fire and dry you out. How are you feeling?"

"By Jeez, Eli, I thought Providence had got me for sure. You saved me three times now—God bless. I think you're my son, I love you so much!"

"We've got Hannah to worry about now, old man. She's gone off alone with the Cannibal. I pray Sorrowful can keep her safe—"

He squatted and set Noodles down. Swinging back to the river, he stared in search of Hannah and the boat . . . but both had drifted out of sight. He stood up, both fists balled up against his hips, his legs spread. He'd never felt more fearful in his life. Please, God, he prayed, keep her well!

PART IV

Deliverance

CHAPTER TWENTY-THREE

Misery

As the boat bounded down the last of Five Finger Rapids, Hannah watched the black tops of heads fade away in the white froth she was leaving behind. Lord, she prayed, what has happened to Eli and my friends? Will they live or die? She pushed the sweep against the force of the river and found she could barely move the oar left or right. The moody flow of currents scared her, wild swirls unlike the calm lake water she had helped sail across before. Why won't the boat behave? she fretted. Then she remembered Eli toiling day after day, paddling, poling, powering the heavy hull by hand toward one side of the Yukon River or the other. The winds had done the work for her over the headwater lakes, but now the mast and sail lay stored.

She peered forward. The river spread wide in front, a large island just ahead, a small one beyond, three choices of channels. Which one should she choose? she wondered. Which one would Eli choose? The more she agonized, the more she felt her faith in herself slip away. Then the thought that she might have sent Eli to his death, that

Naomi, Noodles, Lincoln, and Patches might have all drowned as well, broke her down. She stood still, holding straight on, clinging to the grip of the sweep, crying louder and feeling more frightened than she ever had before.

"Let me loose and I'll help steer the boat."

Sorrowful jumped up and raged his threat against the Cannibal. The voice and Sorrowful's fury shocked her back to the dangers at hand. Lord, she prayed again, protect me against the hazards I've embraced. The reality of traveling alone with a brutal killer hadn't pierced her thinking yet. Her fear deepened as if she were caught up in a dreadful dream—a nightmare of her own choosing.

"Shut up! Leave me be . . . I'll—" She decided to keep to one side of the river until she could stop crying. And she sensed that her tears were the best tonic for her spirit. Her journey away from her father and across the wilderness had taught that her girlish weeping would soon subside and after her tears she could always reach beyond.

The choices of channels continued: islands, sandbars, tangles of deadwood dividing the river into an abundance of possible channels. At last she dried her eyes on her sleeve and looked for a place to run aground, just as she'd promised Eli before he'd jumped overboard to save Noodles. As she studied her surroundings, cold horror rose above her other fears. No other boats sailed alongside now. All the way down the Yukon, she'd seen other stampeders drifting nearby: one boat here, three boats there, dozens of boats in front and behind. Now none floated anywhere. My God, she thought, I've lost myself to some other river. Eli will never find me.

Finally she saw what she wanted—a small, sandy island straight ahead, cluttered with spider-leg stumps along its shore. She aimed for the grounding head-on, heaving on the sweep, moaning through her sniffling nose. Hanging tight, she stuck the nose of the boat onto the dirt bank. The boat hit hard and heaved, lurching downstream. Instantly she felt herself tossed over the side, pitched backward, unable to keep her grip on the sideways-flipping oar.

The cold water shocked her to sudden awareness and sent her splashing back toward the boat. Then she saw there appeared no hope of reaching and pulling herself up the boat's high, slick sides. She swung her arms crazily with the flow of the river toward the sandbank behind and on the other side of the hull. Just before choking on inhaled water, sapping her strength to swim, she clawed into the muddy bottom, grasping thankfully her escape from drowning. Plunging forward, floundering again, she scrambled out of the water onto the island and stood up, looking at Sorrowful and the Cannibal, who both stared back, their faces twisted.

"How you goin' to get back to the boat?" The Cannibal stood nearest to her in the bow, blocking her. The rest of the boat floated too far away, with too much deep and fast water between. If she tried to get back on board, she would be swept downriver once more or attacked by the Cannibal.

"Sorrowful—watch—" She shivered, wondering which felt worse, the dunking from the river or the threat from the killer.

The bearded face grinned, then he said, "I'm goin' to kill the dog. You want to watch? When I get done, I'm goin' to kill you. Then I'll see what Eli's been sleepin' with—except you'll be too dead to feel much. But you'll know what I did forever!"

Before she could speak, the Cannibal spun and challenged Sorrowful, swinging loops of chain, hollering at the top of his voice. Sorrowful leaped in a flash of gray, his fangs bared, raging louder than the madman.

Hannah stood in silent horror as Sorrowful hit the Cannibal, knocking him backward against the bow. Then she saw the chain flip like a noose, arcing around Sorrowful's neck and body. She watched in terror as the killer strangled the dog in one fatal instant, ignoring the snapping, tearing teeth, ignoring the scratching paws, ignoring the hideous growling. She heard Sorrowful's snarling change to yelps, then cries, then gurgles as the last of his life slipped away. Mindless of the gashes, the rips of his hands and face, the blood seeping out of his wounds, the Cannibal tossed Sorrowful's body over the center load into the rear of the boat.

"Now it's your turn!" The madman yanked repeatedly with his manacled wrists on the shackles fastened to the front, trying to pull away the links from the eyebolts that held them in the wood.

Hannah panicked. Whirling around, she ran as fast as she could down the center of the island, jumping dead trees, dashing around stumps and tangled debris. When she got to the far end, she glanced back and saw the Cannibal still yanking wildly at his chains.

She waded through a shallow cut over to a sandbar, sprinted across it, and leaped into water between her and a riverbank with trees covering its slope. Swimming as hard as she could, she saw herself being swept downstream fast, but toward a muddy spit that hooked out from the shore. God, she screamed in her mind, give me just enough strength to swim a little more, and let me reach that awful mud ahead. At last she pawed into the bottom, exhausted, but believing her life had been saved again. She crawled out on her hands and knees but found that she couldn't stand and run anymore. Continuing on all fours, she slopped along until she reached the angle of the shore. When she had worked her way up high enough to roll over and look back toward the boat and the killer, she saw that he was still trying to break free, slower now but chinking away at his bonds without pause. Then, to her further horror, she saw the trail she'd left all across the sand and mud, a path the Cannibal would easily follow the moment he broke free. Feeling betrayed somehow, she staggered to her feet and began picking her way through the trees, not caring about direction or speed. She just wanted to get away from the river as fast and as far as possible.

* * *

Time passes in strange ways here in the North, she thought. Had it been two days since her escape, or had it been more? Daylight always, relentless sunshine beamed down from high overhead. She lived each moment for the energy and hope it added to her soul. And sleep came easily when she needed rest; her dread of the dark didn't matter in this endless wash of light.

An angry numbness had capped her fear—she just felt less afraid of life's terrors. She knew the Cannibal could never find her now. The forest's rubble and her steps from stone to stone, avoiding soft spots, had covered her tracks forever. And she knew she had become pitifully lost without a clue for a course back to the river, so it made sense that he would lose his way, too, if he tried to search for her. With the sun circling above her head at all hours, there seemed to be no way by which to decide on a direction to walk. She had chosen her home for the time being anyway, and she intended to stay regardless of the threats that might appear.

She had accidentally walked into a small lake set among wooded hills. A little brook tumbled over rocks on one hillside and passed near a gnarly spruce that soared a hundred feet into the air. Its green boughs hung down and draped to a perfect canopy to hide herself under after she'd broken off some of the dead bottom branches. A bit of meadow circled the tree and let breezes from the lake chase the insects away. And plenty of dead sticks lay scattered about for the little fire she liked to keep burning, letting the smoke float up through the tall tree and fly with the winds.

Thanks to Eli's reminders to always carry her belt knife and waterproof bottle of matches, she was able to make the shelter she'd discovered into a warm, dry den. And she thanked the Lord for all the nights spent sitting by campfires during the past wintertime listening to tales about wilderness survival. Now her keen interest in the lore that Eli, Noodles, and Lincoln had spoken of kept her busy thinking about weapons and food.

A spear came easy. She selected a slim, straight shaft of wood, skinned it clean, and sharpened the smaller end to a point. Then she sat by her little fire, baking the tip just like the men had explained to harden the wood. Pleased by her handiwork, she jumped around outside of her den, stabbing at a pretended enemy, feeling foolish afterward, even though she knew no one had seen her play. Even so, her weapon made her feel proud, and a little safer as she explored the adjacent area.

The lack of food haunted her during all the hours she spent awake. She couldn't recognize anything tasty to eat among all the plants she had picked and pulled up. She did find roots that worked as strings, and she braided several into a stout cord, even though she didn't need any ties. And she saw plenty of rabbits hopping around, but she kept missing when she threw her spear, damaging the point, and then she had to sharpen and harden the tip again.

Little fish often swam in shallow waters around

the edges of the lake and for short distances up the nearby brook—but she had no lines, hooks, or baits to catch them. Her stomach ached as she sat watching, disheartened. She would eat raw flesh, she thought. She felt so desperately hungry—if only she could get her hands on one.

At last it dawned on her. She had heard Eli tell stories of Indian rock dams, into which fish were herded for spawning harvests. She could do that, she thought, as she surveyed the stream feeding into the lake. Working all afternoon, soaking herself, resting and warming when she couldn't work usefully, she built a little pool and a wing dam from rocks and sticks across part of the brook. After dropping the last stone into place, she waded out into the lake and circled back toward her trap, splashing as she returned upstream. When she peeked down into the pool at the end of her drive, her heart leaped. She had six fat fish inside.

But her heart sank when she tried to spear one. They were much too quick, and she ruined her spear point once more on the first try. Sitting and thinking, she decided the only sensible way to capture them was to use a net. Walking back to her den, she unraveled her cord, gathered more roots, and began to tie one together. When she finished, she fastened it onto a wishbone-shaped alder branch and returned to her little pool.

She caught two on her first pass. Nearly losing both of them in her excitement, she ran back to her fire, smiling for the first time since she'd escaped the Cannibal. She knew exactly how to cook them in a fire; she had listened to Eli and Noodles brag about their favorite wilderness recipes. And the two high-finned, pearly fish looked like they would be delicious when baked that way.

After eating, she slept in her little hollow the best she had since she'd bumped into the lake. When she woke, she returned to her trap with her net and caught two more fish, baking and eating them, too. Then, finally feeling stronger, she decided to explore the margin of the lake all the way around. She repaired the point of her spear again, and began her march along the shore, glancing back at her starting point from time to time. Instantly another idea came to her. She could easily see her trail through the brush and grasses as she plowed along. Crunched stems of plants and broken twigs of brush marked her path backward. If she used her knife to scar trees, she thought, and if she broke brush and faced it in a straight line, she could build trails to and from the lake. This would allow her to search for a course back to the river and to hunt for more food at the same time. And, just as important, it would keep her employed while she was awake; and she wanted to stay as busy as she could, and away from her silent fears as much as possible.

When she reached the opposite end of the lake from her camp, she struck off in a straight line, blazing a trail. After a short distance she walked back to the lake to judge the effectiveness of her plan. Smiling for a second time, she saw that her new wood-craft would succeed, and, if she did the same thing at four right angles, sooner or later she would find the Yukon River again. Perhaps, she hoped, Eli and her friends would be waiting, everyone safe and sound.

CHAPTER TWENTY-FOUR

Grit

Naomi died slowly, her lungs fouled with icy water, her little heart fading. Fighting to save her, Lincoln slanted her body downhill and pumped with his hands trying to empty her lungs. But she had remained underwater for too long. Finally, he gave up his hopeless struggle and sat crying, gripping her cold hand.

When Eli couldn't bear listening anymore, he pulled the black man away and led him to the fire roaring nearby on the riverbank. Noodles, drying and recovering from his own dunking, held Lincoln's hand in turn, and talked softly, keeping his words just between the two of them.

Eli stood waving at passing boats until one rowed over and offered help. One of the men aboard crawled out on the dead spruce that had overturned Lincoln's boat, and by using block and tackle, he and his friends roped the submerged hull downriver and got it back to shore. Part of the gear stored in the bottom still remained, and Eli recovered Noodles' shovel to dig a grave. Then, as the helpful stampeders shoved off, he asked them to watch for Hannah downstream and thanked them for stopping.

He climbed up above the river and selected for Naomi's gravesite a shelf on a slope overlooking bordering lands. This is a pleasant, restful view, he thought, one that offers far-off horizons and morning sunlight. He felt sad to leave the little woman behind, next to the waters that had killed her, but he knew of no other place or means to bury her. He felt even more unsettled by the thought of summoning Lincoln uphill for the burial, for he could see the big man below, still weeping over the loss of his loved one.

As he dug deeper into the soil of the slope, he paused from time to time to look for Patches along the water's edge. The Yukon had swallowed the pickpocket within a moment of the swamping and hadn't let his body rise again. Curiously, Eli sensed a loss, and he wondered why he felt saddened over the death of a man who had stabbed him many months before. He also worried about the aftermath of losing both witnesses against the Cannibal. His mind pictured Jesse Peacock cursing at him again.

When he had finished digging to the same depth as his height, Eli returned to the boat and pulled the stored sail out. He wrapped Naomi's body in it, then went over to the fire and said, "Lincoln, carry Naomi up to her grave. She would want you to lay her to rest . . . not Noodles or me. When you're done saying good-bye, we'll fill the grave and set a cross."

Lincoln moaned as he stood and turned away from the fire to Naomi's body. He trudged uphill clutching her bundled remains close to his breast, sobbing and covering the hill with his lonely sighs.

"Old man, if you're well enough and dry by then, walk up in an hour and help Lincoln as much as you can. I'll bail the boat and lay the leftovers out to dry in the sun. I need to walk the edge of the river, too . . . though I've a notion Patches is lost forever."

"By Jeez, Eli, this is been a bad day. All my life I've seen Providence takin' friends away. Gets tiresome when you're old like me . . . and makes me wonder why I'm kept from my own demise. I would've gived my life up for Naomi's."

"Your Providence has little mercy. I've seen folks like Naomi taken often, and I wonder about the choices no less than you. But now my worry is for Hannah. We need to get downriver and find her. The Cannibal will kill Sorrowful and her the moment he figures to get free."

" 'Cause a Lincoln bein' so sad, I forgot. That Cannibal is crazy—and he's got extra chain that you give 'im. I'll go up and help Lincoln now—"

"Let him say good-bye. His heart is hurt, and only time can heal his trouble. Wait until I'm ready. That will be soon enough to bring him down."

Two hours passed before Eli completed his preparations for their launch back into the Yukon. The submerged boat had spilled most of the food, clothing, and sleeping rolls, but enough tools remained stuck in the bottom to repair the damage done during salvage and to replace the sweep oar. He then watched Noodles lead Lincoln down, the strong, spirited man diminished to a stooping hulk.

After boarding both men, Eli shoved off from shore and pushed out into the middle of the river, watching for Hannah and Sorrowful as the current carried the boat along. He measured one mile by eyesight, then a second, but Hannah and her boat stayed hidden. A chill crept up his spine as he peered around, wishing he had his field glasses to help him search far shorelines and up other channels.

Noodles asked, pawing his whiskers, "You suppose we went too far—could she a stopped already?"

"I don't know, old man. The currents are so strong, I can only think she's up ahead. If we don't find her soon, we'll have to turn back and search again. But getting up against this river will be a nightmare—and it will take days to do it." Eli pinched his lips tight.

"By Jeez, it's my fault. You should've let me drown. I won't want to live if'n I'm the cause of Hannah and Sorrowful bein' lost."

"You deserve no blame for anything. We'll find the boat, Hannah and Sorrowful, too—then we can get you down to the Klondike to find your gold." For the first time since San Francisco, Eli thought, Noodles' eyes didn't dance at the mention of gold.

Lincoln turned from the front of the boat. "It's my fault. If I don't hurry to catch up, if I be careful, I don't break the sweep. But I was stupid . . . and now I killed Na—" His black face broke into tears again.

"Lincoln, you did nothing wrong, and you have no rule over life's prospects. Each of us has spent our time in the wilderness, and each of us has seen these hard losses before. I beg both of you to restore your spirits the best you can and quit the blame. Hannah and Sorrowful need our help now."

In a moment Noodles stood up. "Eli, get up here and stand on the seat. My eyes are old and you can see better than me—I'll do the steerin' from now on so you can watch."

After Eli and Noodles had exchanged places, Lincoln straightened in the bow and wiped his eyes on the back of his hand. He then braced himself, wide-legged, and began to search left and right across the water the same as Eli.

Two hours passed. Then Eli stepped down from his perch. We've gone ten miles or more. Steer to port and beach the boat. We'll have to go back. I've a notion Hannah stayed near the shore she started down. We've missed seeing her for some reason."

"How we goin' to get back up this blessed river? The water's fast, and mostly deep."

"It will take us days. Lincoln and I will have to cut long poles and push back. In places, we'll have to rope ourselves along. You'll have to stay in the back of the boat and steer for us."

They began their return up the Yukon River, staying just off the mainland shore. Eli fixed his spruce pole on the bottom and walked to the back of the boat, pushing. Lincoln waited, then timed his poling to vary with Eli's steps forward to begin again. Hour after hour they struggled—grunting, sweating, Noodles fighting for direction. When the water flowed too deep or too fast, they strung a long line and pulled the boat from shore like odd plow horses, trudging along, swiping at mosquitoes. Sometimes they waded in shallows, towing the bow by hand, splashing through mud and water as they fought their way forward.

On the second afternoon thunderstorms chased them under old spruce trees until the cloudbursts faded, each man silently praying that the crackling lightning would miss his chosen shelter. Then the misty air clouded visibility, slowing them, forcing them to work back and forth across channels so they wouldn't miss Hannah's boat a second time. They slept poorly when they rested before their next day's work, choking on the green wood smoke laid down to keep bugs at bay, wishing their tent had stayed on board.

Suddenly they saw it. A boat beached on a small, flat island offshore, across and upstream from them. They poled as hard as they could to get close, straining to see Hannah, Sorrowful, and the Cannibal. No sign of life appeared as each man hollered and waved, using his hat as a signal.

"By Jeez, Eli, somethin' is bad wrong. There ain't nobody by the boat."

"I see that, old man, and I'm sick to death. Let's get across so I can walk up the island." Eli then remembered he had the only key for the padlock on the Cannibal's chains, and he worried that the killer had gotten away.

As soon as they bumped the end of the island opposite the boat, Eli jumped off the front and raced toward the beached boat. Lincoln chased after him, and Noodles bounced behind them, trying to keep up. At the bow of the boat Eli froze. The Cannibal lay crumpled, looking dead, his skin waxy-white. Then Eli saw Sorrowful, dead in the back.

"Where's Hannah, do you see Hannah? Lord, he's killed Sorrowful!" Eli lunged into the boat and grabbed the Cannibal by the throat, choking and shaking the killer, shouting, "Where's Hannah, you murdering bastard, where's Hannah?"

"Eli, let go—let go, don't bang 'im like that! Lord have mercy, if he ain' dead, don't kill 'im now. We got to find out about Hannah from him." Lincoln leaned over and pried Eli's grip from the Cannibal's throat, pushing hard to stop the throttling. "Get 'way from 'im, you hear, get 'way and let me see!"

Lincoln climbed in and shoved Eli toward the baggage in the center of the hull. In a moment the black man stood up again, hovering over the killer's body.

"Lord, Sorrowful chewed 'im awful bad—and look here at his wrists. He's been tryin' to pull free and couldn't do it. They all wore to the bone. He about dead from losin' blood. We best get 'im patched up, else he be that way pretty soon!"

"I've no wish to keep him alive. Hannah's gone—"

"I've seen enough death to keep me, Eli. You leave 'im be. You a Marshal and supposed to bring 'im for trial. You best remember your duty!"

Noodles panted up to the point of the boat. "Where's Hannah? Lord, he's kill't poor Sorrowful—"

"She's gone, old man, she's gone—" Eli fell back against the heap of freight behind him.

"You don't know, Eli. Might be she's just off close by."

"You two shush up about Hannah. Eli, get back to

Sorrowful and get 'im out for buryin'—and give me the key so I can get the Cannibal out. I need to get 'im bandaged up. Noodles, you help here and get his legs when I lift." Lincoln turned back toward Eli for the key, his hand held out, stiff and demanding.

Eli, his head hanging down, fished the key out of his trousers pocket and handed it to Lincoln. Then he crawled over the load and knelt beside Sorrowful's body, patting the side of the dog's head. Lincoln heaved the Cannibal over the prow of the boat and carried him to a flat, clear space of sand nearby, Noodles struggling to help with both legs. Moments later, Eli stepped out with Sorrowful's body wrapped in canvas, and laid him on an uprooted tree stump.

He then walked sadly over to Lincoln and Noodles. "Noodles, would you help me get the tent set up? I want to rest here for a day or two and give Lincoln enough time to save the Cannibal if he can. Tomorrow I'll cross over and bury Sorrowful on that high hill . . . it will be a fine place for him to look around forever."

The following morning Eli carried Sorrowful away from their camp for burial. Noodles followed with a shovel and a rough board cross that Eli had fashioned during the night. They poled over with the boat to the shore nearest the hill Eli had chosen and trekked up the side, resting often for Noodles to catch his breath. At the top, above the trees, and within a circle of hard ground strewn with stones and gravel, Eli dug Sorrowful's grave, a deep round hole centered on the peak. When he reached the grave's depth, he slid the canvas casket down, settled it, then climbed back out.

Standing there, looking down, he said, "I don't know what to say, old man. This is one of the hardest things I've faced."

"Tell 'im you love him, Eli. That's all you can do. There'll come a day when you'll see 'im again—you can rest certain about that. The Lord'll put you two back together someday."

"I told him a thousand times last night, old man, a thousand times . . ." Slowly Eli picked up the shovel and began filling the hollow around his friend.

When they reached Lincoln's side again late in the day, he still sat nursing and cleaning the Cannibal. Eli saw that the killer had opened his eyes and seemed to be gathering awareness, his color brightened.

"Has he talked of Hannah?" Eli crouched next to the Cannibal's head.

Lincoln stayed busy with his cleaning rag. Finally, after a moment of silence, he answered, "Yes, suh, he says she's drowned in the river. Got throwed over when she hit the shore. Says you should go look for yourself and you'll see. Says it's plain . . ."

After searching the Cannibal's black eyes for long minutes, Eli stood up and walked to the boat that Hannah had beached hard aground, stern angled to the river currents, sweep oar handle pushed over to one side, blade trailing downstream. He stood stone still, watching the river boil behind the boat, ripples slurping, sucking down. It seemed believable that Hannah had been forced overboard, he thought, and clearly the boat had hit the land and jackknifed. Anyone not practiced in piloting a boat into a landing with fast water following would surely have had a similar accident. Yet dim intuition nagged him, a hint of spite in the Cannibal's eyes, and, also, the lessons he'd learned from Hannah as he'd come to love her. She was spirited, clever, determined, and, most of all, faithful to her own ideals. He wondered if it could possibly be true . . . the hope that burned in his heart.

When they roused in the morning, and during their early coffee, Eli said, "Old man, Lincoln, I want you to leave me behind. Take the Cannibal downriver to Dawson. Turn him over to the Mounties or the U.S. Marshals, whomever you find first in that town. Swiftwater's map shows the river as flat from here to there; you've only one more small rapids to run. Sleep in shifts and guard the Cannibal around the clock. Don't trust him an inch. I'll come along later when I'm finished here."

"This is a sad place. You best come with us. You need to get 'way from here like you made me leave Naomi. I has a broken heart from it, yes, suh . . . but you was right in makin' me move along with the river. A man can't be hangin' around graves. No, suh, it ain' good for the soul."

"By Jeez, Lincoln's right, Eli. Don't you be sittin' here feelin' sorry—lookin' for Hannah, pinin' for Sorrowful. I want you to come along. I need you . . . and you promised!" Noodles' eyes grew misty.

"I know, old man, I know. But let me do this thing. You've known about me for many years—I've always lived by myself in the wilderness. Contrary to what Lincoln says, it will be good for my soul. I need to be alone . . . I need to be healed by the peacefulness of—" Eli's voice stopped, and he stared across the Yukon's waters.

Noodles paused, then said, "I owe you my life, Eli, so I guess you ain't askin' for much. If'n you want to stay around here, just promise me you'll come see me soon—that's all I'll say."

Eli held out his hand for Noodles' shake. "You've got my word, old man, and I'll keep my promise."

They split the remaining outfits as sensible for three and one and reloaded each boat. Then, braced against afternoon winds, he watched as Noodles and Lincoln floated away. Waving, he saw them round a bend and disappear, leaving him to recall all the fateful days that had passed since he'd been alone on the land.

Silence squeezed around, yet nature's voices sounded within it: the rising wind through treetops, a red squirrel's chatter across the way, raven caws up above, an eagle's cry higher still, and the timeless whisper from the river beside him. Songs, he remembered, that had soothed him in the past, and sweet harmonies that would help heal him now.

Walking back to the boat that Hannah had vanished from, he poled down and around the end of the island, over to the main shore near the hill where Sorrowful lay. He chose soft sand to camp on, a clear place next to deadwood for campfires, and with wind blowing across and a log to sit on in the mornings. After he pitched a canvas lean-to and stored his gear under it, he climbed to stand on top of the hill again to tell Sorrowful good-bye . . . and to scour all around the country below with his spyglasses.

When his eyes grew tired from searching the land, he promised aloud, "Sorrowful, I'll miss you always and wish you were with me. I'll be back tomorrow and each day after. Speak to your spirits, help me find Hannah."

Each day he climbed up and looked more when the weather and light seemed favorable. The land rolled off in each direction—the Yukon River meandering toward the northwest, high hills bluing horizons far out, spruce and birch and aspen dressing lower parts, and little lakes and fields of berry bushes and bald spots quilting other places east and west. Black bear sows with cubs, cow moose with twin calves, wolves, red foxes, and pine martins hunting squirrels for food stirred during cooler hours. And ducks, beavers, and otters danced and played, leaving wakes and ripples drifting around for him to spy on.

On a day that looked like every other, and after he'd lost track of the number that had passed, he finally saw faint smoke far off. Miles away from him, odd puffs floated up from the forest, joining the summertime haze over the greater hills that stood off against the sky. He focused, his heart pounding as if he were seeing life's resurrection. The smoke grew more plain; then he saw orange flash as a giant tree blazed high above the green below.

He marked the course across using his compass, his mind racing through all the possibilities. No Indian hunting parties had come by, the stampeders on the river had passed days ago, and no lightning storms had rumbled away recently. It had to be Hannah, he thought, but she must be in trouble. Otherwise, why would she burn a spruce tree now rather than when he'd first come up the hill? He grabbed his Winchester and struck out, stretching downhill, measuring his pace so he could last the distance.

After an hour of fighting through underbrush, he found a lightly marked trail slanting a little to his right hand. Someone had scarred the trees and bent the brush in a line through the woods. He followed, tracking as he trotted along. He caught a glint of blue water through the trees; then he caught the scent of wildfire in his nose. Running faster, he suddenly popped out into an open circle. He saw Hannah in the middle, close to a smoldering tree fire, hurling firebrands at a hunting black bear prowling in front of her.

"Hannah, get down!" He saw her spin toward him as she dropped flat, clearing the way for him to aim and fire. The blast from his rifle shook the meadow and lake. Then he saw her leap up after the shot, not looking as afraid as he thought she should be.

"Eli, I've been waiting for you so long . . ." She stood there, holding a long, pointed staff and smiling . . .

CHAPTER TWENTY-FIVE

Dawson

As the steamboat *Victorian* headed upriver, fighting the ceaseless currents of the Yukon River, the incessant beat of the paddle wheel soured Jesse Peacock. Each day he sank a little deeper into a fit of anxiety over whether Eli Bonnet would really be able to capture the killer and convey him downriver to Dawson City. The black dog of worry spoiled all his conscious moments, sending him back and forth on sulky crawls inside the boat. And his mood swings had cost him Etta's patience and chased her off to mix with others who shared her passion for the new frontier.

She rejoiced in the voyage up the roiling river. Miles wide, the Yukon wandered wrong at first, pushing down from the south instead of the northeast, as everyone had supposed. Treeless tundra covered the shoreline for flat miles on end; grassy, shallow marshes stretched off beyond the banks, reminding her of rice fields she had once seen in California. And her greatest thrill came when the skies darkened with flocks of waterfowl, many species more than her borrowed book showed in its illustrations. How could there be a place, she wondered, with millions of ducks and geese milling in the air at the same time, covering even the racket of the thrashing riverboat with their resonant honks and squawks?

More dark, squat people resembling those back in Dutch Harbor in the Aleutians paddled about, hunting and fishing, each of their skin boats stuffed with fathers, mothers, and babies. Waving, they flashed their friendliness with their bright white teeth. Etta waved back, wishing she could somehow stop and talk, get to know their happiness in such a plentiful land.

Then she saw the horse-size animals called moose. With huge, mossy antlers and bulbous noses like camels, they stood dripping and chewing water lilies pulled from pond bottoms. Cowed by the steamboat, they loped up the riverbanks, peeking back, their mule ears flapping in fright. She laughed and pointed when she first saw twin moose calves, tan and long-legged, quick to run with their mother. A wild barnyard, she reflected, a wonderful show of creatures she had never pictured living in such a lovely, green land. Why had she thought it would be barren and forlorn? Why had it ever been said it would be like winter all the time?

She took Jesse's binoculars from his cabin, dismissing his grouching about her haughty manner, and climbed to the top deck next to two stacks that spewed gray smoke. Viewing from there, she learned from Minnesota travelers about beavers, otters, mink, and muskrats. She marveled at the water crea-

tures' ability to slink and splash out of sight in an instant. Then she began to wonder about the imminent hardships when a few of the men talked of
trapping in the coming winter if their gold prospecting went for naught. Judging by the prices of furs she
had shopped back in San Francisco, she decided
that trapping could be worthwhile.

Finally she saw her first brown bears and cried out
in surprise when the sow and cub streaked away with
blinding speed. The Minnesota men claimed that the
bears could run faster than horses; she thought it
more important that they could run three times faster
than a fast man. Despite her shivers over the imagined scene, she still laughed when one of the men
commented he didn't need to run fast enough to better a bear; he just needed to run fast enough to leave
his partner behind.

A few hours later, the *Victorian* blew its whistle
over and over. Angling toward shore against the currents, the steamboat crept near long woodpiles
stacked near the banks of the river. Rough-clothed
men ran about on the lower deck and threw thick
ropes to other men waiting alongside the rows upon
rows of boiler fuel. When the boat had been anchored hard to shore, the deckhands pulled wide
ramps between the ground and the front, and everyone scurried back and forth with carts full of four-
foot lengths of spruce. Etta wondered aloud how
firewood could be waiting for them in treeless surroundings, but then one of her new friends explained
that the timber got rafted downstream, then cut up
and stacked for use.

She went ashore with other passengers who wanted to kick around the supply yard. Again she marveled at the lushness of the land, admiring the tall, waving fields of grass as high as she stood, and the dense thickets of tangled willow and alder, blocking anybody from walking across the land.

Then she learned about the merciless attacks of mosquitoes, small clouds buzzing and stinging in a mad, suicidal haze that ensured some would live and breed in spite of her flurry of slapping and killing. My God, she thought, my body will be sucked dry of blood if I stand still for very long. She ran back aboard to escape the hungry swarms, shivering a second time at her discovery of yet another hazard on the new frontier.

When she reached the cabin, she declared to Jesse, "In the three days since Saint Michael, you've made my life miserable. I've had to spend most of my time alone. I'm not staying with you anymore unless you change. You need to quit your moaning about the Marshal and the man he's supposed to arrest." Etta thought perhaps the bugs had somehow frustrated her into the showdown; she didn't want to be trapped in a stateroom with a grouch for the rest of the river.

"I don't think you understand the consequence of what I've done," he replied. "If I return to San Francisco at the end of this summer without the man that killed the Senator's wife and boy, I'll lose everything."

"I don't understand why you began this trip if that's true. But it makes no difference now. You've spent more than three weeks getting this far, and it's impossible to turn back. Why make us miserable with your silly worries over things that you guess could happen? That makes no sense at all!"

Etta's warning frightened him more than his gnawing anxiety over Eli Bonnet, the killer, and his other nightmares of uncertainty. Somehow he had to pull himself up, he thought, show some kindness and happiness. If he didn't, he knew Etta would leave him. He'd learned to fear her stubbornness and her temper.

"I'll take you to the dining salon tonight. Let's wash and dress. You're right to say I'm silly to worry over things yet to come. I apologize for my behavior, and I'll change it now." He stood and fixed a smile on his face, though he felt sick in his stomach yet.

"Tonight's not my concern, tomorrow is. I said when we sailed into Saint Michael not to spoil my fun. You better remember what I say!"

Jesse could feel his temper rising, thinking it wrong for a woman half his age to correct him. It seemed a matter of respect and appreciation, he thought. But he stayed silent and dressed with the best face he could muster, keeping his promise to behave better. When he was ready and Etta had preened herself to look her best for dinner, he led her out of their room with a show of manners, bowing and opening doors as often as he could.

He entered and seated Etta and himself in the part of the wide belly of the boat that had been made into a dining area. White-painted ceiling beams, paneled sides, walnut furnishings, and bleached and starched tablecloths and napkins reminded him of the grand riverboats he'd ridden many years before, up and down the Mississippi River. He had loved those days before the Civil War—that horrid war that had cost him his arm—and the nation its soul. Now he wished with all his heart for a return to those days of youth when he'd been happy and bright all the time. Somehow growing old soured one's spirits, he thought, spoiling the passion for life as one had tasted it yesterday.

Seeing Etta return the waves of men seated four tables away brought him back from his brooding about days gone by. He smiled and waved at the men as well, remembering that Etta would view friendliness toward others as better manners and that the men across the room would recognize it as a signal of his possession of her for himself. The fear of losing her struck through his belly, and he decided to double his efforts to stay good-natured for the remaining days to Dawson.

After dinner he led her to a sitting room built on the other side of the boat. Wicker and stuffed chairs sat around tables, and coffee and liquor stood ready along an outside wall. Mixing drinks for himself and Etta, he watched as a small-stakes poker game started in a corner. He saw a seat open at the table and got an idea about how to mend his quarrel.

As he rejoined Etta, he asked, "How would you like to play poker with those men? I'm sure they would let you sit in. I'll give you the money and sit behind to teach you how."

"Can I—I'd love to. I want to learn." Etta sprang out of her chair with a schoolgirl's bounce.

Jesse smiled and felt better; he had found a way to win back her desire to spend time with him. He introduced her and himself to the poker players and watched as the men acceded to Etta's request to play, helping her learn the rules and the winning hands. Reminded of her skill in cheering men up with her boundless love of fun, he felt heartened, too, thinking his gloom had been foolish. Eli Bonnet hadn't ever failed to catch killers that had plagued the West. Why worry about misfortunes now? he thought. He slid forward and settled in to help Etta win more money from the boisterous men gathered around.

As the *Victorian* plowed farther upriver and steered around to the northeast, the land lifted a little, and high ground crept closer; the river stayed wide and fast, with two or three waterways to choose from, each rushing by low green islands sometimes several miles long. Stands of dark timber appeared here and there on the shore, contrasting with lumpy highlands beyond, covered by hummocks of grasses, with moss and berries scattered everywhere. Far behind, snowbound mountains thrust up, revealing an eternal country, guarded by great sentinels that man could never push away.

"Jesse, look, look!" Etta cried one sunny evening from the top deck. She pointed off in the distance, motioning with the field glasses.

Peacock took the binoculars and peered toward

the place she had pointed out. He instantly saw tens of thousands of animals covering highlands toward distant white mountains, an unbroken, trotting herd streaming northbound. Grinning, he explained, "They're caribou—like the buffalo used to be in the West not very long ago. I suppose they're migrating north because of spring. You can see their calves running alongside—and wolves hunting behind if you look close." He handed the glasses back.

"Oh . . . they're killing the little ones! Why do they have to do that?"

Jesse wasn't sure of how to answer the obvious, yet on second thought it seemed a sensible question. After pausing, he said, "Every life has its predator. I suppose that's why I'm bound for Dawson City to catch the one of man." He felt proud of his wisdom, though he saw that Etta continued to frown.

"You could have just said it's horrible. I'm never going to believe it's fair." Her lips pinched.

Sensing her displeasure, yet not understanding the reason, he wondered what he would have to do to impress her, instead of just annoying her. They seemed to get along fine while she played poker each evening with the men in the sitting room, a game she was getting good at. But he didn't understand why it was becoming harder and harder to entertain her afterward.

"It wasn't my intention to say it's fair. I simply wanted to tell you about life's facts." He wondered why he seemed always to be pardoning himself lately.

"I'm not here for facts. I'm here for fun. Try to

have some yourself and quit being so serious about things!"

Etta's answer sliced through him. Finally confronted with conflict of attitude as well as age, he interpreted Etta's answer as a third warning to stay cheerful. At least, he admitted, the land around them was spellbinding enough to aid in that effort. He'd never imagined lands so vast and filled with wild game . . . and backed by beauty beyond man's simple description.

As more days slipped by in the timeless shine south of the midnight sun, they watched the river narrow to one mile, folded between banks of eroded, sienna-colored soil and sometimes between honey-hued mountains that pressed close. A broad river named the Koyukuk poured in from the north to join the fierce rush of waters. Then a bright mountain higher and more massive than any other reared above the skyline to the south. Everyone aboard stood in awe for hours on the starboard side, staring, whispering, contemplating how a mountain could be so wondrous, so grand against all the lesser summits.

The summit sat gleaming against a turquoise sky, its white peak and sides shimmering in unsettled sunlight. Gentle mirages danced above the shadowed places, yet those flanks shone enough to show snow sags and buttress rock pushing through. A plume trailed west from its very crown, a flag of misty cloud like smoke from a simmering volcano, provoking many to wonder out loud fearfully if it could be. Others argued about how far away the mountain stood, their judgment confounded by its width and its height.

Jesse left Etta standing next to the railing and climbed into the steamboat's pilothouse. In a few minutes he returned, smiling with his newfound knowledge and proud that he seemed welcome to visit the captain whenever he wished.

"The captain says the Athabaskan Indians living along the river call it Denali, the Great One, their god. I can see why—it's the largest mountain I've seen by far!"

"Seeing this has made it a day that will last me the rest of my life," Etta replied. "I can't imagine a more wonderful mountain. It has to be the tallest in the world."

"If it isn't, it's the nearest to it. I've had many fine experiences in my life—and you're one of them, Etta. But I'll remember this mountain for as long as I remember you. I hope you understand I mean no insult. Seeing such a sight is just that important to me."

Etta turned toward him, smiling, her eyes sparkling, and said, "How could a woman feel hurt by being remembered like that? You've finally said something thoughtful that I like." She then reached up and hugged him close, kissing him on the cheek.

Jesse flushed with pleasure. It had been days since he had felt affection from the young woman he had learned to love so much. He stood against the railing watching the mountain called Denali fade away as the steamboat worked around a bend in the river and calculated that something had been learned by both of them. He wondered what he could say next that would please her as much.

The next day they passed the Tanana River flooding in from the east, a clutch of islands fronting its outlet. After that, the Yukon narrowed more, snaking by mountains that the captain called the White and the Ramparts. Then the boat steamed into a morass of channels looping back and forth, bogs and lakes as far as the eye could see, wild grass and brush fields running off toward mountains in the distance. At last, after days of coasting around in what seemed to be endless loops, the *Victorian* whistled a series of toots, announcing a stop just ahead.

"Why are we stopping here? This can't be Dawson!" Etta stood looking forward toward a cluster of log cabins and tents, with smoke-sullied air hanging over them.

"I believe it's Fort Yukon, the first fur-trading post built this far north, I think. I suppose there's freight on board to unload." Jesse shaded his eyes from the sun with his one hand as he looked toward the small settlement.

"How close are we to Dawson City now?"

"I think we'll get there in two or three days." Jesse looked at Etta, fidgeting like a schoolgirl again. He grinned, thinking he hadn't felt so excited himself for a while.

After leaving the shore at Fort Yukon, the *Victorian* plowed into a river valley bordered by timbered hills and rounded mountains, a few barren of trees on their crests, with blueberry bushes instead. Turning mellow, like a green and sunny dale, the land softened, reminding many of lands they'd lived on before. And everyone marveled at the temperature, seemingly perfect summertime each day. They stayed up on deck, rowdy with the idea that their journey seemed near its end—they were so very close to their Eldorado.

Finally the riverboat's whistle blew without ceasing as the *Victorian* churned up a reach of river with high, wooded hills on each side. The passengers ran to the bow, peered upstream, and saw the boomtown of Dawson City ahead, under an earth slide that scarred the hillside above the town. Thousands of tents, fresh-cut-lumber shacks, log cabins, and white clapboard buildings spread along the muddy shore and up the hill to the north. Thousands more home-built boats bobbed abandoned in the shallows and sat scattered on the downtown waterfront. Four other great steamboats like the *Victorian* lay anchored to shore, their loading ramps aground. And everywhere tens of thousands of men and women dashed about, melting their bustle into a riot of noise and motion, like an army after a victory, a victory of conquering a town.

"This is wonderful—I can't wait!" Etta stared, spellbound.

"It looks much like encampments of the Civil War . . . when people would move in to supply the army. I just can't believe this many could get this far so fast." Jesse stared in disbelief also, his ears numbed by the howling of the stampeders on board, everyone pushing and cheering to get off the boat.

An hour passed while the *Victorian* found a berth

and roped to the pilings; then everyone rushed off to join the crowd who had come to the waterfront to see those just coming ashore.

"The captain told me he'll stay a few days before returning downriver. He has invited us to stay on board as long as we wish—thinks it's hopeless to look for a room in town. I suppose that's why there's so many tents."

"I want to see downtown first."

Jesse looked down the dusty main street, edged with crude boardwalks and jammed with men marching shoulder to shoulder. He frowned. "You need to come along with me. I want to find out if Eli has come in."

"No—you go do your work alone. I'm going to have some fun. I don't want to follow behind when there's so much to see. I'll meet you tonight for supper . . . there." Etta pointed straight toward a sign reading THE LUCKY WISHBONE, painted on a newly constructed vertical-boarded building.

"I don't think you should—not in this town. It's to dangerous for—"

"No. I told you to go. I'll be fine. Now go do your business. Go!"

Jesse stood tongue-tied as Etta whirled around and flew away, her long dress fluffing down the boardwalk. Before he could reach out and grab her and present a reasonable argument, she had disappeared among a thousand others in the same rush.

He turned and wandered along, feeling lost and hurt, thinking the mobs here were worse than those back in San Francisco months before. After an hour he mended his feelings and decided Etta's departure for a few hours didn't seem as disturbing as he'd originally felt. Looking around, he thought to watch for men in the uniform of lawmen. Within a short time, he found one but was told by the Canadian Mountie that no U.S. Marshal and prisoner had ever presented themselves to the headquarters of the Northwest Mounted Police and that there was no other law enforcement in Dawson. He thanked the officer and wandered along again, worrying and wondering if Eli could still be floating down the river.

Late that evening, in the cafe that Etta had pointed out, Jesse met her as directed. He'd waited for two hours and had grown sullen again, astonished by the cost of coffee and the noise along the main street. She swooped in, gay and smiling, the men hungrily eyeing her as she sat down across from him.

"I knew you would be sad, but I've found good news for you! I met a man, a man who says he found the first gold up here. His name is Bill Gates, but everyone calls him Swiftwater. He told me I should tell you not to worry—Eli Bonnet has arrested a man called the Cannibal, and Mr. Gates is sure they'll arrive soon." Etta panted from her swirl of words and hand gestures.

"You've met Swiftwater Bill!" Astonished again, Jesse sat bolt upright, his eyes widened upon learning of Eli's success and imminent arrival.

"You know the man I met?" Etta's face registered surprise as well.

"Swiftwater Bill has been written about in newspapers for more than twenty years. He's been arrested for bigamy and swindling more times than I can count. You stay away from him. I don't want you around a man like that!"

"Jesse, you're not my husband—or my father. I'll meet and talk to whomever I please. Mr. Gates is the most interesting man I've ever met, and he cared enough to give you news. Don't you dare order me around like some—"

"Etta, I love you. Why do you hurt me every time I turn around? Why can't you just stay by my side?"

Etta sat still for a moment. Finally, after smoothing her dress a bit, she said, "Jesse, I know how you feel about me . . . and it pleases me that you care so much. And I care for you . . . but not like you want. You say you love me, but what you really mean is you wish to own me. I'm half your age. I came along to live, to learn, to enjoy myself. I didn't come along to be ordered around like some little fool. Stop it. Do you understand?"

Etta's speech pierced him like a cold, sharp knife. The belief that he had forever lost her fondness crept into his heart, to the center of all his other worries. He felt sickened. The demons of despair had cursed him again.

At last he said, "You've been told how I feel. I've spent a great deal of money on you . . . just remember your debt!" He saw Etta purse her lips and narrow her eyes.

The next morning he climbed to the top deck of the *Victorian* with his field glasses and a padded chair to sit on all day. He searched upriver, watching each late boat float in, having been told by the steamboat's crew that most stampeders had long since arrived from Lake Bennett and Lake Lindeman above. At midmorning he saw Etta leave the boat, waving once as she faded into the crowds.

The previous night, while he lay awake listening to the town howl without rest, he had resolved to accept her ultimatum. And he had accepted deep down that she would choose to stay when he decided to leave with his prisoner. It matched a lesson he'd learned long ago in battle: at some point fear and worry became pointless, worthless—you just had to plow forward with your life no matter how bad it seemed. Short of killing yourself, he thought. Others would do that for you if you just waited.

Now he decided that because of their clash the night before, Etta didn't seem so essential anymore. He would live for Swiftwater's prophecy—that Eli would come downriver today or tomorrow. He would go with that hope instead. What else could he do, he wondered?

The next afternoon he saw them coming from far off. He'd never seen Noodles and had no idea why a black man would be steering the boat, but he could think of no other explanation for a burly, bearded man's being chained up front under the aim of an old man's shotgun. He stood and waved his jacket with his lone arm as hard as he could, then watched as the crude boat sailed his way.

When the three men floated close, he yelled down, "Are you Noodles, the friend of Bonnet, the old prospector he's talked about?"

"By Jeez, I know who you are, you're Jesse Peacock. I should of knowed. Here's the killer Eli's caught for you!" Noodles, with his toothless grin, poked forward with his shotgun.

Jesse couldn't help grinning as well as he yelled, "Tie alongside. Come aboard. Where's Eli? Wait—I'll be down in a minute!" He ran for the stairs below.

When he reached the lower railing, he yelled again, "Where's Eli? Is he coming behind with the other prisoner?"

Noodles and Lincoln exchanged glances, then Noodles hopped aboard the steamboat. "Mr. Peacock, Eli's fine and he'll come along soon. But Hannah's drowned . . . and Naomi and Patches, too, if you know who I mean."

Jesse fell against the railing, clutching at it to hold himself upright. My God, he thought, he'd just pictured his return to San Francisco with the killer, the newspaper articles that would have been printed, the fame, asking Hannah . . .

CHAPTER TWENTY-SIX

Prosperity

"Hannah, why didn't you build a smoky fire before? I've been searching for you for days. Lord, I thought I'd lost you—but I didn't want to believe it could be true!" Eli hugged her so hard he began to worry he would hurt her.

"I was afraid of the Cannibal finding me." She clung to him just as hard. "I never thought to start a signal fire until I accidentally burned down my tree. I was fighting that bear for my fish. I thought you said black bears would be afraid of me!"

Eli laughed. The burst of happiness that filled him seemed the greatest of his life. He wanted to yell, laugh, cry, scream his joy into the sky as loud as he could. After a moment, hoping for a sensible answer in light of his euphoria, he said, "Not when they're starving worse than you. How did you catch all those fish?" He looked down at three fresh ones lying nearby.

"It wasn't so hard. I remembered one of your stories about Montana. I made a net . . . and a spear, too. See?" Hannah pointed to her sharpened stick on the ground by her side.

"It appears that poor bear had met his match before I came along. I'm so proud and surprised. I love you more than ever!"

"Eli, I'm not afraid like I used to be. And I've quit crying so much. I think I can live here now." She smiled and hugged him again. Then she cried, "Oh, my Lord, I forgot—where's Naomi? You must know that Sorrowful's dead?"

Eli held her at arm's length, wishing he could hide the truth of her friend's death. "Hannah, we've lost Naomi. Patches is gone, too . . . but Lincoln and the old man are safe. And we caught the Cannibal before he could get away. I wish with all my heart you didn't need to know . . ."

"Lord . . . I'm going to cry again when I said not . . . I loved her so much, I can't bear . . ." She pulled him close, hanging on again, sobbing a flood of all her sorrow and suffering, and her survival.

Eli held her, cradling and rocking her, in a way glad to see her spill it all out. He began to blink back tears himself, suddenly not able to hold in his own mix of happiness, triumph, and heartbreak. He needed to join her in healing by sharing a secret covenant of tears that he'd never shared with any person before.

They played on the river's shore for days on end. Each as fussy as the other, they pitched a comfortable camp, cleaning and readying their gear for a lengthy stay. Eli taught Hannah how to shoot—first his Colt, then his Winchester—practicing until she shot sure on every trigger pull. He thrilled to talk with her for hours on end over their cooking fires, testing recipes of wild things until she felt filled and her strength came back.

They climbed to Sorrowful's grave together, and Hannah planted wildflowers that she'd dug up, praying with her Bible for a few minutes, misty-eyed as she whispered her final words. Afterward, they stood side by side holding each other, looking over the lands around them. Hannah was pleased by the proximity to the river she'd come to on one of her blazed trails, seeing that she had closed within a mile. Then they slipped back down, huddling, each hushed with special memories of their lost friend.

The next morning Eli saw them coming first, two lean Indians, handsome with sculpted faces and quick black eyes, like hunting hawks on a perch. Stepping ashore, they crept to Eli, then touched his medicine coat and burst into an exchange of words that he couldn't understand. He pointed to Hannah's fire and coffeepot, signing like the Lakota Sioux that they should stay and sit. The hunters signed back their recognition of his signals and sat across from Hannah, nodding their appreciation for her steaming cups.

Eli explained with his hands the death of friends, his finding of Hannah after many sleeps, his wish to help her recover her strength by resting upon the land. Last, after eyeing the cedar-and-canvas canoe they'd paddled in with, he asked for a trade for his larger, clumsy craft, hoping the two hunters would see his bargain. To entice them further, he walked to his boat and took out all the extras, the things he knew he couldn't carry in the canoe, waving his arms over his gifts of food and gear.

The two Indians broke into a chatter between themselves and signed their acceptance. Hurriedly they unloaded their canoe, smiling for the first time since coming ashore. Eli smiled back, feeling good about his trade, wanting to rid himself and Hannah of the work of maneuvering the heavy hull all the remaining miles down to Dawson City.

After the Indians had shoved off and waved their friendship from downriver, Eli took Hannah out on calm waters and played with their new craft. She squealed her fright at first over the canoe's tendency to tip, but then she mastered the bow position, kneeling and flipping her paddle side to side for balance and speed. Eli laughed with pride, shaking his head in disbelief at Hannah's ability to learn and echo his teachings in only a matter of minutes.

The following day they pushed off upriver to visit Naomi's grave before starting down to Dawson. Paddling at a pace that would harden Hannah's muscles over time, they watched the currents slip by for a change, thankful for the ability to cheat the river's bonds with the slim canoe. Partway up, Eli changed positions, letting Hannah learn the twists and flips of paddling from the stern, laughing along as she shouted her side shifts from time to time.

By the afternoon of the next day, they saw Five Finger Rapids ahead once more, and Naomi's resting place up above. They beached the canoe below, anchoring it to a snag that stuck out from shore.

"Eli, please let me go up alone. I'll say good-bye

for a while and then come back down. When I do, I want to leave for Dawson . . . we can paddle all night. I want to put this all behind me."

Eli nodded and squeezed her hand. He watched as she trudged uphill, carrying her Bible under one arm, the wind flagging her hair and clothes.

He turned and walked along the shore looking for Patches' body again, peering under rocks and stumps at the river's edge, hoping the pickpocket's body might have floated to the surface.

Looking up from his search, he saw Hannah kneeling at Naomi's grave, reading, holding the Bible's pages open against the wind. He climbed higher himself and stared up and down the Yukon's channel, sensing its emptiness, seeing no other boats or people. Everyone had passed, he thought, gone on to seek their destiny downriver, and it seemed time for Hannah and him to move on, just as she had said. He felt his spirit soar in anticipation of seeing the rest of the river and what lay beyond.

"The river's taken Patches forever. I can't find any sign of him." He wondered about the wisdom of talking of more death when he reached Hannah's side again, seeing her skid down to the canoe moments earlier.

"I believe it's God's way of hiding him from hell, and I've said a little prayer for him as well." Hannah smiled a little, looking more peaceful than Eli had expected. She then stepped into the canoe's bottom, knelt in her forward position, and added, "Let's go find our two friends and a place to call home. I'm tired of traveling for so long."

Eli shoved off and watched as Hannah turned her face back once, waving her hand toward Naomi's grave up on the slope, flashing good-bye, it seemed, in a fateful way. She then took hold of her paddle and pulled against the water, surprising him with her strength and speed, her head bent down to repeat her swing against the unsettled river.

At midnight Hannah tired, and Eli told her to lie along the bottom and sleep. He kept straight on, eager to pass the miles and reach the boomtown ahead as soon as possible. A short distance below Sorrowful's hill and their old campsite, he shot through the last white water of the river, the Rink Rapids, much less rough than any of the fast water above. Hannah woke because of the stir and noise, and then she paddled again, shooting them faster down the way.

They reached Fort Selkirk late the following day, exhausted from their steady run. The Pelly River flowed in from the east, joining its flood to the Yukon's force, broadening the river more. An old Hudson's Bay trading post stood there, mostly abandoned because of the gold stampede. Eli paid a dollar to an old man for a log cabin with bunks and table, and they slipped into beds with blankets for the first time in many months, both giggling with delight at the change.

The next day they paddled away once more, feeling better for their use of real beds and furnishings. They ran the wide river to the outlet of the Stewart River in two days, stopping for an hour at a Northwest Mounted Police post to sign the record of stampeders kept by the officers assigned to that lonely place. Hannah found the entry of Noodles and Lincoln, showing they had passed safely through with the Cannibal as their prisoner more than a month before.

Excited by the closeness of Dawson City, they set off on the last leg of the river, eager to get it done. Steep dirt shores dropped from nearby highlands, mounds of mountains stood beyond, and hills of green and yellow folded the river's waters in between, giving them a glimpse of a gentle land, less harsh than the country up above, near the headwaters. They sped on by, not stopping, not resting, now determined to reach the boomtown without delay— now eager to rejoin the stampede.

At last they saw it just ahead, downriver, with the Klondike River coming in from their right. Steamboats floated off its front with thousands of small boats beached nearby. Thousands of tents sat pitched all around up the sloping hills. Red, white, and unpainted buildings stood downtown, scattered in rows. And tens of thousands of people thundered about, dusting the air with their puffing feet. Smokestacks streamed murky black eastward from the west winds, flagging the town's enterprise, telling of man's success in building his glory. Finally, rough songs of commerce floated out, calling an end to their long, tearful journey.

When they found Swiftwater Bill sitting in the Lucky Wishbone eating with a blond woman half his age, they smiled and winked at each other before going in. Upon seeing them, Swiftwater gulped down his mouthful, shot upright, and yelled, "Eli, Hannah, Gal-dang! I knew you two would come through. I told that old varmint Noodles you weren't drowned. I know a sturdy woman when I see one. Come on over—did you ever see such a town, Eli? I'm rich and in love once more!"

Eli shook his head in disbelief, smiling his recognition of his friend's old habits. He shook Bill's hand and answered, "Swiftwater, I'm glad to see you. Introduce us to your friend and let us sit down. Hopefully you know where my old varmint friend is, and the man that came with him."

"This is Etta . . . she's got big news for you. You know how she come here? With Jesse Peacock, that's with who. And Peacock's already lost the Cannibal. The Cannibal's already got away down in Fort Yukon!"

Eli fell into a chair next to the table, feeling his heart fall. He sat stunned, unable to ask the hundred questions spinning in his mind. How could it be that Peacock had come this far north and failed so fast—

"Etta, I'm Hannah Twigg. I worked for Jesse Peacock before joining Eli. Why were you with him? Where is he now?"

"I worked for Jesse after you quit the Marshals' office. He asked me to come with him after he wrote Eli to have the prisoner brought here. When Noodles and Lincoln gave the Cannibal to him, he took the same steamboat back downriver the following day. Then, later, he sent me this." Etta reached down and pulled out a wrinkled letter.

Eli reached for it and read the crumpled paper. He saw just two scribbled lines:

Etta,
  I'm in Fort Yukon and sick. I've lost my prisoner and need to see Eli. Please find him for me.
                                        Jesse

After passing the message to Hannah so she could read it as well, he asked, "Etta, what happened to Jesse at the end? Was he well? Why did you choose to stay?"

Etta ducked her head and said, "I met Bill and wanted to . . . I love this town. I've learned to deal poker. Jesse found out I wanted to stay. He seemed in an ugly mood when he sailed, but no more than once before."

"What you goin' to do, Eli? Are you goin' to go down to Fort Yukon and see 'im like he wants?" Swiftwater's face twisted with dark, pitying eyes.

"I don't know, Swiftwater. Before I think it through, tell me how to find my friends. I need to keep a promise I made upriver. And they'll want to see Hannah. They were afraid she had drowned, as you were told."

"Cross the Klondike and follow Bonanza Creek—look in the hills. Noodles and Lincoln are up high diggin' around. Me and everybody are thinkin' they've gone crazy. I hope it ain't true—but there ain't no gold up there."

The next morning they paddled their canoe across the smaller Klondike River and found Bonanza

Creek running southeast up rising ground. A wide road snaked alongside, weaving among mines of piled soil and sluice boxes hundreds of feet long. Thousands of shacks and tents rested among hand-dug pits, waste dumps, flume water, and muddy ponds—each shelter bare and crude, just enough to keep off the rain but not the cold. Thousands of men worked in rows nearby, pitching dirt out of holes and hills, throwing diggings to be washed for gold. Claim owners marched about, bossing, cursing, frenzied by riches and by promises of more. Pack animals hoofed back and forth, up and down, hauling supplies for the crews and bullion for the bosses, tramping with tons of goods to or from Dawson. And the mining ran on and on, higher up the creek, to Eldorado Creek and beyond, as far as their eyes could see.

They found Noodles and Lincoln that evening, working together high on a sidehill, the black man without his shirt, his skin sweaty, glistening in the late sunlight.

Eli turned and led the way up, taking Hannah by her hand, pulling to help her scale the steepness choked with alders and brush. As they began their climb, a miner yelled, lifting his call from the creek water below, "You two crazy like them two. We named that place Chickaloon Hill for that old fool and his nigger friend. Hell, everybody knows you can't find gold up on hills!"

Eli kept climbing without looking back. As he and Hannah gained altitude away from the madness underneath, a peacefulness calmed the air, broken only by Noodles' cackles and Lincoln's grunts drifting down.

When the old prospector saw them coming, he bounded toward them, crying, "Lordee . . . Hannah, you're alive! God bless, Eli, you found her when I didn't believe. Lincoln, come up here. By Jeez, I'm happy this day!"

Lincoln popped his head out, staring from a hole he'd jumped into as deep as he stood tall. "Mizz Hannah, Lord—it's Providence, as Noodles always says. How'd Eli find you when we were sure you got drowned?"

Hannah laughed, hugging Noodles, then Lincoln. She answered, smiling her happiness at seeing her friends again, "I ran away and got lost when I should have stayed and waited. But I'm learning not to be so foolish . . . but that's not what people are telling about you. What are you two doing to cause so much talk?"

"Eli . . . Hannah, lookee!" Noodles snatched a leather poke from under a bedroll. "By Jeez, Lincoln and I are rich—and Eli, I got a claim for you. You don't have to be a Marshal no more. You and Hannah can be richer than bankers."

Eli and Hannah watched as the old man poured his sack of gold out on the dirt all around his feet, nuggets the size of acorns, handfuls of them, coloring the ground bright yellow. Then they watched, stunned, as he danced, whooping again and again, sending his hoots downhill, filling the valley below with odd human sounds bouncing back and forth.

Lincoln bent double with laughter. Then he said,

"They'll be hootin' back pretty soon, makin' fun. They just yell mean things instead of comin' up here. And we been stakin' the best diggin's 'round these parts."

Reaching for Hannah, Eli hugged her close. He stood holding her, shaking his head in wonder, smiling . . . yet not knowing what to say.

CHAPTER TWENTY-SEVEN

Farewell

"Please come back soon." Hannah's quiet words pierced his heart as he walked away, seeing Noodles and Lincoln standing by her side, long-faced as well.

He and Hannah had staked a neighboring claim to the one gifted by Noodles, driving down posts marking parallel lines five hundred feet long by one hundred feet wide. They then journeyed back to Dawson and filed the claim as Chickaloon Number Four, laughing when the clerk shook his head and swore about cheechakos. Hannah laughed even harder when Eli whispered that the word meant "foolish newcomers," as opposed to the seasoned residents of the North called sourdoughs. After completing the registration in her name, he led the way to the Lucky Wishbone and visited with Swiftwater again. Bill said he still courted Etta, but he seemed more interested in a nineteen-year-old dance hall girl named Gussie Lamore. He spit out his coffee and nearly upset the table when Eli showed him the poke of Noodles' nuggets, which Eli had for safekeeping and for deposit in the town's new bank vault, already stuffed with millions of dollars in gold from other rich mines.

The news of Noodles' discovery transformed the hill—and the old prospector, making him a celebrity everywhere he went, an occupation he appreciated more than mining itself. Lincoln remained behind, digging, sluicing, sweating, sacking his gold in pokes without rest, hiding it, worrying Eli and Hannah, who felt they needed to watch out for his well-being.

They ordered lumber and nails to be carried up and, after persuading Lincoln to prepare for the coming winter, built two cabins on their four claims, comfortable and tight against the rising winds and chilling autumn rains. Hannah pitched in with all her muscle, again surprising Eli with her ability to learn and work, to join him as an equal, uncomplaining and uncompromising, determined to do her share. Their love grew stronger, bonded closer by common burdens, their little home, and the sweet joy of touching each day.

Eli at last admitted in his mind that he had to paddle downriver to see Jesse Peacock when new snows frosted tall mountains out on the skyline during the first week of September. Called "termination dust" by the sourdoughs now shoveling crazily all around their mining claims, he conceded that his yesterdays did matter—and that his duty lay with the new frontier and the pioneers pouring into it. His medicine coat swayed him, too, reminding him of his love for the native people whom he now saw being shoved aside, pushed away by greed, making only a little with their hunting and packing for the miners, but not gaining the fabulous wealth they had trod over forever on their own sacred land.

He had made love to Hannah the night before, holding her as close and as long as he could, recalling the two times he had lost her before: once to his own selfishness, once to the wilderness he planned to visit again. Now his ability to go about his business seemed impaired by an ache, an empty place in his heart that only she could keep filled. But he had to go back to his past—and she had talked of it also. She told him it was like her faith: a soulful pledge, a covenant, a path to man's need to devote himself to his God—the God she had learned to love so much and to worship so well. His peace the day of his departure was better than the day before.

Paddling down the Yukon in his canoe, he watched the land turn yellow and red, aspens and birches painted from night frosts and berry bushes blushing their end. The sun swung around to the south again, letting shadows dance once more when he camped at night, sitting lonely near his fire, gazing into its orange spirits, missing Hannah, yet happy to be off again, exploring new boundaries.

On the fifteenth, in a hard, chilling wind, he floated to the foot of Fort Yukon. As he stepped ashore, Indian people, like the two men he'd traded with upriver, ran to his side, touching and chattering about his medicine coat, slowing him from walking to the trading post of the settlement to ask about Peacock.

An ancient man stepped out in front of him, flanked by a boy of ten or twelve, both bright-eyed but solemn. The youth extended his small hand, calling, "Hello, sir. My grandfather's father hears no English but wishes to speak. He asks why you come wearing his brother's medicine. How can you be a warrior and a shaman when you are white? He wishes to know about your home, from where do you walk?"

"Ask your chief if he will sit with me on the shore of this great river and talk. I've come to learn his wisdom, I've come to thank him for the use of his land to nourish and rest me, and I wish to find a white lawman said to be here in his home."

The Indian boy turned to the old man and pointed to several logs lying nearby appearing to be circled for use in ceremonies many years in the past. The two led the way; then the old man sat down with great slowness, other Indians rushing to his side to help lower him, then running to find wood for a fire to warm him.

After sitting down himself, Eli asked, "How is it that you can speak English so well, young man?"

"The fathers are teaching me to be white like you. They say I can be captain of a steamboat someday." The boy pointed to a log church standing across the way.

"Perhaps you should learn to be a chief instead. It will be better for you to lead your own people rather than those that should find their own way."

The boy blinked and remained quiet for a moment. He then spoke to his great-grandfather, gesturing toward Eli as he murmured odd syllables.

"My father's grandfather says you counsel wisely.

He wonders why you would choose to tell a boy about the love of his own people when you are white."

"Tell him I have grown wiser learning from his brothers far south from this place. The land I've come from is wild no more, and I'm sad for its loss. I come searching for peace once more in my life."

After translating, the boy asked, "Why are you wearing medicine—the spirits of our shamans from long ago?"

"I took it from a warrior who was foolish and threw it down. He attacked me with his weapons, but mine were stronger." Eli pointed to his Winchester rifle leaning against the log he sat on. "His medicine coat saved his life from my bullet—but his eyes couldn't see. He got blinded by tears because he'd lost his home."

The wrinkled sage sat listening to the boy's explanation. He remained quiet for a time, searching Eli with his eyes. Then he spoke to the boy passionately for a long moment.

"My father's grandfather says this land will be kept for his people with peace. He tells you to put your weapons down, for there is room in this place for all who wish to come. He tells you to watch the spirits that are now upon the land—that one day soon you will see why the land will be ours forever. He asks that you take only enough to keep strong and leave no fires burning as you walk along."

"Tell your chief I see the reason now . . . and I thank him for his kindness."

The boy squinted with uncertainty, confusion. "Sir,

what did my father's grandfather say? What do his words mean?"

Eli smiled and slipped off his Sioux spirit coat. He handed it to the boy and answered, "You spend time with your father's grandfather every day and wear this medicine. Spend the same hours with him as you do with the priests in the church. Their teachings are important—but his will be better. Listen carefully to his words. That's what I see."

The boy grasped the coat, touching its feathers and beads, his eyes wide with happiness. The Indians standing close by, listening, broke into their dialect, filling the air with noisy chatter. Each of them stepped up to Eli, grasping his hand, shaking it, their eyes round, mouths grinning white.

After speaking again with his great-grandfather, the boy said, "My father's grandfather says his heart is glad to have you upon this land. He says you shall have new medicine soon . . . medicine as strong as you gave away."

"Thank him for his gifts. Now, where is the white man who says he's sick?"

The Indian boy pointed to a log cabin down the high bank of the river without looking up from his keepsake. Eli turned away, walking slowly, looking back once to see all the Indians gathered in a circle around the old man and the boy, everyone still chattering.

He found Jesse sitting out of the wind on the sunny side of a rough cabin with one window and a small portal door. Peacock seemed unaffected by the sudden visit from around the corner of the log structure. He continued to stare across the wideness of the water in front of him.

"I apologize for coming late, Jesse. I didn't receive your message until August; then I needed time to make up my mind to come. The news of you losing the Cannibal upsets me so much—" He stopped, shocked to see Jesse's skeletal, pale face, his torso just sitting, shivering, his hands clutching a bear robe draped around his shoulders.

"I knew you would come—you never fail in your duty, do you, Bonnet?"

"I'm not sure that's true . . . but what do you need? I'm here to help."

"Nothing now. I had wanted to see your face when you found out that I'd lost the Cannibal. I wanted to get even with you for taking Hannah—losing her. But I don't even care about that anymore."

Eli hesitated to answer. The hostility from Jesse had started that long-ago day during the Civil War— Peacock's arm blown to bits, bloody parts lying on the ground beside him. But now Eli saw the fault on both sides through all the many years that had passed . . . the failure to talk about whatever it was that stood between them.

"You've always known I was the bugle boy that stood over you when you lost your arm, haven't you?"

Peacock sat quivering, tears coursing down his cheeks. Finally he whispered, "You Rebels cost me everything, ruined the country with your damn war. I've always wished you would all rot in hell for what you did."

"Jesse, I didn't blow your arm off . . . for all you

know, your own cannon did it. My God, more than thirty thousand soldiers were killed and wounded in that battle. Why hate me for a war I didn't start?"

"You started it—you damn people had to have your slaves!"

"Slavery had nothing to do with it in the beginning. Lincoln said himself he would favor slavery rather than lose the Union. Tell me how freeing people by war is better than the ways of an old Indian I just talked with a few minutes ago!" Eli, embittered by Jesse's indictment, pointed over to the chief, whose people were still standing around him.

Peacock's face remained ashen, with more tears. "I'm not going to talk to some damn Indian!"

"There's the Union I've lived with all my life—kill and cripple more than two million people to free others in the South less fortunate, then refuse to live and work alongside those very same folks. Next, turn the same army and kill and enslave people of another color found in the West. In the end, refuse to talk to some damn Indian. I'm glad to be gone from your Union—and I'll never go back!"

Jesse sat for a moment, then shook his head. "I'll not be returning, either. My life got ruined when I lost the Cannibal. I could have been—"

"Lord, why did you do it, Jesse? You don't seem to be hurt!"

"I felt sorry . . . his wrists were so bloody, he looked so sick. He asked to get off and walk a little when the boat stopped here for freight. I thought I could hold him."

Eli stood, stunned, not believing what he had just

heard. Then, hanging his head and shaking it, he thought back to his exile to Arizona, Jesse's rage about Reuben Tugle being shot in the knee . . . that deluded compassion for killers. He hung his head lower over the riddle, the enigma, sitting in front of him.

He walked to the shore and stared over the dark, stirring waters, hearing Jesse sniffle behind him. Then the sighing began to wear on his heart. All the years of connection seemed, after all, to matter, nonetheless. He couldn't bear to just walk away; he couldn't bear to live with an unjust end.

He turned and faced Peacock. "You're wrong about Hannah. She's not dead."

Jesse stiffened, sitting straight. "Noodles said she got drowned. You're lying!"

"I've never lied to you and wouldn't lie about Hannah. She waiting for us in Dawson now."

His face creased, Jesse asked, "How did you find her if she fell in the Yukon? Even the Cannibal said she was drowned."

"The Cannibal—by now you should know the worth of his word! Hannah ran from him when he killed Sorrowful and tried to yank loose from his chains so he could kill her. That's the reason for his bloody wrists and sickness. I found her lost by a small lake not far from where she'd beached the boat downriver from Five Finger Rapids."

"Even if it's true, it means nothing for me. I know I can't have her, and I wanted to go back to San Francisco with Etta and the Cannibal anyway."

"You can still do that. By the time we get back to

Dawson, I figure Etta will be glad to see you. Swiftwater Bill is already off on another romance."

Jesse Peacock stood up for the first time, peering at Eli, studying, his cheeks dried by the wind. "You would catch the Cannibal again . . . you would turn him over to me?"

"I won't lie to you, Jesse. More for myself and the new land I live in—not so much for you. But do you know where he went? What happened when he escaped?"

"I let him lead me back by the woodpiles. He knocked me down and beat me. I couldn't fight decent with only one arm. He was in leg irons, but that didn't stop him. By the time I woke up, he'd stolen a boat and disappeared downriver. There was no way to search for him the way the river runs back and forth below."

His color looks better, Eli thought. Perhaps the bitterness between us and his despair can end. He turned back from the Yukon's edge and said, "Jesse, clean yourself up and pack your things. Let's go back to Dawson City. When it's winter I'm sure we'll hear of the Cannibal again. We'll go after him together. He won't get away next time."

For the first time, Jesse Peacock's face lifted; he brushed at his ragged, unshaven chin with his one hand, trying to smooth his ratty beard. His eyes stared out from deep hollows but looked clear for a change. Slowly he answered, "Eli, I'll say now I'm sorry. I can't forget my past. I suppose it's too much for either of us to forget. But I'll remember your help from now on. Let me have an hour. I'll be ready by then." He reached out and gripped Eli's hands, then stepped through his cabin door, keeping it open for the sunshine to beam in.

Eli walked along the river, returning to his canoe, feeling whole, sensing peace with the ancient shaman he'd counseled with, seeing peace between himself and Jesse.

He hadn't noticed the wolf-puppy before . . . not until he knelt by the side of his canoe. Tied to the inside, the small white bundle pulled on its leather cord, tugging to get close, wanting to lick his face. His medicine had returned . . .

We invite you to preview
a new, thrilling novel
of adventure and peril
on the Alaskan frontier:

Whispers of the Mountain
by Tom Hron
coming soon from Signet Books

Denali

Athabaskan Indians in Alaska believe that man can never hide from Denali, the great sacred mountain watching over their ancestral land. They say its spirits beckoned from the very beginning—more than a thousand dead shamans back in their past. Coming up from Canada, they describe finding a mother country filled with caribou and salmon and other good things to eat, and an uninhabited place where they could live forever.

Settling along the mighty rivers flowing around their god, they found nuggets of copper and obsidian, birch bark, and warm furs beyond their dreams. They grew and prospered in their new homeland, calling themselves Den'a, the earth's only true people. Inhabitants of the seacoasts, the Aleuts and Eskimos, learned to stay away—the followers of the Great One would kill every unbeliever daring to walk under the mountain's shadow.

Russian explorers were the first to challenge the spirits of the mountain. In 1848 an expedition of eleven men crossed Prince William Sound and paddled up the Copper River toward Mount Drum of the Wrangell Mountains. Many years later, the natives of that region, called Midnooskies by the czar's men, confessed to slaughtering them all, handing over a few remnant journal pages as eulogies for the missing adventurers. Two more fearless parties followed, only to have their heads hacked off with axes at a village named Taral near the mouth of the Chitina River.

The first white men to pass safely through the forbidden land were led by Lieutenant Henry Allen of the Second United States Cavalry. He and two companions crossed almost 2,500 miles of the interior of Alaska, much of it on foot, in 1885, one of the most difficult journeys ever made by man. They fought across stormy seas in Eyak Indian canoes; they poled up coffee-and-cream torrents rushing down the Copper River through deep canyons and past calving glaciers; they hiked on thin ice and waded in deep snow in search of the fabled copper mine of the Chitina and Chitistone Rivers; they backtracked up the Upper Copper River, rounding Mount Sanford for the first time; and they packed over the Alaskan Mountain Range to the Tanana River, starving all the way. Then, desperate, they launched downriver in a moose-hide boat, running thunderous whitewater for days until reaching the Yukon River, finally finding enough food to save themselves from hunger.

After a week's rest, they marched farther north until they sighted the Koyukuk River. Bartering at an Indian camp for two birch-bark canoes, they ran that winding flow down to the Yukon River again. Pushing downstream on the father of Alaska's waters, they learned from natives of a primitive crossing to Norton Sound on the Bering Sea. At last reaching saltwater again after five months of wilderness wanderings, they hired Eskimos to paddle them across to Saint Michael and a ship waiting to return them to San Francisco.

But Denali avenged that brave trespass in 1898 during the Klondike gold rush. Hundreds of men purchased passage to the port of Valdez to join the stampede northward to Dawson City. They began by climbing several thousand feet with their grubstakes to the top of the Valdez Glacier—then by dropping down the Klutina Glacier to the frozen lake and river below. All the way across the surface of the ancient ice, those foolhardy stampeders, one by one, dropped from sight forever in crevices hidden beneath the snow. Then, when springtime came, more cruel disasters took place.

First the prospectors drowned by the dozens while shooting the murderous rapids of the Klutina River as it roared toward the Copper River. Next, coursing along the foot of the smoking, mysterious Mount Wrangell, dozens more drowned by trying to ascend the silty rush pouring from the north. Yielding and forced back, and dying by the hundreds, the survivors retreated from the misadventure, the scurvy, and the heartbreak. Lastly the battered remains staggered back into Valdez, only to be crippled further by sickness, some turning crazy for the rest of their lives from the fear of ever wishing for gold again.

This story is dedicated to those stouthearted men who lost their lives to the giant mountain one hundred years ago—and tells of their courage in searching for every man's dream.

CHAPTER ONE

Trapped

The instant the Newhouse trap snapped on his right hand's fingers, Red Shirt Moses sensed he'd killed himself—he was just not yet dead. He heard the chain slide down, chinking below on the drowning wire, locking its catch forever. He pulled as hard as he could, now feeling how the beaver struggled, dying slowly, a leg clamped by steel teeth. Despite his pulling again with all his strength, the trap stake stayed stuck in the bottom of the pond and frozen on top by ice, telling him to sing his last song. Denali, he cursed, why have you punished me so—the deeds of my past were done to please you.

He rolled off his belly to his right side, fumbled awkwardly with his free hand and gripped his prized skinning knife, laying it next to the hole he'd chopped into the frozen beaver pond. Staring, thinking, he judged the thickness of the ice, then the thickness of his arm. Was it possible, he fretted, to chip away enough to reach his fingers and cut them off? Was it possible to reach and cut his arm off at the elbow—or the shoulder? How long did it take to bleed to death; how much pain could he endure?

Hearing old Wahnie whine, he looked across to his sled dogs anchored nearby. He called sadly to the leader in Athabaskan dialect, "Ah-eeh, old one—I have trapped myself! I will die soon unless you have a miracle. Chew from your harness and save yourself. Those stupid ones behind will kill and eat you tomorrow—then they will eat my body afterward. Run away, old one, run from here. My foolishness today will make this an evil place."

An icy blow fanned snow onto his face, moistening, then freezing his skin; he could see the same white dust frosting the wolverine hair around his parka hood, sinister against the deep brown. What was it? he wondered—five below, ten below—no one could expect to live for long in such cold. The wind hurried again from Denali, north off the Alaskan mountains, those immortals standing overhead.

He looked back down into the boggy water, colored like coffee, puddling around his arm. Why had he been so thoughtless to reach down and feel for his trap? Why had he believed he had caught another beaver to skin? He could see the crinkles of ice freezing from the edges of the hole, soon to lock around his sleeve, then to his arm inside, then to the very marrow of his bones. He angrily splashed with his free hand, breaking back the wicked grip, but feeling numbness already creeping into his shoulder, sensing once more the death that would surely come. Leastways it would be peaceful, he thought, like when he had placed the ancient one to die in the sacred shaman's cave to join the thousand skeletons heaped there before. He would soon sleep, dream of the eagle soaring, dream of the land always.

No—not yet, he decided, his body shivering with the cold. My daughter will never find my bones to take them to the secret place if I die here. Hearing a raven squawk above, he twisted to see six of the black prophets perched above him on a cottonwood branch—waiting to peck his eyes first, then other soft parts bared to their hungry, gray beaks. He knew they would call the magpies and whiskey jacks to join in; next would come the lean fox to tear away his clothing, to bare his belly to ease every creature's winter fast. Wolves would scatter his bones then, hiding everything forever from human eyes. People would wonder what had happened to the last shaman to visit those who had passed on before to the giant mountain.

Clutching his skinning knife, he picked into the ice, enlarging the hole circling his arm. Chipping wildly, the struggle warmed him; his heart pumped with the effort from his pounding the blade's point into the glassy surface. November's covering is thin and soft, he thought, and soon there will be room for me to reach through and cut free. My wrist will be the best choice, severed and pulled off like the skinning of paws of pine martins trapped in the spruce trees. Then Denali's breath will freeze the gush of blood from my arm. Wahnie will dash away, leading the other dogs on a mad chase to my cabin, to my woman and daughter. They will cauterize and bandage the stub. I'll not be crippled much from the loss of just one hand.

Then, suddenly, his hand slipped inside its mitten and lost its grip on the caribou antler handle. Flashing once, the silver blade disappeared below into the beaver's murky, winter home. He stared after his last hope, his spirit sinking like his knife. Why, Denali, why . . . ? What have I done to deserve a death like this, trapped like the beaver, otter, and mink I've caught in the past?

Breaking into a mad struggle for his life, he yanked, kicked, and twisted about, trying to tear off his fingers, trying to break the trap or chain. His shrieks echoed between the valley walls, manically answering his own angry curses against the pain and suffering, against the injustice of dying before he wished to pass away.

Then Wahnie and the other dogs joined their howls to his, filling the mountains with a chorus of calls chilling enough to spook the ravens waiting in the branches overhead, sending them flapping fast for roosts farther off.

At last he tired, unable to thrash any longer. He lay panting, weeping—not cold now, yet feeling the sweat changing into icy drops falling along his ribs. The sickness of exhaustion, of resignation crept into his soul, leaving him helpless to care anymore, leaving him jealous of those he'd shot, of those he'd beheaded with one swing of his ax. That was a much better way to die, he judged, much better than seeing oneself freeze.

His mind drifted to memories of a lifetime spent in the Alaskan wilderness. Born along the Yukon River in the village of Nulato, he'd learned early of fishing and hunting, packing and camping, the most of an Athabaskan's life. Only later had he sampled the ease of the white man's ways. During boyhood, he had been taught by his elders to use the bow and arrow, the spear, nets, snares, and deadfalls, any useful means to harvest the salmon, moose, and caribou living upon the land. And the shaman and leader before him had taught the healing, the sorcery, the calling for spirits of the ancestors and of the great mountain to comfort his soul and the souls of others around him. Life had been good for so long . . .

Just as he'd become skillful as a young man in the lessons of the Den'a chiefs and medicine men, the black robes had come along the river to school his people with other teachings. And those same white preachers had mockingly named him for his favorite color and manner of leadership. Then they had wrested much of his power from him, harming him forever in the eyes of his own people. But they'd paid in blood—he had seen to that. The slaughter in 1851 of the English Naval Lieutenant Barnard and his men near the mouth of the Koyukuk River had been the first punishment for the insults; the death of every unwary trader and prospector afterward had added to his revenge. But now it seemed the spirits were angry with his hateful ways, and they would soon end his life by his own spiteful hand.

He wasn't sure of the time that had passed in his remembering. Stiffness, numbness, dullness were inside him; death was creeping closer. He had seen this in others before. The cold gripped you motionless after the shivers, wrapping around, squashing your heartbeat and stealing your breathing away. Then your eyes glazed, partly from unconsciousness, partly from tears freezing in place. Lastly your body hardened like ice, like the butchered meat of animals exposed to winter winds. Only your spirit could flee, to fly above, dancing here and there upon the land.

Slowly . . . he began to hear Wahnie whine, then yip shrilly, excitedly. The other dogs joined in, starting a chorus of yelps bouncing about the hills. He rolled to his side and stared; he saw a lone figure on snowshoes shuffling fast toward him from the creek leading into the pond. Hot breath puffed behind the jogging stranger like steam from a bubbling tea kettle on a frosty morning. Bundled like a bear, the man looked clumpy in his black beard, gray furs, and earflaps tied under his chin. He is strong, heavy, though not skilled on the snow paws he wears, Red Shirt observed. . . . But, Wahnie, he is the miracle I begged for. You have saved me!

The stranger neared and crouched just above, panting, "What you doin' with your arm stuck down there, Injun? It's colder'n hell!" His forehead wrinkled, perplexed.

Red Shirt endeavored to answer in English. "I caught my hand in beaver trap. Take my ax from sled—cut wood pole out—over there!" He pointed with his left arm to the spruce stake poking above the snow-covered ice.

"You gotta cabin someplace 'round here?" The bundled man stayed hanging overhead.

"Down trail—after dark-time we get there.

Hurry—chop me free!" Red Shirt shifted his arm to point out a packed path through the spruce woods encircling the pond.

"Who's there? You got friends waitin'?" The steam continued to puff, frosting the man's bearded face.

"My woman—daughter girl. They will cook moose and beaver tail to eat—I have whiskey. Hurry, must get out or arm will rot with black sickness!"

"Any more Injuns or white people 'round here close?"

A stab of dread beyond the horror of dying on the ice stuck into Red Shirt's belly. He paused, then decided that truth, lies, words, who would know the difference? He must tell enough to gain freedom.

"No one lives here close. . . . Whites are south by water that never freezes. My people live across land like spirits." He pointed for a third time to the six ravens sitting and watching, overhead again. "Me chief, medicine man. I know many secrets . . . of things white man want as much as life."

Swiping his runny nose with his right mitt, the stranger sneered through the freezing mucus on his mustache, "What've you got more than that sled an' dogs—what've you got I need more than that?"

"I show you gold eagle—more gold than sled can carry—more gold than hundred sleds can carry!"

The wrinkled forehead creased more on the hairy face. "If you know where gold is, why are you trappin' out here in the middle of nowhere? If you got gold—you can be sittin' in Seattle rich an' warm!"

"What I do in city—die on white man foods cooked in white man ways. I only need gold for new

Winchester, maybe new shirt or more bullets. I never leave my land!"

The stranger stood and stared for some time. Abruptly, he turned, snowshoed to the dog sled, then came back with the ax clenched in his mitts, crouching once more. He purred, "We gotta make a deal, Injun. How do I know you're goin' to show me nothin' but your backside once I chop you out? You're goin' to have to tell me more about the gold—or else I'll leave you here!"

"There is cave where all my people's medicine men go to die. The gold is there. . . . But you can't see till hummingbird comes. This place not far . . . but you can't find without me. Me the last medicine man. Chop out—I show you."

"Injun, that's a mighty fancy story—but I ain't believin' it. If there's really gold, why does one need hummingbirds to find it. That's the tallest tale I've ever heard!"

"It is true—I can't lie now. The place is there—above river of ice coming down Great One." Red Shirt pointed with his free arm by laying it on the snowy beaver pond straight toward Denali.

ABOUT THE AUTHOR

Tom Hron grew up in Northern Minnesota loving airplanes, books, and the outdoors. A professional pilot licensed for single- and multi-engine airplanes, helicopters and seaplanes, he has flown from Hudson Bay to Florida, from the Baja to the Bering Sea, and across many mountains in between. He has trained Vietnam War pilots and airline captains, and has owned one of the largest aircraft sales dealerships in the United States. Now he has chosen to write.

A resident of Anchorage, Alaska since 1983, Tom has explored the Great Land with a passion. He loves to walk the old sacred places: Dawson City, Nome, Fortymile, Eagle, Chicken, and Fairbanks. Each of these towns saw many frontiersmen journey from the Old West during the Klondike and Alaskan gold rushes. Wyatt Earp, Calamity Jane, Bat Masterson, and Arizona Charlie Meadows stampeded north in 1897; so did many others of similar character.

Whispers of the River is one of the many stories he intends to tell.

THE DAWN OF FURY
BY RALPH COMPTON

Nathan Stone had experienced the horror of Civil War battlefields. But the worst lay ahead. When he returned to Virginia, to the ruins of what had been his home, his father had been butchered and his mother and sister stripped, ravished, and slain. The seven renegades who had done it had ridden away into the West. Half-starved and afoot, Nathan Stone took their trail. Nathan Stone's deadly oath—blood for blood—would cost him seven long years, as he rode the lawless trails of an untamed frontier. His skill with a Colt would match him equally with the likes of the James and Youngers, Wild Bill Hickok, John Wesley Hardin, and Ben Thompson. Nathan Stone became the greatest gunfighter of them all, shooting his way along the most relentless vengeance trail a man ever rode to the savage end ... and this is how it all began.

from **SIGNET**

Prices slightly higher in Canada.   (0-451-18631-1—$5.50)

TRINITY STRIKE

BY SUZANN LEDBETTER

From the heart of Ireland comes the irrepressible Megan O'Malley, whose own spirit mirrors that of the untamed frontier. With nothing to her name but fierce determination, Megan defies convention and sets out to strike it rich, taking any job—from elevator operator to camp cook—to get out west and become a prospector. In a few short months, she has her very own stake in the Trinity mine—and the attention of more than a few gun-slinging bandits. But shrewd, unscrupulous enemies are lurking, waiting to steal her land—and any kind of courtship must wait. . . .

from Signet

FALCONER'S LAW
BY JASON MANNING

The year is 1837. The fur harvest that bred a generation of dauntless, daring mountain men is growing smaller. The only way for them to survive is the way westward, across the cruelest desert in the West, over the savage mountains, through hostile Indian territory, to a California of wealth, women, wine, and ruthless Mexican authorities.

Only one man can meet that brutal challenge—His name is Hugh Falconer—and his law is that of survival. . . .

from **SIGNET**